Books by
Tracy Hewitt Meyer

The Reformation of Marli Meade

The Blackthorn Peak Duology
Generation Annihilation
Generation Retaliation

The Rowan Slone Novels
A Life, Redefined
A Life, Forward
A Life, Freed

TRACY HEWITT MEYER

GENERATION RETALIATION

bhc press™

Livonia, Michigan

Quotation from Edgar Allan Poe. Public domain.

Jacket/Cover Images:
Title Font (chekart)/Shutterstock, Woods (solarseven)/Shutterstock,
Asylum (berni0004)/Shutterstock, Figures (Kjpargeter)/Shutterstock

GENERATION RETALIATION

Published by BHC Press

Library of Congress Control Number:
2023945953

ISBN: 978-1-64397-400-2 (Hardcover)
ISBN: 978-1-64397-401-9 (Softcover)
ISBN: 978-1-64397-402-6 (Ebook)

For information, write:
BHC Press
885 Penniman #5505
Plymouth, MI 48170

Visit the publisher:
www.bhcpress.com

For Rhys

"All that we see or seem is but a dream within a dream."

— Edgar Allen Poe —

GENER
ATION
RETALI
ATION

1

Ramblings of a Sane Madman

• • • • • •

He stands on the lawn of the Blackthorn Peak Lunatic Asylum, marveling at its beauty. The massive building is a true work of art, an accomplishment in construction that rivals the great churches in Europe. Hand-cut local stone. Skilled masonry. Gothic and Tudor Revival style. Hundreds of perfectly placed windows.

Simply magnificent.

He feels a pang of sadness, though, that someone had the audacity to try and burn it. Of course, so much stone would never burn to the ground, but still. The upstairs section that did burn is blackened and charred where it should be beige, windows shattered where they should be intact. If he wasn't so busy trying to return this building, and its purpose, to its full potential, he would've set about repairs already.

Alas, in due time.

He turns his gaze toward the red building that stands off to the side like the detached smaller line of the letter *L*. This building lacks all the charm and significance of the main structure, but it too has its purpose. Formerly used to house tuberculosis patients, now it will be used for research.

The most important research of his life, of this generation, and likely for generations to come.

That is only his second goal, though. Glory and renown are admirable, but there is a more pressing, *vital* purpose to this red building and the reemergence of the asylum itself.

Blackthorn Peak Lunatic Asylum will literally be the phoenix rising from the ashes.

He releases a soft chuckle. "Maybe I should thank you, Shaun Treadway, for setting that fire after all. How poetic it will be when you are returned to this most symbolic of places."

He inhales the crisp mountain air.

After years spent in Chicago, to return to the area of his birth, his childhood, his shame... His vision darkens with memories. Yes, his shame. To return here triumphant, ready for the ultimate showdown, is such sweet justice.

Yes, he belongs here. Time for the final show.

He counts the windows in the asylum until he finds the one that belongs to the room he will use as his office. It was formerly the office of Dr. Esther Richter, but she will now be in the red building with everyone else. She needs to know her place, and this is a clear sign to her, and to the others, that she is no longer in charge of this place. There is a new sheriff in town. The head of the Agency is here, in person, to take control and move progress swiftly along.

There can be no mistaking who is in charge here. The Agency, yes. But who is in charge of the Agency?

Les Range.

2

The cool breeze ruffles through the dying leaves, both those that have already fallen to the ground, as well as those that still cling to the branches. It's autumn in West Virginia, and I, Shaun Treadway—Baltimore native, redhead, asylum escapee, murderer, avenger, forgotten, forsaken—am alone in the forest surrounding the Blackthorn Peak Lunatic Asylum.

There is a sound that comes with this breeze through the vast forest. It's become as familiar to me as the cool burst of air that awakens me every morning. It's a dry sort of sound, an empty sort of sound, not lush and vibrant like a spring breeze when the leaves are alive and hearty and plush. Rather, it's somber and voided. A sound that evokes the dying and the dead.

The leaves crunch under my shoes as I hike through the forest.

I'm aware of this wind, this solemn sound, but I don't acknowledge it as I walk on. My focus is elsewhere, trained on my destination. That place absorbs every ounce of my attention, though I can't say why. Nothing has happened in the months since my escape from the asylum, so I don't expect any activity there now, but I have visited daily since April when my three friends and I escaped. It's become a habit now, though, and the routine comforts me.

Eventually, I come to the familiar giant rock, and I scamper atop, then sit. This rock rests on one of the mountainsides that overlooks the asylum. The hospital was built in 1830, to house West Virginia's insane, and closed its doors in the 1990s. It didn't stay closed, though, as I'm sure it was intended to do. If only…

I gaze down at the monstrous building. It's about a forty-five-minute hike from my grandfather's cabin, where we—Ryan McComber, Emily Howard, Cassidy Rutherford, and I—have been staying since our escape, along with three other escapees we met that fateful night.

Now it's October, and as each day has rolled into the next and the next, we have all settled into a kind of melancholy that comes with having absolutely no choices in life.

I guess that's not true, I think as I watch a caterpillar maneuver its spiny body over a fallen twig. We decide to get up each morning. Rebuild the fire outside. Eat if we have food. Drink water from the spring. Pee. Shit. Maybe talk, though we don't do that as much as we did over the summer. There's little to talk about, I guess, when you know you have no future.

When I couldn't take the stagnant silences any longer, I started hiking to the asylum, unable to bear our camp's droning existence. Here, on this rock, I spend my days. Sometimes I nap, or I stare at the sky and count the leaves. Mostly I think and remember.

Sometimes Cass joins me, but I think it's mostly to check on me and make sure I'm not planning to off myself. She could just like my titillating company, though I doubt that's the reason.

I think about her now and feel a little warming in my chest. I haven't known her for long—I met her right before I landed in the asylum as a science experiment awaiting certain death—but she's been special to me since I first saw her. Not sure why. Maybe because she was unlike any girl I'd ever come across in my hometown of Baltimore. Who knows? Who really cares?

I wish she was here with me today as oppressive loneliness pushes down on my shoulders, oozes up from the ground, surrounds me as if trying to suffocate me.

I pick up the twig with the caterpillar and study its fat form.

At least I'm not in the asylum.

"Count your blessings," I say to the caterpillar. "It could always be worse."

I snort and lay the twig down on the rock beside me. *It* could *be worse*, I think, *but this is still pretty damned bad.*

My sigh is heavy and loud. I sit on that rock, waiting for time to pass, waiting for something to change, though I know it won't. We are in a self-imposed exile at my grandfather's old cabin, deep in these woods. And there is nowhere for us to go from here.

When I hear footsteps, I don't turn, knowing without looking that it's Cass.

She scrambles onto the rock and claims her place by my side. Cass is a girl of few words, and I appreciate her silence. Today, though, she has something on her mind.

"Shaun?" she asks, her voice hoarse from the rare use of it.

I feel her eyes on my face, but I don't look at her. She knows I'm listening, so there's no need to respond.

"I'm worried about you."

I didn't expect that. "Why?" The word comes out croaky and dry, so I clear my throat, and ask again, "Why?"

"You've been coming here every day for months. You're staying longer, isolating yourself away from the camp—away from us. You hardly talk, eat, or help out. You seem more withdrawn with every passing day."

All of those things are true, so I don't answer.

"Should I be worried?" she presses.

I snort my answer, staring down at the asylum. I suspect it's only late afternoon, but considering the time of year and the vast height of this forest, it'll probably get dark soon. It feels like bedtime even though most people are probably just getting home from school or work. Well, most people save for those around here, because there are no schoolkids or workers here.

The Agency made sure of that.

The asylum below me is as quiet today as it's been since the day I started hiking to this rock. I don't see cars or vans or people. I don't even see animals. This building, and the town that surrounds it, is as dead, proverbially, as we are.

What happened to the Agency? To Dr. Esther Richter and Cass's father, Cyrus Rutherford?

What happened to all those teens who were drugged and kept

inside that massive stone building, awaiting lobotomies and death? Stuck like wooden soldiers behind a glass wall, alive, yet not, until they were led away to meet their fate: to become another freshly dug grave in the cemetery behind the building.

Before we made our escape, we found a list of all the teens housed inside that resting monster. We even found our own names and learned that we had been labeled as dead. Since we are not dead, not in the physical sense anyway, I wonder if the other teens aren't quite dead either.

I shake my head in the growing darkness. It doesn't matter. Nothing matters.

"I'm fine," I manage to say.

She waits several moments for me to continue, but when I remain quiet, she says, "Why don't I believe you?"

"Cass." I look at her out of the corner of my eye, see those big gray eyes staring at me, those full lips downturned, that face as pale as a ghost. Her hair, now a few inches long, has grown in darker than I remember it being before Dr. Richter shaved it off. Then it was light brown with deep purple tips. "Don't ask me questions you don't really want the answers to."

"I do want the answer."

"Why?"

"I'm worried about you, plain and simple. I don't know what I'd do without you."

She pauses again, and I think back to that day when we escaped, when I unexpectedly found her unresponsive form lying on a hospital bed in a straitjacket. I wouldn't leave her that day and ended up dragging her body out of that room toward what I thought was freedom. This sure doesn't feel like freedom, but at least we're not dead.

"I don't know what I'd do if you weren't here," she continues, "and I just have this nagging feeling..."

"I'm not going to hurt myself," I say, "if that's what you're afraid of." I don't really care if my tone doesn't reassure her. I have little feeling left in this body of mine. It's like the medicine we were given during our time in the asylum is still in my system, and it ate away all of my ability to feel anything.

"Again, why don't I believe you?"

I shrug. "I don't know, Cass. I just don't know."

"Something is bound to change. It has to."

There is no hope behind her words, but I appreciate her effort anyway. Nothing has changed in the six months since our escape.

We can't go to the authorities. Of the seven of us living at the cabin, five of us are wanted for some crime or other. Personally, I am wanted for murdering my stepfather, Rodger, after he beat my mother one too many times. Besides, the authorities are working with the Agency and would likely just return us to the asylum—or some other sinister situation—where medication, experimental surgery, and death awaits us. Even our parents are in cahoots with the Agency.

There is literally no one we can turn to for help.

I think of my mom briefly, then shove all emotion down with the force of a sledgehammer. It doesn't take as much force anymore, though. The emotions I used to feel when I thought about how my mom was the one who put my name on the Agency's list are gone. But still. She is my mom and all.

"Maybe we'll hike to Canada," I say.

Cass doesn't laugh at my attempt at a joke. We are hundreds and hundreds of miles away from Canada, deep in these rural Appalachian Mountains. There is nowhere to go. No one to turn to.

"Come back with me," she says, pulling my hand into hers. "It's getting dark, and you shouldn't be out here when the sun goes down."

"I don't need a mother," I snap, the memory of my own mother too close to the surface. Maybe the emotion isn't gone after all.

She drops my hand. After pausing for a moment, she slides off the rock. In my peripheral vision, I see her flashlight come on, and I listen as her footsteps carry her away.

I stare down at the asylum.

When I saw my name, *Shaun Treadway*, with the word *dead* beside it on the computer in the office just before our escape, I never dreamed that it was actually true. But, for all intents and purposes, it is. The Agency has managed to kill us without doing a single experiment.

Now that's an accomplishment.

3

I hike back to camp well after dark. The only feeling inside me, other than the cold from the temperature and my increasing ambivalence toward, well, everything, is a blip of gratitude for the flashlight in my hand and for the batteries that Lith, a fellow escapee who I'd met after my own escape, had found inside an empty cabin not too far from my grandfather's cabin.

I'm met with the outdoor fire's bright crackling as I step out of the dense forest. I see my friends sitting around it, as they do every night, on roughly carved wooden stumps. I tick off their names in my head, always doing a count, always desperate to reassure myself that they're safe: Cass, Emily, Ryan, Lith, Traz, and Celexa.

When we—Cass, Emily, Ryan, and I—met Lith, Traz, and Celexa deep in the forest the night of our escape, those were the names they gave us. And even though we know their real names—Carter, James, and Liza—we stick to the nicknames. They just fit somehow. Lith for the lithium he was given. Traz for trazodone. Celexa for, well, Celexa.

If the rest of us adopted similar nicknames, I'd be Dex for Dexedrine since Lith has already claimed lithium. Cass would be Lex for Lexapro, and Emily would be Pax for Paxil. Ryan would just be Ryan. I don't think he was pumped full of drugs by pediatricians and psychiatrists like we were.

All in an attempt to make us "normal" by society's standards.

Such bullshit, I think as I walk forward. I haven't had that kind of medication—for either my bipolar or ADHD diagnoses—since I ended up in the asylum, and I feel fine.

Well, I feel nothing, but I certainly don't have volatile moods or trouble concentrating.

"There you are," Lith calls out. "We were about to send out the cavalry to find you."

Someone snorts.

I ignore them and sit on the stump between Cass and Emily. I don't touch either of them, but their closeness gives me a pinch of comfort. I can sense Emily studying me, but I don't look at her. Something about those big dark eyes of hers and the way they watch me makes me keep my guard up. It's like she's trying to see into my soul, and I don't want her to. She'd be frightened by what she'd find there—or wouldn't find. I don't know which is worse. I briefly wonder if Cass talked to her after how I acted at the rock.

I glance around the rest of the group. Everyone seems to be waiting on the two rabbits that are roasting on the fire. The smell of meat fills the air, giving both Lith and Traz focused, slightly crazed looks in their eyes. The occasional pop and sizzle of fat hitting the flames are the only sounds other than an owl hooting in the distance. It doesn't look like a lot of meat, though when I look around at our scrawny forms, I think it'll likely be enough.

I don't have an appetite anyway.

"Did you see anything interesting today?" Lith asks. His dark hair is hanging in his eyes, and he blows upward, but the strands settle back in the same place. He and Traz and Celexa all have longer hair than the rest of us, having escaped the asylum—and the Agency's penchant for giving every teen in its care a bold, bald look—long before us.

I stare into the fire, mesmerized by the embers that pop and lift and get carried away with the wind. "Nope. Same old thing. There is nothing going on. It's as quiet and empty as it has been since I first started watching it."

"I don't know why you continue to hike down there. What do you think is going to happen?" Celexa asks. She's sitting unusually close to Traz.

"Dunno." Because I don't. But I can't imagine sitting around this campsite every day like they do.

"I think it's good to keep an occasional eye on the place," Lith says, turning the rabbits. "It makes sense to me."

"What do you think he'll find there?" Emily asks. I look up and study her profile, the teardrop tattoo under her eye barely noticeable in the dim light from the fire.

"Who knows?" Lith shrugs. "Life is unpredictable."

"It seems pretty damned predictable nowadays," I mutter, unable to keep my malaise quiet. Normally, I don't have the energy to say much.

"Ooh, he speaks," Traz taunts. His shitty attitude belies his all-American looks.

I don't even bother to glare.

"Shut up, Traz," Emily snaps.

I feel Cass's eyes cut toward Emily, but I keep my own gaze straight ahead. Ever since our escape, there has been a crackling tension between them. This tension alternates with what seems to be a budding bond that I assume comes from the kind of trauma we've all shared. If frenemies are still a thing in the world, I think they would qualify. They get along. Even gravitate toward each other. But still, there is something between them, an animosity that I don't fully understand.

"Rabbits are ready," Lith says, pulling the animals off the fire. He moves to an old wooden table nearby and starts carving up their little carcasses. Ryan gets the jug of water and passes it around our group. We each have our own red cup, found in the same cabin as the batteries. The water comes from a spring not too far up the mountain.

"Get it while it's hot," Lith says, returning to his stump with a plate dismally bereft of heft. His bit of rabbit is gone before I even stand.

"Hungry, Lith?" Celexa teases.

"You know it. Shaun isn't the only one who's been hiking his days away. I'm determined to find every cabin in these woods and to break into all the empty ones, which, as we know, is most of them. We always need more supplies."

"Have you found any evidence of other people?" Emily asks, returning to her stump with her portion of rabbit.

The Agency bribed or forced the locals to move out of this area, so we never expect to see anyone. The locals had been told that the water was contaminated due to mountaintop removal. What the Agency really wanted was privacy to carry out experimental surgeries, like the lobotomy, and to kill those who survived the surgery. Whether or not they were successful.

In short? The Agency's goal was to kill off our entire generation, operating off the belief that by using us to perfect new psychosurgeries for treatment of behavioral and mental health issues and then killing us, the world would eventually become a utopia. It would be like hitting a nationwide reset button. They would start fresh with younger generations, with new surgeries to use on people if they did develop an issue. Mental illness and behavioral issues would be a thing of the past.

"Not yet," Lith answers.

"Be careful," Traz says. "We don't know who's out there or who we can trust."

"Dude, I don't need a warning. I grew up in mountains like these. I know how to move around," Lith says.

Traz shrugs. Those two never react to each other like Traz and I do...or did. I don't react to anything anymore. Actually, the last time I did, Traz and I got into a fight and ended up knocking Celexa into the fire where she burned the hell out of her hands. That was the first time we really understood how alone we were. We couldn't go to the hospital, or to urgent care, or anywhere for help. We had to assume everyone was allied with the Agency.

We knew, then, we were truly on our own, and we have been ever since.

I close my eyes at the horrible memory, open them, and glance at Celexa. She's watching me with a soft smile as if she knows I'm thinking about that night when her hands blistered and her pain was palpable. I don't smile back, but I don't scowl either, so that's something.

"I know," Traz says to placate Lith. "It just had to be said."

The group plunges into silence, as we do every evening when we sit around this fire. Nothing new happens in our lives, so there is nothing new to talk about. The silence feels oppressive, and I walk into the cabin shortly after thanking Lith for the rabbit.

There is only one bed in the cabin, and Ryan sleeps there. We had to leave his twin sister, Renee, behind when we escaped. He's never recovered from that. Since I basically own this cabin, and I was the one who forced Ryan to leave her in the asylum, I feel like the least I can do is give him the bed.

The rest of us plop onto claimed places on the floor. I sleep between Cass and Emily in the main living space where there is a dusty old couch and a coffee table. We set up our blankets by the wall, near the front door. There was no discussion about the three of us sleeping beside each other. It just happened naturally that first night after we escaped the asylum and hasn't changed. Traz and Celexa sleep in the kitchen. Lith, who goes to bed last and wakes up first, sleeps outside.

I'm just getting settled on my blanket when I hear the screen door open and close. Cass sits down beside me.

"What's wrong?" she asks.

"You're starting to sound like a broken record."

"Shaun…"

"What?"

"Something is wrong."

"What could be wrong?"

"I don't know. You're just…different."

"Of course I'm different." I snort at the absurdity of her observation.

"Don't be a smart-ass."

"Sorry."

"I mean, you've been changing over the past month or two. Withdrawing. You're not yourself."

I don't respond. I'm not sure what there is to say anyway. Besides, I don't have the energy to argue or to determine what it could be. Other than the obvious.

"I know it's not my place to say"—she's speaking so quietly that I have to lean toward her to hear—"but I think you should stop watching the asylum. At least for a while."

Her words shock me. Not only does Cass speak little, but I've never heard her give advice, especially not unsolicited. The fact that she's doing so now makes me pause, even though she doesn't give reasons to support her suggestion. I don't respond, but I do start to think maybe I should consider her advice.

In true Cass fashion, she doesn't keep talking. Instead, she settles down beside me, curling onto her side with her back toward me. I'm too tired to try and decide what that means, if anything, even though she often sleeps in the crook of my arm, her head resting on my shoulder. Emily comes in shortly after, and I pretend to sleep, opening my eyes slightly so I can watch her through the narrowed slits. It looks like she studies Cass, lying in the unusual way she is, then me, on my back as usual. She lies down, facing me but without touching me, which is typical for her. Close, but not connected. I stay on my back and don't fall asleep for hours.

4

The next morning I'm up with the sunrise and am the first one outside. Lith is nowhere to be seen, so I start on the fire. It takes a few moments to get it going because everything is damp with mist. The world is ascending from black to gray, which, if the drizzle is any indication, will remain instead of turning to the colors of a sunny day. I hurry to get the fire going before the drizzle turns to rain.

I usually like these early mornings alone by the fire, before the day turns into another repeat of the day before and the one before that. There is promise with a new day that just speaks to me, and it's really the only time I feel anything at all. This morning, I feel strange.

Cass was still lying with her back to me when I woke up this morning. Emily, on the other hand, had crept closer during the night until she was nestled into my side. Her head didn't end up on my shoulder, but it wouldn't have been a stretch to wrap my arm around her, which a part of me yearned to do. What would Cass think if she woke up to see us cuddled together? Emily lying close to me when Cass herself had put distance between us?

I'm not sure understanding Cass or Emily is something I'll ever achieve. What I do understand is that I like the way we sleep, the three of us together, and don't want it to change.

Trying to figure out Cass and Emily isn't why I feel this strangeness, though. I feel unsettled in a way I'm not used to. Restless energy pulses through me, but I'm not sure what I'm supposed to do with it. Walk to the asylum again? Maybe. But I do that every day. Nothing new there. Maybe it's the changing of the seasons. It's well into October here, though, so that doesn't make sense. Maybe it's Cass's fears for me?

Maybe they're mirroring my own?

I don't know what it is, but as I sit there, the misty rain dampening my short hair, the skin on my face, and my threadbare clothes, I start to shiver. The fire is roaring despite the rain, but holding my hands close to the flames doesn't warm me.

Why this sudden restlessness?

I jump to my feet, unable to stay seated a minute longer, feeling like ants are crawling over my skin. I start walking toward the familiar path to the asylum. Thinking of Cass's words, I turn on my heel and take off in a different direction.

No more than a handful of yards into the forest, I veer back to my regular course. It just feels *right.*

I head toward the asylum.

One last time, I tell myself. This is the last time I'll watch the asylum, and then I'll hike somewhere else tomorrow.

Best-laid plans and all that.

• • • • • •

The overcast sky, the early hour, and the cool, light rain turn the world a somber gray. The forest is so dense in some places my path is dark, even though half the leaves have fallen to the ground. The trees grow close together, their limbs intertwining overhead like long, curled, and knotted fingers that reach and grasp until they create a woven tapestry that blocks the rays of the sun.

But I know this way well. Even when I trip over downed limbs, or slide on wet, moldy leaves, I stay upright and keep going. The smell of the earth is pungent in this damp forest—it smells equally of life and decay.

I see a deer. It sees me. It freezes, large black eyes staring, studying, calculating the risk I present. It bolts. Several yards farther, I see a black bear. It's quite a ways off in the distance. I stop, watch it. It stops, watches me.

"Come and get me," I mutter. "I really don't care."

But the bear decides I am not worth its effort and rambles off in the other direction.

I hear the caw of crows, or ravens as I like to think of them, and watch a particularly large one fly off into the distance. Then all I see are half-bare treetops and a weeping sky.

I find my rock and sit on the cool surface, aware of the cool moistness seeping through the rear of my jeans.

And I watch.

• • • • • •

The grounds around the Blackthorn Peak Lunatic Asylum are flat, despite the soaring mountain peaks that jut up all around. The building is massive, sprawling across the land like something from an Edgar Allan Poe story. Hundreds of windows break up the expanse of stone. I know what is behind those windows, or what was there when I was imprisoned, so I try not to focus on them as the nightmares they invite are still too raw.

The asylum is the only building in the small town of Blackthorn Peak that I've ever seen any sort of activity at. I first drove into town last spring, when I was fleeing from the Baltimore police after setting fire to my childhood home with my stepfather in it, and it was more deserted than a ghost town. I remember so clearly the drive down Main Street—the closed shops, the empty sidewalks, the absolute lack of any life, human or animal. Now there is even less activity in the town since our escape and the subsequent closure of the asylum.

I study the grounds as I pull a crab apple out of the pocket of my shirt and take a bite. Along with the main building of the asylum, there is another to its left. I have no idea what is in or was in that building. The small cottage where Cass lived with her father, Cyrus Rutherford, can't be seen from this point, but I know it's there, situated at the edge of the forest on the far side of the main building. There is a cemetery, dating back to the 1800s, behind the main building, with two weather-beaten statues standing guard at the entrance. Beyond that ancient cemetery lies a newer cemetery where hundreds of teen bodies are buried, only marked by freshly turned earth and small flags with numbers that indicate which death the person was out of the long stream of deaths.

I throw the half-eaten apple at a nearby tree, watching as it slams into the bark; small, squishy bits of flesh burst into the air before it plops to the forest floor. I close my mind to thoughts of the cemetery and return my focus to the building down below.

It is so quiet in these mountains that even the sound of the wind meandering through the half-bare trees is loud. I count the different birdsongs I hear, the tunes mournful and desperate, to pass the time while I sit and watch a building void of activity.

It's this sitting, this listening, that allows me to hear the new sounds.

My back straightens. I train my eyes down below and see nothing other than the expected. But I do hear new sounds. Are they truck engines? The sounds are faint and distant and at first hard to identify. They quickly grow, though, until I know for certain that multiple vehicles are coming…from somewhere.

Are they coming to the asylum?

They can't be.

They have to be.

There is nothing else in this town other than the asylum.

The sound of so many vehicles crescendos as the first white van drives on to the grounds.

I slide off the rock and stand, frozen, stunned. Void of breath or thought. Unease creeping toward me.

For as long as we've been in these woods, I have never seen any activity at the asylum. Not even the passing by of a mangy mutt.

My nerves spark and sizzle as if my veins are connected to a live wire.

The first white van is followed by another and then another. They pull on to the grounds, a long white snake, and drive to the left around the aged angel fountain that rests in the middle of the grounds. There is no discernable label or advertisement. They are nondescript white vans, shiny and clean. Nothing like the handyman vans I saw around Baltimore.

There are at least thirty. The first ten veer toward the back of the redbrick building and disappear from my sight. The others park.

I glance at the clock tower that juts up above the center of the asylum's main entrance. The clock has been stopped since the day I arrived back in the spring, both long black hands hanging woefully at the number six.

My heart skips a beat as I realize the clock is working. The black hands have moved, revealing the time is 7:25 a.m.

"Oh no." The words come out in a guttural burst of fear. Even though there is no way my voice can carry all the way down to the asylum, I clamp my lips closed and slide to the nearest tree to take cover. I peek around the rough bark.

A man gets out of the driver's seat of the first van, and suddenly, all the driver's side doors open, and the drivers exit. Each wears a white uniform, resembling scrubs or painters' clothing.

A moment later, the passenger side doors open along the line of vans and out step people who look like orderlies, dressed in the brown scrubs I know all too well from my time in the asylum. Gibbon, Dr. Richter's assistant, wore scrubs like that. As did every single teenager held there.

Terror makes my stomach churn, creating a dark pit right behind my belly button.

I can hear the van doors slamming shut, creating loud popping sounds even at this distance. Then I hear a slow screeching kind of sound. At first, I'm not sure what it is, then I realize it's the sliding doors of the vans. My breath catches, and that dark pit in my stomach balloons. I don't want to see what comes out of the vans. I know this with every fiber of my being.

"No," I whisper, clutching the tree so hard the bark cuts into my palms.

All too soon, my fears are confirmed. Teenagers exit the vans. They don't spill out like you'd expect teens to do—talking, fighting, laughing, yelling. No, they are dead silent. How can I tell? The sound of the idling engines has stopped. Even the forest wind is quiet. It's as if the entire world is holding its breath.

The teens exit the vans like robots, their motions stiff and jerky. Their heads remain level and forward-facing. Hands by their sides.

Nearly a hundred teens exit the vans. It's far too easy to see that they move with the telltale sign of being medicated into a coma-like state, much like I was, like the others were. It's the most effective way to control this many teens. Dressed in matching brown scrubs and blaringly white sneakers that will never experience scuff or dirt, they all have completely bald heads.

That black ball pushes against my throat, and I swallow against the urge to vomit.

I know that medication all too well. Dr. Esther Richter used it on those of us in the asylum to leave us, for all intents and purposes, alive and breathing, but comatose as we waited. What were we waiting for?

Lobotomy and death.

With nauseating precision, the teens walk in unison toward the asylum where they line up against the wall, facing the entrance.

That pit in my stomach churns, and I feel bile rise in my throat. I cough into my fist and force myself to watch.

I hold my breath, willing the vomit that feels like burning acid in my throat to stay at bay. It's like watching a deadly train wreck. I cannot tear my eyes away.

"Shaun?"

I whip around.

My heart pounds in my chest, my eyes wide, surveying the threat. I'm instantly catapulted back to that day when I dashed into the asylum, chasing Cass's screams, and was plunged into darkness. I couldn't find her—I couldn't even see my hand in front of my face. I also heard nothing…until the whispers started, repeating my name over and over, like a call to arms or a siren song. *Shaun. Shaun. Shaun.* After that, I woke up in a straitjacket and found myself chained to the floor with a maniacal doctor wanting to root around in my brain with a hammer and ice pick.

It takes several moments to recognize that Cass is standing several yards away, and she is the one who whispered my name.

She holds back, as if she knows not to come too close until I've regained my senses. She watches me. What does she see? My hands clenched, ready to fight. My chest heaving. My skin pale from terror.

"Shaun?" she says again, softer this time. "It's me. Cass." She pauses. "I came to check on you. Are you okay?"

She steps toward me.

I put up a hand asking for a minute as my mind and body struggle to de-escalate. I know enough about psychology to know that I suffer from PTSD. Not that that information matters. We all do, so it's not a badge of honor. It's just what I'm struggling with right now.

Eventually, I straighten. "You scared the shit out of me."

She nods and continues moving toward me, the dead leaves crunching beneath her shoes.

I motion for her to join me.

"What is this?" Her husky voice is barely above a whisper. I glance at her profile and see eyes that are enormous with disbelief, skin that has lost all color.

"I don't know. The vans just arrived. All these teens got out of them and then lined up against the wall. Clearly medicated."

She shivers beside me. I don't offer her comfort, though, and we stand in silence, waiting and watching.

Finally, the doors to the asylum open, and Dr. Esther Richter steps onto the landing.

She's dressed in black slacks, a red top, and a white lab coat. Her bright red-orange hair is unmistakable, even in the overcast light. Following her is a tall, pale, bald man in street clothes.

"Do you recognize him?" Cass whispers.

I shake my head.

Dr. Richter moves down those stone steps, past the two resting dragon sentinels at the bottom, and toward a man in white scrubs. They talk for several minutes before Dr. Richter returns to the landing. She and the tall man hold open the main doors while the teens start to file into the bowels of the asylum. In no time, every teen has disappeared inside, followed by Dr. Richter and the man. The doors shut behind them.

Out of my peripheral vision, I see Cass raise her hand to her mouth.

My teeth are clenched, and through that obstruction, I state what we're both thinking.

"They're starting again."

5

If this operation is starting back up, if they are able to bring teens in by the van load and just start right back up, then there's no hope. There is no hope for those of us who escaped. No hope for the teens in the asylum. No hope for anyone, anywhere.

My fear has descended into despondence.

It's time to give up.

I've been fighting for so long—for my mom's life after years of abuse from my stepfather, against other kids in juvie, for survival in the asylum.

When we escaped, I still had fight left in me. I just knew there would be help on the outside, somewhere. That we'd find that help and dismantle this maniacal program. Dr. Richter would be in jail, as would every member of the Agency. Maybe they'd all get the death penalty.

The only thing we found after our escape, though, was another sort of prison: the forest.

This area is so rural and isolated, and since we had no form of transportation, there was nowhere to go. We couldn't just walk to another town. On my drive into Blackthorn Peak, all those months ago, I went miles and miles without seeing any road signs or other towns.

I think of my truck that I drove into town. Where is it? I had parked it outside the asylum when I went to pick up Cass for our date. That night had ended with me being lured into the asylum and drugged. I woke up in a straitjacket, chained to the floor, and never saw my truck again.

Soon after our escape, I snuck out of the forest and over to Main Street where I'd parked it that fateful night. It wasn't there.

Is the Agency using it?

The thought makes me want to cry. I loved that truck. Had worked for two years to be able to afford it.

There was no one else to ask for a ride out of town, or even a car to steal, which was Lith's area of expertise. The Agency had run off all the locals, and thus every vehicle. We were left stranded in the forest surrounding Blackthorn Peak.

When we escaped, we managed to get to my grandfather's cabin and foraged for food in the forest and abandoned cabins along the mountainside. But without transportation or phones, we were, and still are, prisoners.

It's very clear to me now that we will not escape this world we've found ourselves in. We will never escape. Never find help. Never live to adulthood.

We are destined for a life of hiding, or worse—death. Or maybe death will be a welcome relief.

I used to have hope—that faulty notion that makes fools of us all. Now, I know there is no hope.

"Shaun?"

I forgot Cass is by my side.

She slides her hand into mine. Gives my arm a gentle tug. "Are you okay?"

My eyes cut her way and see her brows pursed in bewilderment. Before I bark, "No, of course I'm not okay," I clench my teeth together and just stare at her. Unable to answer, I return my gaze to the asylum. I wish she'd stop asking me that.

"Something will change…at some point. It has to," she says, reaching for any hope she can muster.

"I'm sure that's true," I say, my tone deadpan. "What will change is that they'll get tired of letting us live up in these mountains, and they'll come and find us. Then put us back"—I point at the massive building—"there."

I turn my head to study her. Desperate to see if she gets it—the truth. We are still prisoners, and we always will be. Until they decide to kill us.

She is studying me in turn, something unsaid wafting from her closed lips and challenging eyes. The dark patches beneath those eyes give her such a vulnerable look that I find it hard not to wrap her up in a blanket and shield her with my body from...everything.

Yet I can shield her from nothing.

"You've given up." Her words form a statement rather than a question. Or an accusation.

I break our eye contact and turn away from her toward the asylum.

"You have. You've given up." Her voice comes from behind me now. "Why?"

"Because there's no point. Don't you get it? We can't escape—" My throat slams closed, and I force myself to swallow several times. I throw my hand out toward the asylum, not bothering to see if she is following my movements or my gaze. What else is there to look at anyway? The asylum is the only thing that matters. That building. When will we end up back in there, held against our will? The Agency runs this operation. There is no way to escape the Agency or the asylum.

"Did you say something?" she asks.

I try to recall if I've spoken aloud. I don't know and don't care. "There is no escape," I say. "Surely you know this by now. It's October. Going to be full-on winter soon. We have shelter, but how long before our food runs out? Before there are no animals left to hunt, and all the abandoned cabins have been pillaged? I'm sure it gets awfully cold here in these mountains and probably snows. A lot. We don't have winter clothing, winter boots."

"God, could you sound more negative?" She moves into my field of vision, not obstructing my view of the asylum but standing in a way that forces my eyes to choose which to focus on: the asylum or her. "Shaun, look at me."

With effort, I do.

"You brought us this far, helped us escape, demanded I not be left behind, and for what? To just give up and die here in this lonely forest? To let the Agency get ahold of you again and finally fulfill their desire to kill you? To kill all of us?"

I avert my eyes, but she sidesteps back into my field of vision. "This is not the Shaun I know."

Anger swells in my chest. "Saving the world is not my responsibility."

She blanches. "What's happened to you?"

"What's happened to me? How can you ask that?" I grab her shoulders. Lean close to her face. "There is no hope here, Cass. None. You're not naïve. I know you know this."

"There's always hope."

I snort and release her arms. "Yeah. Right. What exactly does hope look like to you? Starvation? Lobotomy? Freezing to death?"

She shakes her head, glancing to the ground as if answers can be found there.

We've never gotten angry at each other before. Mostly we exist in companionable silence. But I can't ignore the proof right in front of us. Those of us who escaped the asylum—me, Cass, Emily, Ryan, Lith, Traz, and Celexa—have zero chance of survival. The Agency hasn't come looking for us yet, likely because they know we are no threat. We've been hiding out in this forest since our escape months ago. Has anyone come looking for us? No. Why not?

"There is no hope here," I state firmly. "None. And I don't have the energy to pretend that there is anymore. I'm not the champion here. Not yours, theirs"—I point at the path toward the cabin—"or my own. Don't ask of me what I can't give. Because I wouldn't try to give it anyway."

She's watching me again, her eyes burning into me.

I continue, "We can't...we can't compete with this, with the Agency. We have to assume they have every social worker, police officer, doctor, and anyone else who might help a teenager on their payroll. And guess what?" Anger is rising in me like lava. "I'm wanted for *murder*. Do you think I have anywhere else to go? Even if there is an adult out there willing to help, I am wanted for murder, Cass. Do you understand that? If they find me, I could be charged as an adult. We're talking life in prison. The death penalty."

I shove my hand through my inch-long hair and tug at the ends.

"There's no hope. Not for me. They'll find us eventually. Or they already know where we are and are just waiting until the right time to get us. If they don't bother to do that, then we'll die here on this mountain, having wasted away. They could always send the police to arrest me. Don't forget Emily is also wanted for manslaughter. Traz for statutory rape. Lith for grand theft, or whatever it was he did, and Celexa for dealing. None of us are innocent. Well, except maybe you and Ryan."

"I can't believe you."

"Why not?" I snap. "What can't you possibly believe?"

Her gray eyes narrow. "I'll wait for you back at the camp."

She stomps away.

There is no part of me that wants to run after her, to console her. There's no point in prolonging the inevitable: we've lost. They're revamping the program, filling that massive building with enough teenagers to supply an endless stream of specimens.

But Dr. Richter had said—I can't remember if it was to me or if I just overheard—that the lobotomy was almost ready for mainstream use. That means they shouldn't need more specimens. So those teens, who were just led into that massive building, aren't there to be guinea pigs in the name of psychosurgical research but to die. Plain and simple.

Their bodies will be laid to rest in the cemetery behind the asylum, along with the bodies already there. Gathered, killed, buried. Boom. Boom. Boom.

How can we compete against that? We have no money, barely enough food, no way to leave. No one to talk to or solicit help from. We have no future. Why pretend otherwise?

I step toward the asylum, ignoring the sound of Cass's feet crunching the dead leaves as she walks away.

The clock reads ten minutes after nine now. The drizzle has

turned to cool rain, and the sound of millions of drops hitting millions of leaves creates a sort of drumming sound across the vast forest.

Time passes, and the cold sets in. My nose starts to run, and my fingertips have gone numb. Just as I am about to turn and leave, I see movement at the entrance to the asylum; one of the heavy black doors at the entrance is swinging open.

Out steps a long and lean giraffe-esque figure. The shocking orange hair is unmistakable.

The door swings closed behind her. She doesn't walk down the concrete steps to the lawn. Rather, she stands as still as an obelisk and gazes outward. Then, with a smooth swing of her long neck, her head pivots toward the right, toward the mountains that surround this side of the asylum, toward where I stand hidden in the millions of trees that cover this landscape. There is no way she can see me standing here. I can barely see her from this distance, and that's only thanks to the light that hangs over her head.

But her head pivots, and when it stops, a cold shiver marches down my spine, and I know it's not from the cold. I can't see her face, but I don't need to. She and I are intertwined somehow, and I can feel energy, dark and charged, emanating off her like a vibration. Her hands hang by her sides until one arm raises, the one closest to the mountains. And she waves. As if she can see me. As if she knows I am here watching her.

She can't possibly see me.

There's no way. It is physically impossible for the human eye to pick out my thin body in these masses of trees and from this distance.

Yet she waves. And the terror is so real and so potent, my knees buckle and I fall to them on the dank forest floor. As quickly as the terror comes, it subsides, and I collapse to the ground, curling into myself, suddenly feeling nothing.

Why would I? It's only a matter of time. There is no escaping the asylum. The Agency. Death.

There is no hope.

There is no hope.

There. Is. No. Hope.

The words play in my mind like a broken record. I don't even bother to try to change them, to distract myself, to contradict. It's only a matter of time until…

Until what?

Until the end.

I close my eyes.

6

Thus Speaks Cassidy Rutherford

• • • • • •

I'm standing in the shadows, between a handful of trees, watching Shaun watch the asylum. I never left this lookout point he's claimed, but he doesn't know that. He seems so lost in thought or memories or, more likely, nightmares that I doubt he's aware of anything other than that sinister and ominous building down below. In my opinion he's become obsessed with the asylum, hiking to it on a daily basis. And for what?

Yes, the Agency seems to have started back up. But we've managed to exist for six months out here in the wild. So what if we have to move to a new location or hike farther away?

I refuse to believe that it's time for us to surrender and die.

It's ironic that I am the one holding on to hope when I am the one, out of all of us, who has tried to take my own life. But that was then, and I'm not the same girl anymore.

Shaun has changed in many ways. I know it's not my place to state that fact, especially since I didn't really know him before he landed in the asylum. But he was different before that, and he was different after. He was full of life, and fight, and swagger. A real-life Robin Hood. He could do anything.

It wasn't until about six weeks after our escape that he started to change.

Now he barely sleeps, even though he often goes to bed early.

He barely eats. That's no surprise. Our diets are meager here in this remote wilderness, and growing more so every day as supplies dwindle.

He barely talks. He used to have passion, especially when it came to helping others. He wouldn't leave the asylum, for God's sake, if he couldn't take me with him, putting not only his life at risk but Emily and Ryan's as well.

It's as if a light has dimmed in him, to the point of teetering on extinction.

I study his back. His shoulders are hunched in a way I don't recall seeing during that brief time I knew him before he was locked up in the asylum. I remember him being tall, broad-shouldered, proud, a little defiant. A shock of dark red hair and freckles gave him a Shaun White look. I never asked him if anyone had told him that he looks like the famous snowboarder. Somehow, considering all that has happened, it seems irrelevant. What isn't irrelevant is how much he's changed.

I'm worried about him.

Not only are his shoulders stooped, he is too thin. Of course, we all are, but he was built like a swimmer: slim yet powerful. Now he's just skinny, hollowed out in the torso. That's what a diet of foraged food and beans will do. Occasionally, Lith or Traz kill a rabbit or squirrel. Once a deer. Mostly, we barely eat. When we do have food, Shaun barely eats.

Something has changed in him beyond his physical appearance.

When he first stumbled upon the asylum, he'd been fleeing the Baltimore police after killing his stepfather. But he didn't seem afraid. He'd been self-assured, confident. Not cocky, but not quite *not* cocky either. Self-righteous in what he'd done.

Now he seems like not even a shadow of his former self. He's just a shadow.

The asylum didn't take his physical life, but it definitely took something. His passion, maybe. Certainly, his confidence. His fire, outrage. His Robin Hood complex. All of those things that were there before the asylum, and briefly after our escape, are gone now.

There is no fire behind those blue eyes. No fight.

Shaun was made to fight for others—the underdogs, the weaker, the less fortunate. Now he can't seem to even fight for himself.

He's given up. He doesn't think we'll survive much longer. He might have a point. How can we continue to go on like this?

But something will happen. I choose to believe that we'll get out of this diabolical mess one way or another. At night I dream about the FBI or the CIA or the state police coming to our rescue. Maybe the men on horseback in Canada. Someone, anyone, coming to our rescue, freeing us and all the other teenagers, and putting Dr. Richter and everyone at the Agency behind bars.

I know this would include my dad, Cyrus Rutherford, who used to work for the Agency. I didn't know about his personal connection to the asylum and its purpose when we lived in the cottage, though I could tell something strange was going on with him; that something strange was going on within those walls. But my dad was a strange man. I often wonder what he would've been like had he, himself, not been lobotomized as a small boy by Dr. Richter's famous grandfather.

Maybe he would've been a loving and attentive father instead of a punitive and detached one. Maybe he would have seen how horrific lobotomies are if he hadn't been convinced that the one he'd been given had improved his life. Maybe he'd have seen the importance of life and not death, of help and not punishment, of love and not fear.

I wish my mother was alive. I wish I had a normal father. I don't even know where he is—haven't seen him since we escaped. He likely wouldn't want to see me anyway. I was never anything but a disappointment to him. A painful reminder of my mother and all the ways she'd hurt him.

Shutting down these thoughts, I focus on Shaun.

He has moved forward a few paces, toward the asylum. It's well into morning now, but still gray and gloomy, and the mist is growing thicker through the forest. I can't see the asylum from here, but I can tell he's watching it. Like he always is.

Suddenly, something changes in his posture. Something changes in the air. I don't know why. I can't see anything but Shaun, but the energy has suddenly sparked and become charged like a live wire.

Shaun's shoulders tense. What does he see? Just as I start to move to rejoin him, he falls to his knees, stays there a beat, and then crumbles to the ground. He coils into a fetal position, so tightly wrapped around himself that I can't see his face.

I dart forward, putting my arms around his cold and rigid body.

"Leave me alone." His words are guttural and coarse, barely audible.

"What did you say?" I ask, leaning forward so my ear is closer to his mouth.

He's shaking all over. "Leave me alone," he says again. "I want to just die. Die here. Die now."

"I'm not leaving you here to die, Shaun Treadway." I pause, lift my gaze, and look around. Glance down at the asylum that is illuminated by the industrial freestanding lights. "What happened? Did you see something?"

"Dr. Richter."

"You saw Dr. Richter again?"

"She saw me."

"That's impossible. She couldn't see you this far away."

"She did. She waved."

He lifts his head, his features contorted into an agony that makes my heart hurt. Stoic, bold, and brave Shaun is weeping. Shaun is weeping. I hold him close as he cries, wondering if the bipolar psychosis he always said he didn't have is actually happening.

There's no way the doctor could see him from this far away.

7

I'm shivering even though I'm wrapped in a blanket by the fire. I don't remember hiking back to camp or finding my way to this stump. Nor do I remember someone wrapping me in a blanket or putting a cup of water in my hands. I don't remember someone restarting the fire or coaxing its flames higher, but they must have, trying to ward off the encroaching cold that stems from more than the temperature.

The fire. Flames pop and crackle. The size of it is bigger than we've ever allowed ourselves to have. Smoke billows and swirls high into the gloomy sky.

The fire. The smoke.

I jump to my feet. "Stop! Put the fire out," I yell. I stamp the burning embers. "Fools! Do you want them to find us?"

"Shaun, what the hell, man?" Traz comes running from behind the cabin, followed by Celexa.

"Fools," I scream again.

Cass jumps to her feet from the stump beside me. "Shaun."

Emily darts out of the cabin. Ryan walks out behind her.

I'm suddenly yanked off my feet, and I know, in the back of my mind, that it must be Lith. The others are standing before me.

I thrash. "Fools," I keep saying over and over. "You're all fools."

"What the hell is going on here?" Traz demands.

My breath comes in panicked bursts. Lith's grasp is tight, but I fight anyway. "Put it out!"

Tears and snot and sweat cover my face.

"Shaun?" Cass moves in front of me. "Shaun, look at me. You're in shock." She puts her hands on my face. I see three of her and struggle to get my eyes to focus.

Emily looks at Cass. "Did something happen during his hike?"

"Unfortunately, yes. I was going to give Shaun a minute to regroup before I called you all over here," Cass answers.

Lith is holding me so tight I can barely breathe.

"The asylum. It's up and running again. But what caused this"—Cass glances at me—"is that Dr. Richter waved at him. Or that's what he said, though there's no way she could see us from that distance—she was standing on the landing at the entrance to the asylum. He collapsed after that, though, and I finally managed to get him to walk back here. He's been unresponsive since. Until now."

"That's not possible," Emily says. "None of it."

"The asylum is open again?" Celexa asks, her eyes wide with fear.

"Tell us exactly what happened," Traz says, trying to exert his imaginary authority.

I hear my own breath, and I sound like a bull. "Let me go," I snap, trying to shake Lith off.

Traz steps close, getting in my face. "Not till you calm down. You're going to set yourself on fire, dumbass."

Lith's arms are like iron clamps, but I thrash anyway. "Call me a dumbass again, pretty boy, and I'll feed you to the dogs." Spittle shoots out of my mouth with my words.

Anger flashes across Traz's face. For several moments we glare at each other. Eventually, he throws his hands up and steps back.

"You gonna quit trying to jump into the fire?" Lith asks.

With only a grunt for an answer, he slowly releases his hold, and I jump away.

"You stupid fools." I'm back in control now, my senses restored. I feel like I've been dissociating and am now back to reality—reality that feels like a gut punch.

"Shaun, just explain what's going on, man," Lith says. He stands between me and the fire, arms crossed. Lith is a big guy, lean but muscular, even with our pitiful food supply, and he exudes a hostile undertone that leaves me glad we're friends. I focus on his face and try to gather my thoughts.

"The asylum," I say.

"What about it?" Lith asks.

I look at the group around me, their expressions afraid, weary, irritated, angry. Ryan's is pained because any time the asylum is mentioned, he thinks of his sister, Renee, who we left behind when we escaped.

"They're at it again," I say, still not quite able to get my brain to accept what I saw.

"At it again?" Celexa asks, moving closer to Traz's side.

"I saw vans," I say. "Ten went around the red building and out of sight. Twenty parked in front of the red building, facing the asylum."

They wait in silence for me to gather my thoughts and put them into words. Eventually, I continue, "Dozens of teens piled out of these vans under armed guard. At least a hundred."

"And where did the teens go?" Emily asks, her words sounding like she's holding her breath, preparing herself for the words I'm about to speak.

"Into the asylum."

Silence descends over our group. I stare into the fire, at the burning wood that had only moments ago sent me into a rage. Now, that old familiar void is licking at my rage, threatening me with numbness.

I realize none of these things matter. The asylum. The teens. The fire.

The Agency knows we are hiding in these trees. Dr. Richter's wave said as much. I doubt the big fire tipped them off to anything they didn't already know.

My shoulders drop. My back hunches. I plop down on the stump and put my head in my hands. As quickly as my rage flared, it's been snuffed out.

The group stands frozen for several moments—I don't know how long. They eventually start talking, their voices low, mixed with fear and urgency. No one adds wood to the fire, and soon the flames reduce.

"What do we do?" Emily asks.

"We should move to a new camp," Traz says.

"Move to where?" Celexa asks, sitting on the stump beside me.

"We go anywhere but here," Lith says. "I came across another abandoned cabin about thirty minutes away."

"Won't we have the same problem there?" Emily asks, sitting on the stump to my other side. I glance at her profile while she looks between Traz and Lith. The whites of her eyes are glassy.

Cass rubs my shoulder. I reach out my hand and rest it on her knee, the only comfort I can offer.

They continue to talk. Ryan, as always, stays quiet. Cass, for her part, does too. My focus weaves in and out. At times, I'm listening; at others, I'm lost in my own world.

I can't believe this is my life.

Mom always told me to control my imagination, because I always had such grandiose ideas. Even my imagination couldn't cook up this life.

I don't know if the group has come to any conclusions, but I can't sit there anymore, so I go inside the cabin. It's likely only late afternoon, but facing another minute of this day isn't an option.

I fix my blankets, lie down, and go to sleep. I'm vaguely aware of Cass, then Emily checking on me throughout the evening. I can tell who it is because they each say my name softly, pause for a response, and when I don't give one, go back out the door. I think Ryan comes in at one point and touches my shoulder. I don't wake up enough to respond to any of them.

I sleep the rest of that day, then all that night, and don't wake up until sunrise the next day.

I feel exhausted beyond measure, despite the long slumber, yet restless at the same time. I'm used to my daily hikes to the asylum, getting up and immediately setting off. I don't want to return to the asylum today. No way. But I can't sit here in this camp either, and there's no way I can go back to sleep.

I ease off the floor without waking Emily and Cass, both facing me as they sleep, and step onto the front porch.

Dew is thick on the ground; the autumn air is cold. The mist is heavy on the mountain, and it feels like rain again. I take off in the direction opposite the asylum, with the faint intention of walking and walking and walking and maybe, just maybe, never returning to this cabin. I don't care if I die walking. Get eaten by a bear. Get killed by the elements. Who cares? At least I'm doing something. I'm walking. Walking away.

When I get thirsty, I cup my hands in a stream of spring water. It's frigid and gives me a slight energy boost. I haven't explored this direction before, and I feel almost giddy at coming across this water source. Whereas the hike to the asylum is straight along the side of the mountain to a point where the forest clears enough to see the asylum down below, this hike takes me up the mountain, and I struggle with the ascent. My breath comes in bursts, and it feels like my heart might explode, and I stop often to rest.

The trees grow closely together, blocking any warmth that the sun might offer, though this late in the year the warmth is all but nonexistent. I slip a few times, with the sharp ascent and the dew-moistened ground, but manage to stay upright. I use the trees for stability and sturdy bushes to help me catapult myself up when the incline is too steep.

I reach the mountain peak. There are huge rocks up here that interrupt the heavy tree line. I scramble onto the largest rock, the tip jutting out over a plummet to the bottom. From here, I can see three hundred and sixty-five degrees. What do I see? Trees. Trees. More trees. What don't I see? Towns.

Up here, on top of the world, I feel something I haven't felt in months. The air is so crisp it burns my nostrils, then my lungs. Several deep breaths only exacerbate the rush until I'm light-headed. It's freezing up here, and the cloudy sky doesn't help. What I feel is not fear or isolation, but a little teeny tiny blip of freedom. I feel free.

I relish the feeling. As the sun continues its ascent, it manages to increase the temperature a little. I lie down on the rock and try to make shapes out of the clouds. I don't ever want to leave this spot.

It's well into the afternoon by the time my hollowed-out stomach growls, and I force myself to stand. The sun is still high at the top of this mountain, but I know this area well enough to know that as soon as I start to descend into this thick forest, the rays will quickly become obliterated by treetops and mountain peaks. I slide off the rock and forage for crab apples or blackberries but find nothing.

I have a choice—stay here, hike on, or return to camp.

The thought of returning to the same people in the same spot doing the same thing brings a blackness to my vision and a sour acid to my mouth. I do feel a pinch in my heart when I think of Cass, and then Emily, knowing how worried they'll be if I don't return. But I can't go back there and have my newfound sense of freedom eclipsed, so I rise and start down the other side of the mountain.

It's near twilight by the time I near the base of this mountain, having stopped several more times to rest or to find a water source. The land is starting to flatten. I can see a break in the trees ahead, indicating a possible clearing. The cloudy skies and rain of yesterday are gone, leaving a full moon easing up into the sky—I can just see it peeking over the next mountain—as the sun simultaneously begins to dip behind the tree line.

The world around me descends into a pinkish-gray as I slow my steps, pondering the clearing and what that could mean. *Who* it could mean.

But still I walk on, feeling separate from my body—tingly all over, light-headed, suspended from a sense of reality...suspended from a sense of consequences. Starvation and excursion will do that, I guess.

I pass a flowering plant of moonseeds. I recall Lith's tutelage about what to eat and what not to eat and remember that these are poisonous. I think of Katniss and shove a handful into my pocket.

I will not be put in the asylum again. No matter what.

I hike on.

8

At first, I think I've walked in an arc and have come back around to the asylum. That I've grown delirious and have ended up going in a circle rather than in the opposite direction.

But that can't be. I went up the mountain, down the mountain. Never veering off course.

Still… My body is frozen with sudden terror as flashbacks of that hated building pound my mind. Straitjacket. The "wall." The needles. Gibbon. Owen. Dr. Richter.

Sweat breaks out over my body, and I start to tremble. Then shake.

I blink several times, urging my mind to catch up with my eyes. I am not looking at what I think I'm looking at. I need to focus outward, not inward, and calm my body. Where is the out-of-body feeling I had just moments ago?

I will my hands to raise and rub my eyes.

It's not the asylum, but rather a building made in its likeness, far smaller, but so similar it takes several minutes of blinking to convince my mind that they aren't one and the same.

I use the breathing techniques I was taught in juvie to settle my nervous system. Who knew anything productive would come out of that horrid experience when I was twelve?

Breathe in. I count to five. *Breathe out.* I count to five. Focus on the air filling my lungs, the air leaving them.

I shake my head and feel mostly immersed in the present, and I can fully acknowledge that I am not looking at the asylum.

This building is made from the same beige stone blocks as the asylum, but they are more weathered with a black tint that reminds me of smoke damage. I see no other evidence of fire though. Maybe it's just shadowing caused by this haunting twilight hour.

It has the same imposing entrance—five concrete steps, guarded by dragon sentinels, that lead to double black doors with heavy door knockers shaped like dragons' heads.

It's the same shape as the asylum, with the entrance in the center of the building, then the walls sprawling out from there, to the right and to the left, like wings. If the asylum was a resting dragon, this building would be a bat. I'm not sure it's any less sinister or imposing though.

The windows are the same, but instead of hundreds like in the asylum, there are dozens. Rectangular, thin, seemingly opaque. Bars cover every window.

The grounds around the building are flat but not as expansive as at the asylum. Not as well-kept, as the grass is overgrown and reaches waist-high in some places. The grass sways with the same breeze that brushes over my sweaty face. I feel oddly comforted by this overgrowth. If there was regular activity here, wouldn't it be obvious? A road, maybe. A well-worn path from foot traffic. Maybe I'm being foolish, but I allow myself that blip of comfort anyway.

Barbed wire snakes along the roofline, and I wonder if this building was associated with the asylum in its heyday. Maybe this was where the really psychotic and violent patients were kept. Maybe the criminally insane. Maybe it's just an old prison?

There are no cars or white vans. No red roses, perfectly attended to, like at the asylum. Cass's father, Cyrus, had seemed to care about his roses more than he cared about his own daughter. I remember how much they looked like blood splatters against the walls.

This place looks abandoned.

I thank the gods above that it's still light enough to see before the shadows of night set in.

Am I a fool? My body pulses with the urge to move forward, to explore.

My mind stops me midstep, though. What am I doing? Have I learned nothing after what happened in the asylum?

A glance behind me tells me I can quickly be under cover of the blackened forest if I turn around and run. A glance ahead shows me what appears to be an abandoned building. Why would I want to explore it? Haven't I accumulated enough reasons not to step toward that building?

I've always had a problem with impulsivity and right now is no different.

Curiosity wins over fear, and I start forward, emboldened by the deadly moonseeds in my pocket.

There is no sign of light or life behind those windows, not that that means the building is empty. But I have nothing to risk at this point, and I continue until I am standing in front of the main entrance where the words *Blackthorn Peak Penitentiary* are posted in black iron letters with the year, 1864, listed below. So, this building is thirty-four years newer than the asylum.

I turn full circle and see no other buildings or signs of life. Off to my right is what looks like a path that used to be a road. It's unpaved, but the grass is slightly shorter and bare in patches, indicating a path no longer used. That comforts me. If the ground that leads to this building isn't trampled or crushed, then that means no one is coming here, at least not vans full of people. The rest of the area is surrounded by the mountains, so that is the only way in.

I walk around the building, keeping close to the tree line just in case, and confirm there are no people or vans. The moon continues its ascent, and its rays cast a silver sheen on everything they touch.

After a full search, I stop near the front doors, several yards back. I look to the right, left, up, even down. I calculate the seconds it would take to get to the cover of the forest from where I stand. I finger the moonseeds in my pocket.

I realize my heart rate is only slightly elevated now. Maybe this not caring quality I've adopted is good for the ole blood pressure.

I march up to the front doors and try one of the handles. It doesn't turn. Then I try the one to its left. This handle looks like it's been tampered with and hangs loose from the door. Did someone try to break in? Wouldn't someone with the Agency have a key?

I jiggle then turn the knob. The door swings open.

I pause. Listen. Focus on what I can see in front of me, which, with no artificial lighting inside the walls, isn't much. But it's not completely pitch-dark because of all the windows. I look to the right and left. Nothing. I scan the grounds to both sides and behind me. I look up at the moon and see golden stars starting to peek out. It's a cloudless night, which is rare for this area, and bright, offering me nature's best illumination despite the sun having fully set.

What am I thinking? What am I doing? Fear circles me again, this time like a shroud I want to discard.

I step inside the building. Before I allow the door to close behind me, I prop it open with a rock that rests just outside, allowing moonlight to seep in. In front of me is what looks like a cage built of metal bars, preventing me from moving straight through. It looks like a revolving door, made of tarnished bars that were painted blue, but most of the paint is chipped off. The door is met on each side by floor-to-ceiling bars that jut out to the right and left for a few yards before meeting brown tiled walls.

The revolving door opens into what looks like a small reception area, where I'd bet intakes were done. This room has a door at the back that is opened, allowing me to see across a hallway to what must be an office with another desk straight ahead, sitting directly in front of a window that allows more moonlight to stream in.

I reach out and push against the revolving door to see if it moves. It's the only way into the bowels of this building, and I realize I'm just interested enough, and insane enough, to try it out.

At first it doesn't budge, but with a little more effort, it creaks and starts to jerk around.

I'm comforted by the fact that this doesn't seem to have been used in years. If the Agency was using this building, wouldn't they have restored it to working order, like the asylum?

The creaking turns to a high-pitched squeal, but I'm invested now, my impulsive nature running the show, and push it all the way around. When I come out on the other side, I am standing in the reception area. I stop and listen.

There isn't a sound anywhere.

The silence of this building feels different than the silence in the asylum. That silence was loud somehow—between the moans and groans of the ancient building to the consistent squeak of Gibbon's medicine cart to the rasp of voices those few times someone actually spoke. This silence is more ancient and pervasive. Heavy. This building sounds like no one has been here in decades.

A quick look around shows two plastic chairs to my right, one fallen on its side, one upright. To the left is a bathroom, the door leaning off the top hinges. The floor is covered in dust, cracked tile and plaster, and cobwebs. I peek inside and find a toilet and a sink. I don't check the water.

The reception desk looks ancient, beaten by time and circumstance. The surface is covered with dead bugs, dust, gashes on the surface that look like they came from a knife, and what look like cigarette burns. There is no office chair, and I wonder what happened to it.

The door that opens to the back hallway is laden with deadbolts that run up and down the side. Old school security, I guess. A far cry from the more automated building that I was in during my stint in juvie.

I peek my head around the door frame, glancing up and down that back hallway and see the office straight ahead with prison cells spanning both sides of the hall to the right and left. All the cell doors, with bars similar to those out front, are open. The windows allow in more light than I would have expected, and I appreciate that.

Still not moving forward, I stare into the office. I can see most of it from this vantage point.

On quiet feet, I tiptoe across the hall and confirm there is no one hiding inside. Then I walk down the hallway to my right, peering into the cells on each side. Most are made for one inmate—with one bed, one toilet, one sink. One desk and chair. One window. A few have bunk beds. There are no personal items in any of the cells. I head down the other end of the hall. There is no evidence that anyone has been here. On this floor, at least.

The one and only office must have been the warden's.

I'm very aware that it's odd that I am as comfortable and relaxed as I am, considering what happened to me at the asylum. But I am. Maybe it's the moonseeds, reassuring me that I will never be locked up again. Maybe it's my confidence that this place is empty and has been for a very long time. Maybe it's finally being out of the forest, indoors and alone. Maybe it's being somewhere new when I thought I'd never be somewhere new.

Maybe I'm just a fool.

I step inside the office.

It's a boring room, covered in dust and dead bugs. Metal desk. Wooden chair. I quickly discern that all the files have been cleared out. Two chairs sit opposite the desk, for visitors, I assume, and I envision crying, distressed relatives feeling lower and lower as the warden delivers nothing but negative feedback about their poor, suffering relative turned violent inmate.

Imagination, Shaun.

I walk around the desk and look out the window. The thick tree line keeps the forest dark, but the land leading up to it is nicely lit by the moon. There is no hint of another person.

I take a seat. Feeling particularly full of myself, I prop my feet up on the desk and look around. I listen to the quiet.

9

The static is shrill.

The screech startles me awake. I fall out of the chair, hit the floor hard. I jump to my feet. Dart into the corner.

Where am I?

Where's the danger?

How do I escape?

What is that noise?

It's completely dark outside the window, with dim moonlight filtering in through the cloudy sky. I must've fallen asleep in that chair. How could I be so stupid?

I take quick stock of my surroundings. No one in the office with me. No one outside the window. No one in the reception area.

But that noise? It sounds like a radio or television that can't be tuned. It's coming from close by.

I yank open drawers but find nothing.

The shrill spikes again.

I look under the desk and find a radio taped to the underside. I pull it free from the duct tape and stare at it.

It's black, narrow, and rectangular with an antenna. Like something out of the 1960s.

Why is it turned on?

I lift the radio, maneuver the antenna, and walk around the room. Right at the window, I hear a woman's voice just barely breaking through, though not in complete sentences.

I hear what sounds like a name. *Teagan.* Something about a meeting. Safety. Survival.

I curse because I feel I've missed so much of what is being said.

Maneuvering the antennae in micromovements, I finally hit the right spot for clarity.

"There is a doctor from San Francisco who is known for his interest in bloodletting," the woman's voice is saying. "A common form of this is called leeching. His name is Hans Wolford, and he is sixty-three years old. He had a son who was also a doctor before he was killed in a drive-by shooting in Washington, D.C."

Confusion muddies my brain. What's she talking about? Is this an old broadcast? Like a repeat message from World War II?

My hands shake, and I clutch the radio until my fingertips turn white.

"We are unsure of how far along in his progress he is, but it is safe to assume he is getting victims off the 'list' from the Agency."

Static erupts and abruptly clears.

"We can also assume that the Agency's work is going into Phase II."

Phase II?

I scan the grounds behind the prison. It's dark now, but the full moon casts a yellowish-white sheen on the overgrown grass.

"I've heard of another doctor, this one from New Orleans, who is using similar methods. I don't know if they're working together or if they're just working on variations of similar procedures. This doctor's name is Emerson Waters. Female. Age forty-nine.

"I'm sure you know that the asylum is up and running again," she continues, "as is the research lab in the red building next door to it. Or maybe you don't. I don't know how often you're able to get out. They've ramped things up far quicker and more swiftly than I expected."

She pauses. "Please stay safe, honey. Lay low until I can figure out how to come and get you."

The static breaks through, obscuring her voice. I dart to the other side of the window and fiddle with the antenna again.

"Remember, only contact me if it's an emergency. I'll try to reach out again as soon as possible. I love you."

It's not a World War II message. She's talking about the Agency. She's transmitting in real time. But from where? How?

And who is Teagan?

Where is Teagan?

The radio grows hot in my palm while the rest of my body tingles. With purpose, I plunge into the thick forest.

• • • • • •

As if in a trance, I stare into space. My brain can't process what I just heard. Soon, I've almost convinced myself it was a dream.

At some point, I stand and start to move. I stretch my neck and shoulders. Stretch my arms out wide, all while listening to the pervasive silence. I take a few laps around the desk, then walk into the hall. Listen. Hear nothing and start strolling. I move down each hallway again, imagining them filled with violent prisoners.

I imagine myself locked in a cell, and the image sends a violent shudder through me.

When I was in juvie—after the second time I tried to kill my stepdad, Rodger—it was more like a dorm. I had three roommates, and we were free to move up and down the hall. The hall was locked, of course, but that was only at night. During the day, we could go outside during our allotted time, or to the library. We walked to the cafeteria three times a day. Had sessions, so many sessions, with therapists—both individual and group therapy.

It was no picnic, and I got into several fights—not to mention what assholes the guards were—but it wasn't like adult prison.

If I'm caught, charged, and convicted for Rodger's murder, of which I am one hundred percent guilty, then I'll end up in an adult prison. Like this one. I'm almost eighteen, and Rodger was a cop. I have little doubt they'd try me as an adult because of that simple fact. Would they hand me over to death row?

I think of the moonseeds in my pocket and reach in that dirty fabric to confirm they haven't been squished. They haven't.

I hurry back to the office, suddenly eager to get as far away from those cells as possible. I move through the reception area, through the revolving metal bars, and out into the fresh night air of Blackthorn Peak.

I do a full scan of the area. When I see nothing unexpected or alarming in the darkness, I head off toward the cabin, thankful I remembered a flashlight. I have no idea what time it is, or how long I slept, but I need to get back to the others.

If it's possible we are not alone, that someone somewhere is trying to divulge useful information, then they need to know.

I feel a flicker of *something* deep in my chest, almost too buried to feel, but the ignition of that something is unmistakable.

With purpose, I plunge into the thick forest, the radio in my back pocket.

• • • • • •

"Where the hell have you been?" Traz demands, chest puffed. He's standing in the middle of the yard with Celexa by his side. A jagged hunting knife is clutched in his right hand.

It's likely well after midnight, and I wonder, fleetingly, why Traz and Celexa are still awake.

"Get everyone around the fire," I say, struggling to catch my breath. "Hey!" I shout. "Everyone, come here!"

"Where have you been?" Traz demands again.

"We've been worried sick," Celexa says.

Cass runs out of the cabin, not stopping until she's thrown her arms around me. "Shaun, is everything okay?"

Lith appears from behind the cabin and strolls over. "Dude, where were you?"

"I've found something." I move to the stumps around the fire and sit, catching my breath. "Wake everyone up."

Lith makes quick time turning the dying fire into light and warmth.

Traz marches over. Stands over me. I look up at him with a deliberate look of annoyed impatience.

Emily comes out of the cabin, breaking into a sprint when she sees me. "Shaun, where have you been?"

She sits by my side, and Cass is on my other side. Ryan lingers on the porch while Lith and Celexa settle down. Traz sits last, and only after another puff of his chest and an annoyingly heavy sigh.

Whatever. I roll my eyes. Cass hands me a cup of water, and I drain it.

"What's going on?" Emily asks. The firelight catches her tattoo, casting a shadow that makes her look like she's crying one giant tear.

I look at Cass. Her cheekbones could cut glass, making her mouth appear wider than it used to. The dark circles under her eyes have smudges of black, and I note, for the first time, that she looks like a heroin addict.

Lith appears relaxed, ankle casually resting on his knee. His arms are bent, fingers intertwined and lying on top of his flat stomach. His biceps have grown, if that's even possible with our meager diets. He looks like a fighter, patiently waiting for the right moment to strike. Someone you wouldn't want to meet in a back alley. The "resting smirk face" only adds to his air of danger. He's the last person you'd want to get into a bar fight with.

Traz is Traz, and I don't even bother to look at him.

Celexa, by Traz's side as usual, is chewing the side of her lip, and I'm struck by how muscular she's grown. There is a clear difference between those who stay close to the cabin, who are just wasting away, and those who are out hunting and hiking.

"Well?" Traz snaps. "Some of us would like to go to sleep."

"I found something." I take a moment to organize my thoughts as this information could be a game changer.

Traz huffs.

Cass puts a hand gently on my knee. "Shaun, what is it?"

I lean my elbows on my knees and look around the group, noting that I have everyone's, including Traz's, rapt attention.

I reach around to my back pocket and pull out the radio.

"Where the hell did you get that?" Traz jumps to his feet.

"I found a place," I say. "A miniature version of the asylum that's off in the other direction. It used to be the state penitentiary."

"You *found* a place?" Traz sneers. "What does that mean?"

Lith's eyes narrow.

Ryan takes one step closer to the group.

"It means, there is an abandoned building that we didn't know existed," I say.

"Did you go into this place?" Emily asks.

"I did. There was zero evidence of anyone being there or having been there any time recently. Except for this." I hold up the radio.

"You idiot, what if that's bugged?" Anger and a healthy dose of fear flash across Traz's features.

I jump to my feet. Hold his gaze. Wait to see if he's going to take this any further.

"Sit down," Celexa says to Traz, tugging his arm, "and let him speak."

When Traz finally clenches his jaw and clamps his lips, I say, "A woman is trying to contact someone through this radio. It was the only thing in the office. I can't imagine it's chance. Strange thing was it didn't seem like anyone was there. Maybe someone is supposed to go there at some point and retrieve the radio. I don't know."

"You stole someone else's radio?" Emily asks. "I don't understand. What did she say?"

I sit on my stump at the same time Traz sits on his.

"It sounds crazy—especially after how isolated we've been—but someone, she sounded like an adult female, is trying to get ahold of someone named Teagan."

"Teagan?" Lith leans forward.

"You know him?" Celexa asks.

"I was in the asylum with a Teagan. I wonder if it's him. He disappeared one day." Lith pauses. "Like so many others did."

"You never saw him again?" Celexa asks.

"No," Lith answers. "I wonder if that's his mother. She was a scientist or something."

"How do you know that?" Traz asks.

Lith shrugs. "Gibbon used to share secrets with me. Remember?"

Lith had done favors for Gibbon of the kind that we don't talk about. He'd get moments of freedom and information during these dalliances while he was in the asylum.

"So, he wasn't in the prison"—Emily turns to face me—"when you went in?"

"No. There was no one on the first floor," I answer. "It was so quiet I didn't explore the other two floors. Just assumed they were empty. I literally heard nothing."

"It's possible he was in there the whole time?" Celexa wonders.

"Anything is possible." I shrug, not wanting to think about the possibility that I was being watched when I thought I was alone.

"He's not going to be happy that you took his lifeline to his mom, you stupid ass," Traz says. "Why would you do that?"

My eyes narrow, and I struggle to keep control of my anger. I do, just barely. "She said something about other procedures being performed across the country. Something about bloodletting."

"That's the same as leeching," Emily says. "It used to be a form of treatment for mental illness back in the day. The medieval day, that is. Drain the blood to drain the sickness."

"Right up there with the lobotomy," Cass offers. "What else did she say?"

"For him to stay safe wherever he was, and that she would dial back in as soon as she could. Or something like that." I shrug.

"Was this a recording?" Emily asks.

"I don't know," I say, "but I don't think so."

"How do you know?" Celexa asks.

I shrug again. "I don't. I mean, I guess it could be a recording."

"What are the chances that this Teagan is alive and living in this prison, and that he has contact with his mother?" Lith wonders. "It's possible, but that would be crazy. It means that not only is there another escapee out there, but an escapee who has contact with the outside world."

The group falls silent for several minutes, all staring at the little black box. Ryan moves forward to stand behind Cass's left shoulder.

"What should we do?" Celexa asks eventually.

"If there's any chance that someone knows what's going on and is sharing information with this Teagan person, then we need to make contact," I say. "We need to go back to the prison, maybe even relocate there since Dr. Richter knows our general location, and monitor that radio every day, all day. Maybe even find this Teagan guy."

"Relocate?" Celexa asks. "How do you know it's safe?"

"We're not going anywhere," Traz snaps, full of authority.

"I did a thorough search of the first floor and the grounds surrounding the place. There was no evidence of foot or vehicle traffic. The area is overgrown and dilapidated," I say. "We just need to search the top two floors and basement if there is one. I'm telling you, no one has been there. Maybe this Teagan guy, but that's one person. A mass of people is not going in and out of that building. Nothing like at the asylum."

Traz snorts. "The first floor? We were held on the third floor of the asylum. Did it never occur to you that something could be going on in the rest of the building? That it was a trap?" He stands slowly, unfolding his tall frame until he's upright with arms flexed. "You're such a dumbass."

I shoot to my feet again and have his hole-filled shirt in my fist before he can react. "Shut the fuck up. This is the first possible breakthrough we've had in months." No one moves to pull me away. "So, sit down, and shut. The. Fuck. Up." I release his shirt with a push.

He hesitates, then throws his hands up. "Whatever," Traz mutters, and though he doesn't sit, he doesn't say another word.

"It does sound risky," Lith says neutrally. "Before we move camp, let's make sure that it isn't a trap. I'm happy to go with you when the sun comes up to scout the scene."

"That makes sense," Emily says. "But I don't think I could go. Even the thought of being near another building makes my skin crawl." A visible shudder runs through her body.

"Maybe just me and Lith go. Keep it to a smaller party and then report back. It'll be less threatening if this Teagan guy happens to be there."

I scan the group. Cass watches me with serious eyes. I see concern there, and fear. Eventually, she nods.

"That makes sense," Celexa says. "I agree with Emily that I don't think I can willingly go back into any sort of prison or building or anything that remotely resembles the asylum. But I'm happy to gather weapons and supplies for the two of you."

We wait for Traz's response, and I pray he doesn't offer to go too. He doesn't. Instead, he says, "You'll leave at sunup."

I roll my eyes. Always trying to exert control. But that buried spark in my chest I first felt at the prison is pulsating, and I'm so eager to get back there that I don't rise to the bait.

Lith is watching me. I meet his gaze. We offer each other a brief nod.

"That's settled, then," Traz states. "Go in the morning. Explore this building. Hike back in the evening. We'll want a report ASAP."

Neither Lith nor I respond to Traz. We just walk off a short distance and start planning.

10

"Want to go for a walk?" I ask Cass after Lith and I are done talking.

Emily is talking to Ryan by the porch, but I can feel her eyes keeping tabs on me. I'm not in a relationship with either her or Cass, though I have kissed Emily. One night after we'd just escaped the asylum, she confessed she'd never been kissed and asked me to kiss her. And I did. We thought we were looking death in the eye at that point, and it was important that she get her wish. It certainly was no hardship.

Right now, I want to kiss Cass, whom I've never kissed. I want to feel alive, take advantage of this sudden sense of life pulsing through me, regardless of how fleeting it's likely to be. It makes me feel bold, and I want to share that with her.

She puts her hand in mine, and we walk off toward the forest, our path illuminated by my flashlight.

"What's going on?" she asks quietly. The only sounds until this moment have been our breath and the crunch of earth beneath our feet.

"I don't know," I say, hedging. "I just feel…a nervous energy, I guess."

"After finding the prison and the radio?"

"That has to be it." And the asylum, Dr. Richter, the feeling that we are standing on the edge of a precipice.

"Makes sense. Several new factors hitting us all at once."

I pull her to a stop deep inside the forest. I lay the flashlight down on the ground and turn to look at her.

She gazes back at me, curiosity making her eyes appear even larger. She looks so vulnerable right now, and I realize I'd do anything to protect her.

Feeling an ancient, forgotten energy beat inside me, I cup her face in my hands. Her brows purse briefly, as if she is wondering what I'm doing, but then her brows relax. A faint smile curves those lips upward.

I kiss her.

The first touch of my lips to hers sends shock waves through me.

She leans into me.

After several soft touches with lips closed, I urge her lips to part and slip my tongue inside her mouth. She meets me halfway as her arms weave around my waist. I feel a gentle pull of my hips toward hers, and I'm more than willing to oblige.

She tastes fresh, like spring water and new leaves, and her mouth is warm. So warm, it's almost hot, which surprises me and makes me melt at the same time.

Emily's mouth was warm too, but she tasted different. Like cinnamon.

I release her face and run my hands over her shoulders and then down her arms until I'm cupping her butt. She pulls me closer still and we deepen the kiss. I pull back and kiss her neck. She allows her head to fall back, giving me more access.

I release her and lie down on the cool earth. She stands above me, gazing down. That soft smile returns, and she lowers herself down on top of me.

The earth is cool against my back. Her body is warm against my front.

I suddenly feel alive in a way I haven't in a year.

The asylum, the prison, the radio—everything—is all but forgotten.

• • • • • •

Lith and I are quiet as we hike. Neither of us slept, so we were able to leave before any hint of sunrise. We stop and drink from the spring we pass.

When we come upon the plant with the moonseeds, I stop.

Lith, a few steps ahead of me, senses I'm no longer following and turns. "What's up?"

"These things. When I hiked here before, I took a pocketful."

"You trying to off yourself?"

"Remember *The Hunger Games*? At the end they decided to take their fate into their own hands versus waiting on the government to kill them. I'll never be a victim of the Agency again, so I pocketed a fistful of these babies when I was out walking yesterday. It's better to be prepared if things go south. I won't be put in that asylum again."

"I thought you said the prison was empty."

"I said it seemed to be, and I still feel pretty confident about that. But there is always a risk, especially in this area." I start plucking the moonseeds off and dropping them into my pocket. "So, I'm taking some, just in case." I raise my brows and hold out my hand. "Want any?"

He strolls forward, grabs a stem, and pops off several of the grapelike fruit. He lifts one to smell it, looks like he's going to lick it, but drops a handful into his pocket.

We set off again and are soon overlooking the overgrown grounds of the Blackthorn Peak Penitentiary.

"It does look abandoned," Lith says.

"We can walk right in, which is crazy."

"Not to mention suspish."

"Be sure to keep those seeds handy."

We go to the front door. As expected, it's unlocked. Out of the corner of my eye, I see Lith lift his homemade knuckles, the tips whittled to a sharp point.

My body is so tense, I feel my insides coil.

We step inside the prison.

It's light outside, any threat of rain staying at bay at least for now, and the sun brightens the interior.

Thank the stars for small blessings.

We pause and listen for several moments. The only sound is Lith's breath just behind my shoulder.

"Come on," I say, leading him through the revolving door,

through the reception area. Just before stepping into the hall, we stop again. Listen. Hear nothing. I lean forward, my eyes focused as I scan to the right and then left, my mind alert. Seeing and hearing nothing, I step into the hall and cross over into the office. I go to the desk and show Lith where I found the radio. He studies the underside of the desk. The air is warm and stagnant in this ancient building. Sweat beads on his forehead. A drop snakes down my back. He straightens and scans the room. Looks out the window. I watch him, silent.

When he pivots back toward me, I turn the radio on and am met with nothing but static. I play around with it for several moments.

"We're here earlier than you were yesterday, right?" Lith asks.

I nod.

"Give it another minute, then turn it off. We can check it every so often, but we don't want to run out the batteries."

"Good point. Let's look around, and we check it after."

Quietly, I allow Lith to lead and follow him down each corridor of the first floor. His weapons are clutched in his hands, fingers white from the pressure. Besides the wooden knuckles, he's carrying a knife, and a chain dangles from his belt loop. His chest is puffed, biceps tense, making him look like a very dangerous man.

I'm glad we're on the same side.

"Is there a basement?" he asks after we've walked through the entire floor.

"Not that I've found. Maybe there's an entrance outside? The stairs at the end of the hall lead upstairs."

We head back toward the center of the building, pausing at each cell, looking for any doors or stairwells that we might've missed. We see nothing.

"Okay," Lith says, standing in the reception area. "I think we can assume there's no basement."

"Let's check out the rest of the building."

We walk to the stairwell and start a slow ascent, keeping our footsteps light and barely audible. I pat the hilt of the knife in my belt loop.

The second floor looks exactly like the first, minus the reception area and office. It's rows of cells, rusted metal doors open. Zero evidence of anyone having been here.

The third floor proves to be the same.

"I do think it's abandoned, at least right now." I study Lith for his reaction.

"That doesn't explain the radio. Someone has been here."

We walk to a window and gaze out at the backyard of the prison.

"You know," I say finally, "for a building that has three floors and cells to fit a hundred people, why don't they have a cafeteria? A kitchen? Where are the showers?"

"That, my man, is a very good question."

"There has to be a basement."

"Has to be," he agrees. "But where?"

"Outside entrance?"

"Did you search outside the building?"

"I did, but I was so focused on looking for evidence of people, it's possible I overlooked something. I vaguely remember a door but can't say for sure."

"Well, what are we waiting for?"

We head outside and turn left. I breathe in deeply, my lungs starved for fresh air. We walk around the side of the building and start down the back of it. Three-quarters of the way down, we come upon a door.

"Why would they have a cafeteria with an outside entrance?" I say out loud, to Lith as much as to myself.

"A form of torture?" Lith guesses. "Have to brave all the elements to get the reward of a maggot-filled bowl of oatmeal?"

"Gross."

There is a way for a chain and padlock to seal the door, but I don't see either.

I push against the door. It squeaks open.

"Bingo," Lith says.

• • • • • •

With breath held and three quiet steps, I ease into the building. I can feel Lith directly behind me, and I am grateful for his presence. Scanning right and left, weapons clutched tightly, I listen as I seek.

I turn toward Lith. Motion for him to prop open the door, which he does with a nearby rock.

It looks like a standard cafeteria. Rows of rectangular tables with attached benches are screwed into the ground. To the far left is what must be the kitchen. From where we're standing, I can see the long counter where the inmates likely filled their trays with delectable treats.

For several minutes, we don't move. We listen. We watch. At one point, Lith turns around, eases open the door, and studies the surrounding area while I continue watching the room. With caution, we move into the room.

We don't speak as we each head in different directions.

Lith takes off to the right, down a hallway with wooden doors. At first glance, it looks like a typical school's hallway. His weapons are raised.

I turn toward the cafeteria, moving toward the kitchen on silent feet, my own weapons raised.

It is, in fact, a kitchen, filled with closed cabinet doors. Someone could, feasibly, be hiding in any of them. I start to open them one by one, braced for an attack with my knife raised.

They're all empty...of people, that is. What they are filled with is food.

I inhale sharply, Lith's name ready to burst out of my mouth in excitement. I catch myself just before and continue to take stock: canned foods, and more than just beans. There are cans of soup—large cans—boxes of pasta, jars of sauce, cans of tuna, crackers, beef jerky, containers of applesauce. I pull a jar of marinara off the shelf. There is no dust on the top.

I turn. Lith is standing on the other side of the counter, watching me with eyes as round as the plates that I find in another cabinet.

There are pots, pans, olive oil, cooking spray, salt, pepper, hot sauce, ketchup, mayo, mustard.

What is this place?

Lith comes to my side, and we stare at each other. I don't know what he's thinking, so I say, "What is going on here?"

"Check the expiration date on the pastas, and I'll check the cans," Lith says. "If these expired years ago, then there's no reason to think someone is bringing fresh supplies here."

I already know the answer before we each confirm it. The expiration dates are a year and more in the future. Someone has stocked this kitchen recently.

"Holy shit," Lith says. "What have we stumbled on?"

"What did you find in the rooms down the hall?"

"There's one room with a door closed. Let's check it out together."

I hesitate to leave the kitchen. After months of starvation, stepping away from this food is more difficult than I'm prepared to admit. Eventually, I follow, though not before grabbing a chocolate chip granola bar and another one for Lith.

One room is large, like a small conference room. The others are the size of classrooms, reminding me of the rooms we had group therapy in when I was in juvie. Then there's one more room, the door closed.

We exchange glances. Lith counts down from three with his fingers, not making a noise.

He pushes the door open.

There is a desk straight ahead. And a guy standing behind it. "Can I help you?"

11

I gasp. Adrenaline shoots through me. Time seems to stop.

We haven't seen another person in months, other than that day down at the asylum, that is.

I listen for the sound of footsteps, of an ambush from others unseen.

I hear nothing but Lith's breathing.

Standing behind the desk, arms crossed and focus intense, is a young man. His sandy hair has a military cut, and though he's shorter than me or Lith, he's muscular. Built like a tank. He's wearing fatigue bottoms with a belt and a beige, well-worn T-shirt.

"Who the hell are you?" I demand.

Lith takes one step forward, weapons raised. Then he lowers them.

"Hey," Lith says. "You're Teagan, right?"

"Who are you?" The other guy studies Lith.

"We were in the asylum together. You *are* Teagan, right?" Lith presses.

He shrugs. "My name is Teagan, yes."

"Is that your mom on the radio?" I blurt out.

Teagan narrows his eyes and refuses to answer.

"Were you here when I was yesterday?" I ask.

"Yes," Teagan replies.

"Did you know..." I pause.

"That you were here?" says Teagan.

I nod.

"Yes," Teagan says. "I can't afford to be lazy."

"Who...how...what?"

Lith nudges my shoulder and whispers, "Spit it out, man."

My brain feels muddled and confused yet alert and focused at the same time. "Was that your mom? If not, who was that woman on the radio? Is there anyone else who dials in with information? Is there help out there? Are you the only one here?"

Teagan shrugs. I don't think it's a shrug of ignorance but of omission. "You answer questions before I answer questions."

"My name is Shaun, and this is Lith," I offer, instantly deciding to trust him. For now.

"Lith?" asks Teagan.

"Short for lithium." Lith must agree. "My real name is Carter Phillips."

"Huh," Teagan says with a slight nod.

"Can you tell us more about what's going on?" I can't quit asking questions. My knife falls to my side. "I mean, we haven't seen anyone in months. I find this place just as the asylum is up and running again, hear your mom or whoever that woman was on the radio, and realize there are people out there—people who might be able to help us. Then we find you here the next day."

"Could you possibly stop word vomiting?" Lith mutters.

Teagan smirks. "Like I said, I need information before I divulge information." He seems strangely relaxed, and I wonder if he has a gun. But by the way his arms are crossed, I don't think he's holding it if he does.

My eyes cut sideways to Lith who looks back at me, and with a barely discernable nod, he prompts me to speak.

"Thanks for the permission," I snap, then start talking. "We escaped from the Blackthorn Peak Lunatic Asylum several months ago."

Teagan does not look surprised.

"We've been hiding in the mountains since then. My grandfather—he's dead now—had a cabin nearby, and we've been staying there. Doing nothing. Literally nothing but surviving. We have no one to turn to. We have nowhere to go, and certainly no way to get there." I shudder at my own acknowledgment of just how dire our situation is.

"Your turn," Lith says.

Teagan looks at me. "How much did you hear yesterday?"

"I heard something about two different doctors performing similar procedures—bloodletting, I think one was called. I heard a woman telling you to be careful."

Please tell me we're not alone. Please. Please. Please.

I'm surprised by the urgency of my internal pleas, as if Teagan has a lifeline to throw to me in my darkest hour. Just when I was starting to understand my grandfather's suicide in these haunted mountains and feeling the inkling of an urge to join him.

"We're pretty much alone," Teagan says, and my knees go weak. "But not completely. The woman on the radio is trying to help. Me, at least. And she knows others who would like to help, who aren't happy with how things are and who are afraid where things might go. But it's complicated. Nothing is ever as easy as simply choosing to do what's right."

"Others who would like to help… Do you mean people who work for the Agency but aren't happy with their mission?" I ask.

Teagan shrugs.

Lith takes a step forward. "Or do you mean parents of these teenagers who are being kidnapped off the streets and used for experiments and then murdered? Are they the ones who aren't happy with what's going on at the Agency? If so, does that mean parents actually know about it? Know the nitty-gritty details?"

My mom put my name on the list. Dr. Richter said so. Did she know what she was doing to me? Where she was sending me?

A vice squeezes my heart, as it does any time I think about my mom.

"No. Not all parents do. In fact, some parents lost their kids to the Agency against their will," Teagan explains.

"How so?" Lith asks.

Teagan shakes his head. "Look, I don't know you. I believe you are who you say you are, but I'm also aware of how fragile my freedom is and how far the Agency's reach is. No more trade secrets, so to speak. Not right now, at least." He looks at me. "Did you return my radio?"

"I did. It's upstairs in the office."

"Thank you," Teagan says. "Please don't take it again."

The way he says *please* makes it sound like less of a request than a threat.

"I won't. But I sure would love to hear more of what that woman has to say," I say.

Teagan doesn't answer, and the three of us stand motionless. My mind is whirling around like birds flying in a circle. I never expected this—to find someone here—and am trying to process it. Trying to keep any hint of hope at bay, but the questions keep swirling. Is there help? Will this woman and these people be our saviors? How soon can they help?

I'm trying to weave through these spinning thoughts to get to my gut instinct, to decide if I feel threatened or safe here with this guy in this prison. And to not get too far ahead of myself. I can't take more disappointment.

Eventually, Teagan claps his hands together and says, "I bet you're hungry, thirsty, and maybe in need of a shower. I"—he mimics a bow—"can provide all three."

"Let's start with the food," Lith says as he strides toward the kitchen.

• • • • • •

We eat crackers with tuna salad—premade from a package like kids used to carry in their lunch boxes—a bag of pretzels with peanut butter, beef jerky, and as much water as we want. My stomach starts hurting long before I stop gorging, and I wonder if I'll just puke it all up. *If I do*, I think as I look around at the filled cabinets, *I'll just do it all over again.*

"How do you get these supplies?" I ask, rubbing my distended stomach.

Teagan looks at me, expressionless, before answering, "Again, and I hate to sound like a broken record, but I don't know you two at all. I'm not divulging any more information. I think you're who you say you are, but I can't take the risk that you're spies."

"I get you don't trust us," I say, impatient. "No one seems to be able to trust anyone around here, but you gotta give us something. It's possible we're all telling the truth, that we're who we say we are, came from where we said we did, and can work together."

When he doesn't answer, Lith leans forward. "We're asking you to trust us, but how do we know we can trust you? Are *you* working for the Agency?"

"I promise you," Teagan says, his blue eyes glowing with seriousness, "that I am not connected with the Agency in any way other than I used to be on their list and was in their asylum."

After several minutes pass, Teagan shakes his head, as if shaking away the memories. I know that reaction all too well. All of us react that way on a regular basis. A memory is triggered. A dissociation happens. A struggle to come back to the present occurs.

"Shaun and I, and those back at our camp, were all in the asylum as well. We all escaped before they—Dr. Richter—could perform lobotomies on us. Before they could kill us. Like Shaun said, we've just been hiding out in the forest since."

Teagan nods. "I escaped several months ago."

"How?" I ask.

Teagan shakes his head. "Not yet. Let's just stick with the fact that I did. Thank goodness I have this place. I know it's hard to believe, but no one comes here. Not once, before the two of you, has someone shown up here. I don't get it, but I don't look a gift horse in the mouth either."

"Where are you from?" Lith asks.

Teagan says, "Maryland."

"Baltimore?" The word pops out of my mouth.

Just as I think he's about to say that, yes, he's from Baltimore, Teagan shakes his head. "No. Lancaster County. Amish country."

"You're Amish?" Lith asks.

Those blue eyes plant on Lith. "No."

Lith shrugs.

"How did you end up here?" I ask.

"Tell me about how you escaped and about those who escaped with you," Teagan says instead of answering. "I believe you mentioned others at your camp. How many of you are there?"

Lith and I glance at each other. He shrugs again, and I start talking. Because, why not? It's clear that if we want answers from this guy, we have to give information.

"There are seven of us. I escaped with three others. We ran out the front door, into the forest behind the asylum, and through the cemetery. Deep in the forest, we ran into Lith and his two friends, Traz and Celexa."

"What is up with these names?" asks Teagan.

Lith smirks. "Nicknames from the meds they used to pump into us. It was more irony in the beginning, and also a way to maintain some secrecy as we got to know each other, but it just stuck. I was given a bipolar diagnosis for some reason. I wasn't manic or depressed. But they saw fit to force me to take these medicines—my pediatrician, my mom, the school. I haven't taken a pill in over a year, so clearly their diagnosis was off the mark."

Lith falls quiet for a minute, his eyes taking on that distant look. He shudders, returns to us, and says, "I still call Shaun and his friends by their names, though, because that was how they introduced themselves to us, and they call each other by their real names." He looks at me. "Would you prefer to be called Dex?"

"Dex for Dexedrine?" Teagan asks. "ADHD?"

"Yeah. I could've been called Lith as well, because for some reason I was given that diagnosis and medication like Lith was. Maybe because my mom is bipolar, they assumed I was too. Who the hell knows? Sometimes I think these doctors just like to pump kids full of meds because they don't know of any other way to control us. Or our parents can't handle us, or we don't conform at school. How about giving us more freedom, more time outside, less school, and less demands? Anyway, the ADHD diagnosis was probably more accurate, but school just sucks. It's boring and trite and just a slog fest. Who doesn't have trouble concentrating and sitting still for eight hours?"

"Tell us how you really feel." Lith laughs, and Teagan smirks.

"Just call me Shaun," I continue. "We have built a camp at the old cabin my grandfather owned before he died. It's not that far from the asylum, all things considered, and I'm pretty sure the Agency, or at least Dr. Richter, knows we're still in the area. But we don't have anywhere to go. We don't know who to trust. Plus, most of us are wanted for something or other, so what authorities can we trust?"

At the mention of our crimes, Lith brings his foot down on mine.

"Ouch!" I yank my foot out from under his.

"Shut your mouth, jabber jaws," Lith snaps. "We don't know this guy any more than he knows us."

Teagan looks amused as he nods. "True statement."

"Anyway," I continue, rubbing my foot. "We're nearby."

"Now you can answer some questions," Lith says. "Quid pro quo."

"I'm the only one in this area that I know of, like I said," explains Teagan.

"How did you escape?" Lith asks.

Teagan shakes his head. "Not that question. I won't divulge information about anyone else. Not yet."

"For another time, then," Lith says.

"You're here all alone," I say. "And somehow you get food, or got food at some point."

Teagan shrugs. "Maybe it was already here when I found the place."

"Uh-huh. Right," I say, growing weary of this runaround. "Well, I guess we'll head back. Do you mind if we take some food with us? We're near starved out there."

Teagan studies us for so long, I think he's going to refuse. But then he surprises me by saying, "Bring your friends back here. The one thing I will admit is that I'm lonely. But only those you mentioned."

"Those are the only ones we know," Lith says.

"Fine. Come back tomorrow then. And plan to bring your stuff. If you'd like, you can stay here. If it's true what you said, and the doctor knows where you are, it's only a matter of time before they come looking for you." He waves his hand upward, toward the floors above. "I clearly have enough rooms."

He chuckles, and Lith chuckles, and I force a half-assed smile, wondering if it's a good idea for all of us to congregate here in this prison with this guy we just met. What if it's a trap? His one claim to fame, so to speak, is that Lith recognizes him from the asylum. And he is the right age. It's doubtful he's a traitor working for the Agency, but one never knows.

"We need something, though," I tell him. "Some information given in good faith. I think we're all on the same page, but I'd like a smidge more reassurance before we consider dragging our friends here."

He surprises me again by saying, "The woman on the radio is my mom."

"Okay," I say, startled. "Uh, thank you for sharing. You've thrown me by being so blunt all of a sudden, but I appreciate it."

"How does she know so much?" Lith asks.

Teagan shakes his head. "I'm not giving up all my secrets on our first date."

Satisfied on all fronts, we agree to talk to the others and likely return the next day. We take the food we can carry, but the amount of food we leave behind is reason enough to return.

Beyond the food and the more fortresslike feel of the prison, it's not a good idea to stay at the cabin, so I think we should return. Get away from the cabin at least for a little while. We don't know if the Agency knows about the prison, but we do know that Dr. Richter knows I'm hiding out in these mountains. She likely knows all about my grandfather's cabin. And if she knows, the Agency knows.

12

October is cold in the mountains, and our hike back to the cabin leaves me shivering despite the physical exertion. After Lith and I have debriefed about Teagan, the radio, the prison, and the Agency, Lith starts to talk about his childhood. The conversation is a welcome distraction.

"I was raised in what old folks called a holler," he says, stepping over a fallen tree.

"A holler?"

"Yes, city boy. A holler. It's kind of an area between mountains where the landscape is V-shaped. A steep climb to get there, and an even steeper climb up to the top of the mountain. It's rural and isolated. A great place for thinking and not a great place for socializing. We were dirt-poor—my dad worked the mines, my mom stayed home. When I was fourteen, though, my dad died in a mine collapse, and my mom remarried. To a real son of a bitch. A preacher, God help us, who believed in preaching to others what they should do rather than taking his own advice. Anyway, we moved into town, and suddenly I had friends and things to do. I loved it. Then I caught him cheating."

"Cheating on your mom?"

"Yeah. Like I said, a real son of a bitch. Mom needed me to take something to the church where he was preparing for the next service. I walked in the main entrance. Didn't see him. Went back to his office. His secretary was down on her knees in front of him, if you know what I mean. To keep me quiet, he bought me an Xbox and the game Grand Theft Auto. And that, my friend, is what gave me and my friends the inspiration for what got us in so much trouble. Man, did we have fun, though."

"You never told her?"

"I didn't have to. She caught him herself a week later."

"Would you have told her?"

He's quiet for a minute as he pauses to pick up a twig. He starts to chew one end. "Yeah. I would've told her. I would've told her sooner, but I wasn't sure how. I suspect she already knew, though."

"How so?"

"Just things I picked up on."

"Why are men such asshats?" I ask, more to the wind than to Lith, thinking about my stepdad, Rodger. My dead stepdad. Rage charges through my body until I remember the fire, and it's cushioned with a healthy dose of satisfaction.

"I don't know," Lith says. "I hope I don't turn out like him. My own dad was a good man, though. I plan to be more like him. If I ever get out of this mess we're in."

"You only stole one car, right?" I try to remember back to that night we first met when we all told our stories.

"Armed robbery. Yeah. I had a gun."

"Was it loaded?"

His gaze slides my way. "Of course. And I stole more than one car. I only got caught with the one."

I must look surprised because he laughs. "It didn't shoot bullets, but pellets. Looked real enough, though, and definitely would've hurt if I shot it close range."

"But you didn't?"

"Nah. I'm not a murderer."

Silence plummets between us. Lith stops. "Look, sorry, man. I would've killed my stepdad too if he did to my mom what yours did. I didn't mean any disrespect."

I study his eyes a moment before I nod. "No worries. It's not like I go around killing people. He was a unique case."

"I got you," he says as he starts walking again.

"I didn't really know my real dad," I continue. "He died too, before I was born. The only father I ever knew was my stepdad. You talk about a man being a mean son of a bitch. If I hadn't killed him, he would've killed my mom. Would've beat her to death."

"Yeah, I remember you saying," he says, the twig protruding from his mouth.

"Do you think we actually have control over how we turn out? I mean, did your stepdad and mine decide one day to be asshats, or were they born that way? And if they were born that way, what was wrong with our mothers that they thought it a good idea to marry the bastards?"

"That, man, is a question for someone other than me. I don't know."

"Maybe we are all born evil."

"Okay," he says, "this took a dark turn."

I don't respond. If we're all born bad, not just this generation of teenagers but everyone, then is there some merit to what the Agency is trying to do? By eliminating our generation, society can start over. By seeking alternative treatment methods for bad behavior and mental illness, can they keep bad things from happening? Is there justification for such drastic treatment methods?

I think of what I know of the lobotomy and can't help but wonder…

How much pain is caused by people's actions? Is there a way for the Agency to take away all the pain in the world? The younger generations will have these procedures the Agency is perfecting to correct whatever goes wrong in the brain to cause people to do things that hurt others. The goal being that no one will harm anyone else with their actions.

There's so much pain in the world. Generational, situational, occupational, etc. Is this what the world needs—a fresh start?

Are they actually on to something?

I must've moaned or groaned, because suddenly Lith is close to my side and watching me with intent eyes. I glance his way but resolutely turn my face forward and march on. These thoughts leave a trail of oily refuse in the recesses of my brain that I'm afraid will haunt me forever.

Whatever that means to a teenager in a world hell-bent on annihilating him.

• • • • • •

"What did you see?" Emily rushes up to meet us as we come into the clearing. "What happened?" She throws her arms around me in a big hug, kisses my cheek, then does the same to Lith, minus the kiss.

Cass stands slowly from the stump by the fire, watching. I wave. She hesitates, then waves in return.

"Get everyone," Lith says, "and we'll tell you all about it. There's food there, a lot of it, and we brought some back. And you won't believe this—we met someone. The guy named Teagan who was in the asylum with me—it is him. He's staying at the prison. We have a lot to discuss."

Emily jogs toward the back of the cabin. "Traz! Celexa!"

Ryan is standing on the porch and slowly makes his way down. He doesn't sit but lingers just behind Cass.

It's dark out already. We spent more time at the prison than we expected. Not to mention that hiking up and down a mountain isn't a speed race. It's cloudier than it was last night, but the fire is going, and I sit down on a stump, relieved to be off my feet.

When everyone is gathered around the fire, Lith gives the recap. My thoughts are still a jumbled mess as I try to process not only the prison and Teagan, but my errant thoughts on the hike back. Did part of me actually find merit in what the Agency is doing?

How can I even begin to think that what they're doing is a good thing? That there might be an honorable reason behind it? Have I actually...*finally* lost my mind?

I think of my bipolar diagnosis and the lithium I used to take. I'm not crazy. I haven't had a manic episode even once. Ever. Depressive, maybe, but aren't we all depressed? At least every teen I know is. I don't think that counts. I don't think I'm psychotic right now. Then where is this coming from?

I become vaguely aware of my stomach cramping and wonder if

it's the food. I listen as the group starts to ask questions but suddenly feel oddly detached.

• • • • • •

The debate about whether or not to take our belongings and hike back to the prison is a heated one. I'm now fully present mentally, having been able to pull myself out of my haunted thoughts. This reality is barely any better, though. Tension is high around the camp. I can almost hear it pop and sizzle like the fire.

Traz is a hard *no*.

Celexa agrees to whatever Traz does. *No.*

Ryan abstains from offering an opinion.

Emily is skeptical. Cass is too, though she doesn't say much.

Lith and I plead our case: it's a fortress; one entrance in the main part of the building, so it's easy to guard; food; showers; *food.*

"I'm tempted," Cass says finally, "but I do have a concern. What if it's a trap?"

"Legit concern. I just don't think it is, though," I say. "Not only from talking with him, but from listening to the radio. That woman was his mother. She wasn't talking about the Agency and their work in any glorified way. She sounded afraid. Don't forget, I wasn't supposed to hear the radio message. It was meant for Teagan's ears only. She gave him a recap of new information she'd learned and told him to be careful. It was meant to be a confidential conversation from mother to son."

Lith nods, so I know his vote is to go. But I already knew that.

"Ryan, what do you think?" I ask.

He's about four yards away from the group, but everyone is quiet, and my voice travels in the night.

He offers a shrug, then retreats into the cabin.

"It might be a good idea to give Ryan a change of scenery," Emily says softly, watching the door close behind him. "He is not doing well."

"You have a good point," Celexa says, ignoring the look Traz shoots her.

"I'm in," Cass states. "I could use a change of scenery too."

"The question, then, is..." I look at each person around the group. "Do we take our stuff and plan to stay at the prison? At least for a while. My vote is yes. After seeing Dr. Richter the other day, I want to put some distance between myself and this cabin."

"I agree," Lith says.

"It makes me nervous, though," Emily says. "I mean, we haven't seen another soul in months, and suddenly, this Teagan guy is in the picture."

"True," I say, "but no one has really hiked anywhere other than to the asylum and to hunt. We haven't ever gone in that direction."

"How about this," Celexa says, casting a quick side glance at Traz. "Let's go tomorrow. We can even take our stuff. But there's nothing that says we have to stay. If we're not comfortable, let's come back here."

Traz is staring at her, his expression unreadable.

"I'm starving," she says, placating. "All they had to say was the word *food*."

"I know," Traz says softly, as if for her ears only. "It would be nice to eat something besides beans and squirrel or rabbit."

It's nice to know Traz has a heart, even if he only shows it to Celexa.

"I don't think it's safe here anymore, so we might want to consider moving camp anyway," I say. "Even if we don't stay." I glance at Lith. "You've seen some other abandoned cabins, right?"

Lith nods. He gazes at the fire without looking up.

"That's settled, then." Traz stands, ever the voice of authority, acting as if he hadn't just been against the idea one minute ago. "We'll pack up what we can carry and hike to the prison. We can decide to stay or go on from there. For now, we should get what sleep we can." He looks at Celexa. "Let's go to bed."

She follows him into the cabin.

"What is going on with the two of them?" I ask as I watch their retreating forms.

"What do you think?" Lith responds.

• • • • • •

It's getting colder outside, and even though the cabin has a wood-burning stove, it can get chilly near the wall where our blankets lay. As Cass and Emily struggle to get warm, I pull them each to me and wrap them in my arms, the three of us sharing all the blankets. Soon our body heat rises, and I hear Cass's soft, sleepy breathing.

"You like her, don't you?" Emily whispers.

"Who?" I ask into the dark, having a pretty good idea where this is going but choosing to play dumb.

"Cass."

"Of course I like her."

"I mean, as more than friends."

I hesitate, listening to Cass's regular breathing while I decide what to say. "I do."

"Have you kissed her?"

"I have."

"Does she know you kissed me?"

"She doesn't. At least not to my knowledge."

"Do you think she'd mind?"

"I don't know. I doubt it."

"Do you regret kissing me?"

I pause again before saying, "Not at all." I taste cinnamon as if her lips are still on mine.

She raises up a few inches and brings her lips down on mine. It is a chaste kiss that doesn't develop but leaves me confused nonetheless. She settles back against my shoulder and is soon fast asleep.

13

We allow ourselves to sleep as long as we want, knowing we will need strength for the hike, not to mention for what might meet us upon arrival. Then, in silence, we take off from my grandfather's cabin. The hike seems longer with the larger group, with few of us used to steep climbs, especially Ryan. We stop several times, rest at one point to eat apples, and shut our eyes. We don't arrive at the edge of the forest until dusk.

It's the coldest day yet, and I can see my breath. The sky is clear, allowing the rising moon and starlight to reflect off the first frost. The dark forest is cast in a silver sheen that is at once haunting and beautiful. It reminds me of a scene out of a fairy tale. Everyone knows that fairy tales, in their raw form, are dark and twisted. More nightmare than happily ever after.

Which scenario does our future hold?

My nose is running, and my fingertips are numb. I yearn for the warmth of Cass's and Emily's bodies sleeping next to mine on the floor of my grandfather's cabin and wonder what it'll be like once we get to the prison if we decide to stay. There are endless cells to sleep in. Will one or both of them decide to sleep alone?

We can always return to the cabin, I tell myself, and that brings me comfort. Then I think about the food, and that also brings me comfort. As does the fortresslike building. The cabin seems so flimsy after being inside the stone structure.

Just wait and see, I guess.

Lith draws the group to a stop inside the cover of the trees. Gives everyone a minute to take in what lies before us: a mock asylum, though much smaller. Swaying grass, tall and capped in ice crystals, causes the overgrown lawn to sparkle in the changing light. It's so quiet I can hear the frost crackling.

We sip water. Use nature's facilities. Check our weapons. Study the prison and the surrounding landscape.

On the way in, I pocketed a handful of moonseeds. I pull them out of my pocket now.

"What are those?" Emily asks, reaching for one.

I pull my hand back.

"Insurance. It's best not to handle them too much."

"What are they for?" she asks as the group gathers around.

"Lith and I both think that this place is safe. We also know that we can take nothing for granted. These are an insurance policy I've been carrying around."

"Insurance for what?" Celexa asks.

Lith reaches out and takes a few. Puts them in his pocket. Wipes his hands on the grass.

"They're poisonous, aren't they?" Cass asks. "I recognize them. They get mistaken for wild grapes, but they can kill you."

"They are," I say. "I refuse to be imprisoned again. If it comes to that, I'll eat these first."

The group falls silent for a few moments, looking at me, the seeds, each other. Lith steps away and finishes repacking his bag. Each hand reaches out, takes a few. They wipe their hands, then make final preparations to cross the lawn to the prison.

Ryan doesn't reach for any.

"You don't want a few?" I ask him. "No pressure. Just making sure."

He shakes his head no, and I pocket the remainder, wondering what he is thinking. It's useless to ask, though, so I don't.

Nervous excitement pulses through the group. With confidence I find admirable, Lith leads the group forward.

"Do we just walk in there?" Cass asks by my side.

"That's what I did and what we did yesterday," I say. "Teagan is expecting us."

"Again, I have to ask. What if it's a trap?" She pulls me to a stop, her hand lingering on my arm. "What if he's lying...is a spy...and is supposed to lure us in there?"

"I don't think he is."

"Are your instincts always spot-on?"

"What are you insinuating?"

"I'm not insinuating anything. It just seems dangerous to me. After everything we've been through, you don't agree?"

I sigh, swallowing my irritation. "I get what you're saying. But I'm not the only one who thinks it's safe—Lith does too. Do you trust him?"

"I trust you," she says. "But why was the front door unlocked both times you went? I mean, someone who is afraid of the Agency wouldn't just leave themselves exposed like this Teagan seems to have done."

"Good point," I say. "I guess I want so much for this to work out, I missed that little detail."

"I'm afraid," Cass continues. "There are too many unanswered questions."

Emily and Celexa have doubled back. "What's wrong?" Emily asks, looking between me and Cass.

"I don't think we should all just go barreling in there," Cass says. "It seems risky. What if it's a trap?"

"I thought about that," Celexa says, "but got so excited about the idea of food that I chose to ignore it."

Traz and Lith, then Ryan, join us.

"What's up?" Lith asks.

"Cass is having second thoughts," Emily offers. Cass shoots her a look that I'm not sure Emily sees.

"I'm just concerned that it could be a trap. We don't know this guy. It's awfully close to the asylum, which is operating again. Dr. Richter knows we're nearby. Shaun can't answer why the door has been unlocked. I don't think we should all just barge in there."

"Shaun and I will go in," Lith says. "Scope the joint again, like yesterday. Y'all wait just inside the tree line. If the coast is clear, as expected, we'll come get you. Won't take more than ten minutes, so you shouldn't get too cold."

"I'll come too," Traz says.

I resist the urge to roll my eyes. "Fine," I say. "You all wait here, and we'll be right back."

The girls and Ryan huddle together for warmth as the three of us take off for the main entrance.

As expected, we walk straight in the front door.

A flashlight flips on. Teagan is sitting behind the desk, waiting for us.

"I keep the lights off as much as possible," Teagan says, rising. He walks forward, and we meet in the reception area.

"This is Traz," Lith says.

The two nod as they eye each other.

"Where is everyone else? I thought there were seven of you," Teagan says.

"Just being cautious," Lith says.

"Got it. Feel free to have a look around. Like I said, I don't turn the lights on much, but you can take the flashlight. I'll wait in the office. It'll get light in there pretty quick once the sun rises, but that isn't for hours. If we go to the basement, we can turn on the light."

"Why is the front door unlocked?" I ask him.

Teagan meets my eyes. "I'm afraid for my mom and want her to be able to come right in if she needs to."

I mull that over while we search the floors, finding them as empty as they were yesterday.

"Lith, why don't you show Traz the upper two floors and then the basement, and I'll stay here with Teagan."

They leave.

"Any new messages on your radio?" I ask, moving to the window in the office. All seems quiet outside.

"No. Not since the last one you heard. She doesn't have the chance to make regular contact."

"Did you hear her message yesterday? I didn't see you, so I assume you didn't."

"I did actually. You had left the door propped open, so I listened from the outside."

"Huh." The idea of someone watching me sends a chill up my spine.

Traz and Lith return, and they have the others with them. The quiet prison is suddenly full of energy as introductions are made. Cass moves to my side. Emily is at my other side. Ryan huddles by the revolving door.

"I assume y'all are hungry?" Teagan slaps his hands together in an oddly ebullient way. "Let's go raid the kitchen. Well, not raid. We don't have unlimited resources, but we do have food, and from what Shaun and Lith said, you all are near starved."

Lith and I explain the layout of the prison as we walk outside and head toward the basement.

"There's no way to get to the basement without going outside?" Celexa asks.

"No. Not well planned, is it?" Teagan says.

"Definitely not," Celexa says.

"How did you find this place?" Emily asks him.

"My mom found it," says Teagan. "She had some suspicions before we came to this area. Thought she might need a place to escape to. Turns out I did."

No one responds. It's all a lot to process, I guess.

"Let's get downstairs," Teagan says. "Get to know each other a little more before all the secrets are spilled."

He holds the door open while we pass through.

For the next several minutes, there are cries and moans as everyone discovers the food.

Celexa has a granola bar unwrapped and half-eaten before I even make it to the kitchen.

I laugh, feeling a bubble of joy at the happiness I see on the faces of these friends who've been through so much.

Emily has her fingers shoved into a jar of peanut butter and is alternately feeding herself and Cass.

It's surprisingly erotic to watch, and I'm struck motionless for several minutes.

Lith starts laughing, punches me in the arm, and hands me a box of crackers. I glance back at Cass and Emily, and they're laughing as Cass wipes peanut butter off Emily's chin.

When did those two become such good friends? Guess food will do that to you.

Traz dives into the olives, and Ryan opens a package of freeze-dried green apples.

"I think we stay here," Emily states, watching Cass lick peanut butter off her fingers. "I feel safer here for some reason."

"It's the food," I tell her. "Having food makes a place feel safe."

"Not to mention it's a fortress," Celexa says, taking an olive from Traz. "Even though it's similar to the asylum, it feels different. Less threatening, somehow."

"It certainly offers more protection than the cabin. Someone could break in there with a swift kick to the front door," Lith says.

"The only entrance upstairs is through the main entrance?" Traz asks.

"Yes, so it's pretty easy to batten down the hatches, so to speak," Teagan answers. "Of course, we're exposed any time we want to come downstairs and eat, and the showers are down here. But I haven't seen a soul around since I moved in."

"And when was that?" Traz asks.

I glance at Teagan. At some point, he's got to get tired of all the questions and start answering them.

"Let's sit," Teagan says instead. "And we can talk." He walks over to the nearest table, and slides onto the bench.

We join him, and the talking starts.

14

"You were in a gang?" Teagan leans forward, staring at Emily with wide eyes.

I watch his face closely, my interest piqued at his interest in Emily.

"I was friends with gang members—I wasn't a full member; more of a satellite, I guess. I probably would've become one, though, had we all not gotten arrested. They were like family. We spent all our free time together and had each other's backs, no matter what. Loyalty is worth a lot. And we found far more loyalty within the group than we did at home with our own families. You know what I mean?"

"I do," Teagan answers. "I wasn't in a gang. I grew up in Amish country, so we didn't exactly have exposure to a lot. But I did have a group of friends I was really close to. I've always been close to my mom, though, so home life was fine enough. No dad around, big surprise."

Someone snorts. Did any of us have a valid father figure?

"I had exposure to too much too early. Drugs. Sex. Crime," says Emily.

"Did you do all that?" Teagan asks. "Take drugs, do crimes." He blushes and doesn't mention the other.

Emily gazes down at the table, scratching at imaginary dirt. "Some, yeah. We weren't like some of the gangs you hear about on the news. Mostly petty crime, like theft. Drank and smoked some marijuana."

"Why the teardrop tattoo?" Teagan asks.

She doesn't answer for several heartbeats. Finally, she says, "I… we…" The silence is heavy as we wait for her to finish. "We killed someone. We didn't mean to." Her voice drops off. A real tear slides over the tattoo. "The tattoo is so we never forget."

Eventually, those dark eyes lift, planting on Teagan, unblinking. "How did you end up in the asylum?" Emily asks.

We all lean forward. Obviously, I'm not the only one who wants more information about our new friend.

"Aggravated assault." Teagan's eyes take on that far-off look. I know that look all too well, that tumble into the painful past and the dissociation that can come with it.

"What did you do?" Emily's voice is soft, nonconfrontational, luring him back.

"Those friends of mine and I beat up an Amish kid."

Teagan is straddling the past and the present. The rest of us keep a respectful silence. We might be wary of this guy, but we all understand the traumatization of reliving the past.

"He assaulted my friend's sister." The look of pain on his face is painful to see. "She was my girlfriend." Teagan clears his throat. Forces his emotions to the bottom of a very deep hole. Straightens. "She was never the same."

"So, you and your friends beat him up?" Emily asks.

"Within an inch of his miserable life." He looks around the group. "I would've killed him if they hadn't stopped me. But I did kick him so hard in the head that he'll never be a rocket scientist, if you know what I mean."

After that revelation of violence, the mood plummets, and we all go quiet.

Finally, I say, "Well, you're in good company. I killed my stepfather after he beat my mom one too many times."

Teagan stares at me a moment, as if he's struggling to process my words, still straddling memories and this moment. Then he nods.

No judgment there.

"I stole a stop sign," Emily says as tears well in her eyes. "We were bored one night. Just bored. That was it. Not out to get anyone. To hurt anyone. Just bored, looking for something fun to do. We stole the sign, and then a tractor trailer hit a minivan at an intersection." She pauses, swallows. "Killing Dr. Richter's sister and her children."

Cass touches her hand.

"Is that why you were put in the asylum?" Teagan asks gently.

Emily nods.

"I didn't kill anyone," Lith says neutrally. "Just grand theft auto. Guess I was a bored teen too, and I liked the video game. You could also say I had some anger issues. Impulsive. Didn't think before I acted. Standard stuff like that. Some assault. I was an all-around menace to society. The video game was far more fun than the reality I found myself in after I stole that car, believe me. Wasn't worth it."

Traz snorts. "They got me for statutory rape."

I glance at Teagan. His fists clench at the mention of assault. Traz doesn't seem to notice.

"It was consensual," Traz states. "She even testified to that. Said that she'd lied about her age. That she had initiated it. For some reason, it didn't matter to the courts. Or to the Agency."

Teagan's hands relax.

"They got me on drugs," Celexa says simply. "Selling more than doing. I had a whole operation going and was making bank. A large portion of the money went to helping my mom and my younger siblings. We were so poor, and she couldn't feed all of us. Something needed to be done. I took matters into my own hands. Guess I chose the wrong profession." She smirks, but there is no humor behind her eyes.

"What about you?" Teagan asks Ryan. "You're awfully quiet."

Celexa and I exchange glances.

"I didn't do anything," Ryan says finally, quietly. "My sister and I didn't do anything but be born to drug-addicted parents who overdosed and died. We got put into the foster care system. We were older. No one wanted us."

He gets up and walks down the hall.

"Is he okay?" Teagan asks.

I shake my head. "No. His twin got left behind in the asylum when we escaped." I inhale deeply. Exhale. "I left her behind."

"You couldn't save all of us, Shaun. You know that." Cass puts her hand on my back. Her other hand is still holding Emily's, connecting the three of us together.

Teagan stands. "Let's clean up and go back upstairs. I could use a minute of fresh air."

• • • • • •

After having our fill of food, we go upstairs and sit in a circle on the floor in the hall between the reception area and the office. Ryan has moved down to a cell and disappeared from view.

"So, we all know the asylum is up and running again," Teagan says.

"Yep." I sit cross-legged between Cass and Emily.

"Did you also know that the program is nationwide?" Teagan asks. "And that other locations, as far away as Alaska, are working on a variety of treatments—not just the lobotomy?"

"Tell us what you know," Traz says. "We have some information but not much."

"Different areas of the country, different doctors, are doing different experiments. Here, it was the lobotomy, run by Dr. Richter. But the other places? Various surgeries, experiments, procedures—whatever you want to call them."

"Can you be more specific?" Emily asks.

"For instance, in New Orleans, there is a doctor working on what's called bloodletting. Basically, it's draining out a certain amount of blood, assumed to be contaminated, in hopes that it will reduce whatever ailment is happening to the person," Teagen explains.

"That's what your mom was talking about on the radio the other day," I say to Teagan.

Teagan nods. "Yeah. She tells me what she knows. Not sure why other than to keep me informed. Maybe to keep me scared enough to stay hidden. She's known for a while that the operation is nationwide and that they're working on new treatments. She's only just now learning what those treatments are, and when she finds out new information, she tells me over the radio."

"Is that what she does—gives you information about what the Agency is up to?" I ask.

"She gives me any information she can, and yes, that's part of it," says Teagan.

"You're saying that in my case, for instance, I'd be leeched," Celexa asks, "as treatment for selling drugs?"

"Sounds crazy, but yes," Teagan replies. "These treatments are meant to treat deviant behavior, mental illness, and substance abuse. You name it, they treat it with these treatments. As for the bloodletting, they believe the blood holds the toxins that lead us to make poor decisions, and selling drugs is deviant behavior. At least that's the reasoning I can gather. Quite archaic if you ask me. Really, anyone who got put on the list can be subjected to any of these treatments. I'm sure you know about the list."

We nod.

Cass's hands are clasped tight in her lap, her fingers clenched together until I unwind them and pull one hand into mine. Emily glances down out of the corner of her eye, before planting her gaze back on Teagan. I resist the urge to hold her hand too.

"Other places are doing electroshock therapy or hydrotherapy. Some are cutting off part of the skull to relieve brain pressure or something like that. It's all very medieval. Like, literally medieval. I'm sure you learned about some of this stuff in history class, or psychology class if you took one. These are ancient treatments they're doing. And the list of procedures being done seems to grow all the time. I love hearing from my mom, because it means she's okay, but I always cringe when I hear her voice. I never know what she's going to tell me," says Teagan.

"That's it," Celexa says. "They're reimagining medieval methods of mental health treatment because they feel that the modern methods are no longer working. Sick."

Emily touches her teardrop tattoo. "I remember Dr. Richter saying that medicine no longer works for mental health treatment like it used to and that the medical community is desperately trying to find new treatments. Instead of just creating more medicine, they're going back in time."

"What else can you tell us?" Traz asks. He puts his arm around Celexa's shoulders, and she leans into him.

Teagan looks at Emily. "You're right. They're bringing back medieval practices. Modern science is no longer serving the community, so to speak. Medications don't work. Nothing new is on the horizon, other than more medications." He leans forward and plants those baby blues on each of us in turn. "I can tell you that this is personal. Each and every member of the Agency has been affected by a teenager's actions in some painful, catastrophic, or deadly way." He pokes the floor with his finger as he repeats, "This is personal." He breaks eye contact and straightens. "That's why they'll never stop."

"I guess we already knew that," I say. "Dr. Richter alluded to as much if she didn't just say it outright. I can't remember."

"But what we didn't know," Emily says from my side, "is that they're doing more than just lobotomies. That this is so pervasive and widespread."

Teagan offers her a sympathetic smile. Their eyes lock for several moments.

"Is there nothing we can do then?" Celexa asks, completely deflated, her shoulders hunched, her back rounded, as if she's trying to curve into herself and disappear.

"As of right now, there doesn't seem to be," Teagan says. "It's just really hard. Especially being in this area. We have such a lack of resources here, and getting information is extremely challenging. Besides, Mom doesn't seem to know who to trust, and in this kind of situation, you have to be careful who you talk to and what you say."

"They want a better society," I say, thinking aloud. "Modern medicine isn't working to eliminate crime, murder, assault, drug use, you name it. Not to mention, it's personal for every single one of them. What can we possibly do when the motivation is really, simply, revenge?"

Cass looks at me sharply. "Could you sound any more defeated?"

Her words shock me. She seldom speaks and rarely in such an acid tone. I see the challenge in those gray eyes and break contact, gazing down the empty hallway.

"I'm just trying to be honest," I say softly. "To have a clear understanding of what's going on and why."

"He's got a point," Teagan says. "I'll not deny that. It's personal, and they want revenge. At least whoever is in charge does. But we aren't giving up."

"We?" Traz asks.

"Well, I guess my mom and me. I assume now"—his gaze sweeps across our group—"us. We aren't giving up. Are we?"

"What's the plan, then?" Traz pushes, not answering Teagan's question. "Do you have one?"

"No. No plan as of now," Teagan says, "other than staying alive."

Any time I feel a blip of hope, it's almost immediately shattered by the reality of our situation. The thrill of finding this prison? The food? Shattered by Teagan's words that there is basically no way to change our situation.

Then those black thoughts about any merit the Agency might have hover at the edges of my mind. I don't want to acknowledge them because that would mean the Agency is doing some good. But as I reflect back on our stories, including Teagan's about the severe assault and the now brain-damaged boy, I can't help but allow those black thoughts to creep a little closer to consciousness.

Would the world be better off if the Agency continued its work? Will the Agency find a way to prevent pain and suffering in the world?

In a new world, would they treat a person like Rodger with, say, bloodletting, and take away any violent urges he had? Would they be able to prevent someone else's mother from being beaten nearly to death?

I feel like a wounded little bird, wing broken, lying on the ground while an eagle soars over my head. Circling. Circling. Circling. There is nothing I can do but watch and wait until the eagle decides to descend. And devour.

And I wonder, would we all be better off if the eagle succeeds?

15

Teagan gets up and heads into the office. Lith stands and follows him when static from the radio pierces the quiet.

The rest of our group disperses. The others start exploring the cells, but I move into the hallway. I contemplate doing some push-ups to try and get my strength back while I listen to what is happening in the office. Which isn't hard considering how sound travels within these stone walls.

"Any new info?" I hear Lith ask.

"No," Teagan says. "Nothing so far today, but that's not unusual. I feel better sticking close to the radio, though."

"I'd think there'd be more information," Lith says, "with the asylum up and running again and the assumption that other locations are doing the same."

Both are quiet for a moment before Teagan says, "I found a deck of cards right after I arrived. I forgot all about them, being here by myself, but anyone is welcome to them." I hear what sounds like cards shuffling. Traz and Celexa exit a cell toward the end of the hall and walk toward me.

"Do you ever send messages over the radio?" Lith asks.

"No. I don't know who might be listening," Teagan says. "We agreed I wouldn't reach out unless it's an emergency."

"We?" Traz asks, looking at me with brows raised. He moves past me and steps into the office, Celexa by his side. I step in behind them.

Teagan sighs. "My mom and I."

"Where is your mom?" I ask.

"Here."

"Here?" I repeat.

"In Blackthorn Peak."

"Ready to tell us exactly what she does?" I fold my arms, ready for answers. "I think it's time."

Emily and Cass come out of a cell and walk toward us. I see a hint of Ryan's shoulder in the doorway of the nearest cell and know he's eased forward, likely so he can hear too. Looks like we all are ready for the answers.

Teagan looks at each of us in turn. Puts his hands in his pockets. Sighs. "She works at the research facility. It's the red building on the asylum grounds."

"Your mother works for the Agency?" Traz demands.

"She does," Teagan responds calmly.

"What does she do?" Lith asks.

"It's a research facility. She does research," Teagan says.

"You're telling me that she works for the enemy?" Traz presses, that chest of his puffing up.

Teagan says, "She does. But not willingly."

"What do you mean?" Celexa prompts.

"She works for them to keep me safe. Many of the scientists and doctors who work for the Agency do so to protect their own children."

Teagan sighs again, a heavy, weighted sound. "Let's sit. I'll tell you the rest, or at least what I know. Which isn't a lot."

We sit. Ryan even comes out of the cell he was in but keeps his distance and stands against the wall. Lith stays standing as well, leaning against the door to the office.

"I told you how I got into trouble," Teagan says. "In a nutshell, she went to work for the Agency once she realized what I'd done and what the consequences were going to be."

"What do you mean? She knew about the Agency before you got into trouble?" Celexa asks.

"Right after I was arrested, someone came to see her, touting this program. Said it would keep me out of prison. I was sixteen when the assault happened. They were talking about charging me as an adult. There was a huge uproar over Amish rights, and their counsel got involved. It was a particularly vicious attack, I admit."

"What about the vicious attack on your girlfriend?" Emily asks.

"Well," Teagan says with a snort, "boys will be boys was the refrain at the time. It wasn't that long ago, but that area of the world is behind the times. Plus, another local boy had raped one of the Amish girls, so they felt those crimes canceled each other out. The injuries I gave to that asshole were deemed too violent, though, despite the violence he'd inflicted on my girlfriend. So, I was in a heap of trouble."

"I feel sick," Celexa says.

"Yep. Anyway, whoever came to see Mom convinced her to send me to this program. I ended up, as you might expect, in the asylum. When my mom found out...when she discovered that the program wasn't what she thought it was—that it was more of a prison, a hospital, and a morgue all rolled into one—she worked night and day to get a job with the Agency."

"How did she find out?" I ask.

Teagan snorts again and shakes his head. "It wasn't even a secret. She was at the grocery store in our hometown. Ran into the parent of the Amish kid. He knew where I'd been sent and told her all about it. He could've been gloating. I'm not sure. She only gave me minimal information about how she discovered the truth. I'm sure, hopefully, that I'll find out more at some point."

"She found work with the Agency...and then what?" Celexa prompts.

"They renovated the red building and opened it for research. Her background is in research—she's a psychopharmacologist, and she was working on a new medication for the treatment of schizophrenia. The Agency wanted people with her background to come work here, and she managed to apply and get the job."

"Did they know who she was? I mean, that they'd taken her child?" Emily asks.

Teagan says, "We think they do know, but her research is invaluable to their mission, so they have allowed it to slide."

"The Agency doesn't believe in medication," Lith says. "Why is she invaluable?"

"Some of the procedures do require meds afterward," Teagan explains. "To help the body heal. Minimize or eliminate side effects, like seizures or migraines."

"This is so disturbing," Cass whispers. "Are we sure that it's not all just a dream?"

"It's not a dream," Ryan says quietly. "It's a nightmare."

We fall silent, not sure how to respond. Eventually, Emily motions for him to come sit, but he shakes his head, then retreats into his cell.

Teagan looks around the group, then continues, "Gibbon—is he still there?"

Traz shakes his head.

"He died," I answer. "Dr. Richter killed him after he helped us escape."

"He helped my mom get me out too. I was in the wall. You know...*the wall*," says Teagan.

"Yeah." Lith snorts. "We know of it."

Teagan continues, "Anyway, I don't know how, but Mom was able to get inside the asylum and get me out."

"I don't understand the timing," Lith says. "You were in the asylum when I was there. When did your mom start working at the research facility?"

"She came to this area right after I started the program," says Teagan. "I went straight into the asylum, so I don't know any details except that. It's not like we're able to sit around and chat. We have quick communication when we do talk, but it's mostly her sending me messages."

"So, she came here and then helped you escape?" Lith asks. "One day you were there. The next you weren't."

"Gibbon did," says Teagan.

I think of that large man-child, and my heart hurts.

Teagan continues, "Gibbon worked with my mom to get me out of there."

"I'm still confused," Emily says.

"Like I said, the timing... Everything that happened during

that time is vague for me. Once Gibbon helped her get me out, they brought me to the prison. Mom didn't stick around. She made sure I was set up here and left me alone while she returned to the red building. She didn't want to draw further attention to herself."

"But her own son went missing..." Emily asks, "Wouldn't she be the first suspect?"

"Yeah. I mean, I'm sure she was. But her research was invaluable. Only I went missing from the asylum. I assume they thought it was worth it—letting me go to keep her on."

I think of my own mom who put me in that demonic place and did nothing to get me out.

Teagan looks around the group. "That's it."

"She doesn't know enough yet to create a plan?" Lith asks.

Teagan says, "No. They just got the research facility up and running again, and she's trying not to make waves, so to speak. Especially after my rescue. She's trying to quietly get a read on who is there willingly and who is being blackmailed with their child's safety. Those are the ones she will try to ally herself with. But everyone is so afraid. If you threaten someone's child, parents will do just about anything to ensure their safety. In this case, they'll go to work for the very agency that put their kids in the asylum."

"And be complicit in the killing of teens," Celexa says. "No judgment. Well, some judgment. That's the trade-off, I guess. Harm someone else's loved one to keep your own safe."

Teagan doesn't answer. His unblinking stare is answer enough.

"So, you just wait here for her to contact you?" Traz asks.

"That's what I've been doing these past months," says Teagan. "It's not ideal, but I have shelter and food and a warm shower, though why there's running water in this old, abandoned building, I'll never know. Likely they just never turned it off when the prison was shut down, and then whoever was in charge forgot about it. But it beats the hell out of the asylum. The most important thing, though, is I'm still alive. I can be patient when it comes to a literal matter of life and death."

"Amen to that," I mutter.

"So, we wait," Celexa says.

"We wait," Teagan repeats. "I have a feeling something will happen soon, though. The asylum has started back up. The research facility is up and running. More people seem to be coming into the area, more doctors and staff."

"And teens," I say, remembering the white vans.

Teagan nods. "I don't take risks here. I keep the lights off. Leave no footprints. I'm not on edge all the time, but I never drop my guard."

"You saw me coming the other day?" I ask.

Teagan says, "I did. I calculated your age, how starved and weak you looked, what you were wearing, your hair. Everything pointed to an asylum escapee, but I wasn't going to make myself known. There was a good chance you'd never come back. But you did, and here we are."

"Makes sense," I say. "I feel like we'll be on guard for the rest of our lives…however long that will be."

"Dark turn," Emily snaps.

I shrug.

"Something is brewing," Traz says. "We all agree on that."

"You can feel it in the air," Celexa says.

"I think so," I say. "Phase I of their plan was to start experimenting with the medieval surgeries, killing off everyone they experimented on. Phase II is simply killing."

"The extermination of our generation," Emily confirms.

"That's my understanding," I say quietly.

Teagan glances at my hands, clasped with Cass's and Emily's, and says, "The expectation is that soon, they will come looking for us. If it's Phase II, they won't leave any of us alive. It'll come to a head at some point."

"Annihilation," Lith states, his usually stoic face pale and his features reflecting the terror the word instills.

• • • • • •

Since it's likely well past midnight by the time we stop talking, we decide to stay in the prison. Teagan shows us where blankets and pillows are kept in the basement, and we each grab some bedding, then walk back upstairs and claim our cell. Teagan sleeps in the first cell by the office.

Lith takes the cell next to his.

Ryan the one after.

Traz and Celexa head to the end of the hall and slide into the last cell together.

Cass and Emily stand uncertainly by my side.

We've been sleeping side by side since our escape from the asylum. Huddled so close together that we provided each other with warmth and security. Oftentimes I'd wake up with Cass curled into one shoulder, Emily in the other, and my arms around both. Those were the nights I slept the best, the nights the nightmares stayed at bay.

But these are typical cells with narrow metal beds. A few in the middle have bunk beds, but that means one of us would have to sleep alone.

Quietly, I say, "There are enough blankets here to make a bed on the floor of one of these cells. The beds aren't big enough, so let's just sleep on the floor like at the cabin."

Since there seems to be no other answer, the girls nod, and we head to a cell in the middle of the hallway, ignoring the empty bunk beds inside.

We take turns using the small bathroom, flushing a toilet and using water to wash our hands and rinse our mouths.

Before slipping into his cell, Teagan calls down the hall, "Keep your weapons handy. It's best to be prepared for the worst."

• • • • • •

That night I can't sleep, even though both Cass and Emily lie tight against my sides. Their warmth doesn't go unnoticed, but I still feel cold despite the two blankets that cover us.

Complete annihilation.

Phase II.

I already knew these things. Why is it plaguing me tonight?

I killed my stepfather.

Escaped a lunatic asylum.

My heart squeezes painfully at the memory of Renee's unconscious form in the hallway of the asylum.

We just left her.

We had no choice.

My mind is racing with memories: Trevor, Owen, Gibbon; the table, Dr. Richter, the wall; the straitjacket, the chain to the floor, the feeling of the medicine in my body.

The escape. I can't think of the escape without thinking of how we left Renee behind and destroyed Ryan in the process.

Memories are like demons. Their dark and sinister presence drifts along the periphery of the wakened mind, only to dive-bomb peace when the mind is at rest.

I'm not at rest right now, though. I can't rest. My shoulders are up to my ears. My stomach and jaw are clenched. It takes every ounce of effort I have to uncurl my fingers from fists and wrap them instead around Cass's and Emily's shoulders.

I knew the Agency was killing us. That their goal was the annihilation of my entire generation. Why am I bothered now, hearing it from Teagan's own mouth?

Because I still couldn't believe it.

Or maybe I did, which is why I'd already given up.

Cass has been accusing me of giving up for days, weeks even. Challenging the limp and weak guy before her to return to the strong and battle-hungry guy who helped her escape the asylum. I've felt glimpses of him. Since finding the prison. Teagan. The food. Learning we have a contact on the inside.

But none of that seems to matter. The odds are still stacked against us.

That battle-hungry guy? Simply doesn't exist anymore.

The Agency and Dr. Richter made sure of that.

What's left then?

A blob of desolation? A waste of a human heartbeat?

That's what I feel like.

I have no energy. It's like someone extinguished my light bulb, leaving barely enough energy to try to ignite, with the end result being nothing but more darkness.

More darkness. Everything is darkness. Always darkness, and it always will be.

Complete annihilation.

Dr. Richter knew where I was. Or at least that I was in the general vicinity of the cabin. Hell, I'm sure she's known the exact location of my grandfather's cabin, as well as the fact that we've been hiding out there.

She had no need to find us because she knew we had nowhere to run. No one to help us. Nowhere to escape to. So why bother? She'd get us eventually.

And she will.

She and the Agency will find us. Then kill us. How will they do it this time?

Their treatments are violent, but I don't think their mode of death is. I never heard gun shots or anything like that, so I assume they gave all the teens at the asylum medication to permanently put them to sleep.

A small gift, I guess.

The ground is hard against my back, and I'm surprised at the difference between a wooden floor like at the cabin and a concrete floor like here. Both are hard. This one feels harder.

My hands are growing numb, but I don't move my arms from around the girls' shoulders.

I'm going to die anyway, so why not cut off all the circulation in my arms doing something I love?

I pause at the word. *Love.* Do I love Cass and Emily sleeping next to me? Do I love them? Can I even feel love anymore?

One thing I always knew was that I loved my mom. I loved her so much I killed for her. And then she betrayed me. The one person who should have loved me no matter what sent me to my death. I don't know what she knew, but she sent me away. Do I still love her?

Tears build behind my eyes until they seep out, sliding down my temples.

Will I ever love again?

I pull both girls tight. Turn to the left and kiss Cass's head. Turn to the right and kiss Emily's.

I've always felt a pull toward Cass, but the truth is I feel a pull toward Emily too. I don't want to lose either of them. I'm not sure about love, but I am sure that these two are the most important people in my life right now. What that means, I simply don't know.

I sniff. I want to wipe my tears but don't dare move my arms.

At some point, my erratic thoughts settle enough to carry me into a fitful quasi sleep.

I tumble into a nightmare.

• • • • • •

I'm home in Baltimore. I'm a young child again, walking in a haze down the hall where the bedrooms are. The light is gray and fuzzy all around me.

I hear crying. My mom is crying. Again.

I stop outside my mom and Rodger's bedroom door.

I hear his voice. He is speaking low, but his deep voice is angry, words shoved through clenched teeth.

My mom's cries grow louder until I hear a thump and a whimper. And then silence for a beat before I hear Rodger say, "You stupid bitch."

Rodger leaves the bedroom, but it's not Rodger. It's Cyrus Rutherford, Cass's father. His knuckles are bloody. He walks past me as if he doesn't see me.

I peek around the door to the bedroom, dreading what I will see.

It's not my mom on the floor. It's Dr. Richter, bloodied and beaten, eyes swollen shut, lip busted, orange-red hair matted bloodred. She is crying as she looks up at me.

"I deserved it," she whimpers. "Just like you do."

"Shaun?" a voice calls, and I turn. Emily is standing there, her pale skin making the teardrop tattoo glow in its blackness. "Teagan will protect

us now," she says. "He will end this. Not you."

Cass floats into view, her hair cut short with purple-dyed ends, like it was when I first met her. The lip ring is there, and I wonder, briefly, how it would feel to tug on that ring with my teeth.

"You've given up," Cass says. "We need a new savior."

I want to protest, but I don't, because she's right. I have given up.

Teagan comes behind Emily and wraps his arms around her waist, pulling her against him. Cass is wrapped in Emily's arms. The three of them stand as one.

A pang of jealousy, of loneliness pinches my soul.

"You took us as far as you could," Emily continues. "Teagan will see this through."

I look back into the bedroom, but it's my mom again, exactly how I remember her after a beating when I was eight.

"Shaun?" She reaches her hand out, and it's shaking. "Come to me. You don't need to fight anymore. Come to me."

She's encased in glowing white light.

Did my mom die, and I don't know it? I'm vaguely aware that this is a dream, and my mom is alive, but the dream is just real enough to make me question what I think I know.

"Mom, is that really you?" I ask.

"Shaun, come to me. There's nothing left to do here."

Blood starts seeping out of her head wound, running down her face and into her eyes.

I recoil in horror.

Cass is by my side. "Shaun, it's okay. You can go to her."

I step toward my mother. Glance back at Cass who is now wrapped in Teagan's arms. Emily is close by their sides. They move as one unit.

"Go, Shaun," Emily says. "It's okay. You've lost your fight. Given up. It's time for you to go."

Traz appears, smirking, before his face grows serious. "We are going to battle. We need warriors. Not weaklings. You're weak. You always have been."

My fists clench as I turn away from my mom's weeping form. Her whispered chant of "Come, come, come," plays on repeat while Emily's whispered chant of "Go, go, go," mirrors it.

Cass remains silent, watching me with those big gray eyes.

"I always wanted to feel that lip ring against my tongue," I tell her.

She doesn't respond at first. Then eventually pulls Teagan's face toward hers and allows him to kiss her. I watch as he gently tugs at the ring.

Rage shoots through me. I step forward to pull her away from him, but they're gone, and I'm standing in front of my mom's bloody body. Now she's lying in a coffin, face cakey with makeup, pale, with lips overly lined and overly pink. Like fuchsia. She's wearing her wedding dress, and her hair is splayed out on the white silk pillow on which her head rests.

She has no bruises on her face and looks like a teenager despite the poorly applied makeup.

She looks peaceful.

Is death the only way to gain peace? Is that what this dream is trying to tell me?

Death.

No more struggle. No more fear. Terror. Rage.

There is a peacefulness that comes with the thought of living with a void of emotions.

As I stare down at her, though, the makeup fades away, and in its place is a bloody, pulpy mess. She is disfigured, and those fine bones are broken. Her nose is crooked; her mouth falls open to reveal missing and broken teeth. Blood seeps out of the sides of her mouth.

I've never seen her like this. In all the beatings I've witnessed, I've never seen this.

I recoil. Horror fills me.

"You did this to her," a voice says, though whose voice or where it comes from, I can't say. I look around. I'm standing in an empty funeral home, the chairs unfilled, the vases flowerless, the pulpit void of a preacher. "You gave up," the voice continues. "This is what would've happened if you hadn't killed Rodger. He would've killed her."

I feel a swell of pride and justice. I knew I'd done the right thing when I burned my house down with Rodger inside.

"But now you're giving up," the voice says.

Is it God? The devil?

"And because of that, all will die."

"I can't be responsible for everyone," I shout into the emptiness. "That's not my job!"

"It is," the voice answers calmly. "It is your destiny to fight. But you're turning from your destiny, and now all will die."

Die.

Die.

Die.

• • • • • •

I bolt upright, sweat pouring down my body. I'm panting, unable to catch a breath.

"Shaun?" Cass sits up by my side. Emily leans up on an elbow.

"What's wrong?" Emily asks.

But I can't breathe. Cass puts a hand on my back. Emily places a hand on mine.

Lith shows up in the doorway. "Everything okay?"

"I think he had a nightmare," Emily says.

Lith lingers a moment longer, then walks away.

"Can you talk about it?" Cass asks.

"I'm ready," I pant.

"Ready for what?" Cass asks.

"To fight."

16

Midmorning the next day, Teagan is in the office with the radio. The shrill metallic sound of static draws us all into the room, except for Traz and Celexa, who have gone off into another part of the building.

"How can you tell if she's trying to make contact?" Emily asks.

"I check it every day at five o'clock, for starters. That's when she has a dinner break, and if she can, she makes contact. Honestly, though, I often check it throughout the day because a few times she's tried to reach me when she's not on a scheduled break. It's not a good system, and I can't leave it on all the time, or it'll waste batteries. But I know which station she uses and just try it periodically in case there's an emergency," says Teagan. "If I haven't heard from her in a day or two, I start checking every hour on the hour."

The only sound that fills the room is the radio's static, but suddenly, that changes.

"T, it's me. I'm fine. I pray every minute of every day that you are too." Her voice crackles over the radio. "Things are amping up here. I'm not completely sure what's going on. There are reports of kids—teens—going missing, and it's starting to get noticed. There are no locals in Blackthorn Peak, but a fellow scientist had to go to Charleston the other day and heard rumblings on the street. Too many teens are going missing now to not be noticed, in West Virginia, but also in Maryland, Virginia, Kentucky, Pennsylvania. I don't know what this means, or if this will get any traction, so I'll keep you updated. But it does make sense, because they have decided to roll out Phase II in record time."

Static.

"Can you hear me?" She chuckles, humorlessly. "I guess I won't know if you can or can't. Anyway, they plan to move into Phase III by the end of next year. That means just over twelve months until they start the last phase. That means—" This time it isn't static that interrupts her words, it's emotion. "That means," she says again, "that your generation will be annihilated, completely, within the year. They've already started mass killings—that's been going on awhile—but the experiment phase is over. Now it's just killing."

You could hear a pin drop in the office.

"I'll try to come see you soon, but don't plan on it. Preserve the batteries and food. Don't turn on any lights or go outside. Keep that place looking as abandoned as possible, and don't raise any alarms. I'll be in touch soon. I love you. Stay safe."

Static fills the room.

"Phase III in one year?" Emily says, her voice shrill. "That means they want us all dead, our entire generation, by next Christmas?"

At the mention of the holiday, Emily breaks down, sobbing. I fold her into my arms, this feeling all too familiar, like when I held her after our escape from the asylum. I even feel my shirt becoming saturated with her tears again.

I glance at Cass. Tears are silently rolling down her cheeks as she gazes out the window. The others look, simply, stunned.

After a while, Teagan turns the radio off.

Rage simmers in my blood, and the feeling isn't empowering. It's overwhelming, because I just do not know what we can do.

The Agency's reach feels so massive. Pervasive.

My body starts to shake, and soon Emily's body is shaking in response.

"We need a plan," I say, looking everyone in the eye in turn. "Let's start focusing on a plan of action. Dr. Richter knows we're in the area. At least that I am. I'm sure she and the Agency know our whereabouts. Hell, they probably even know we're in this building now and no longer at the cabin. We have to assume they know everything."

"Where do we start?" Lith asks.

"I don't know," I say. "Fortifying this place would be a good start."

"Shouldn't we move somewhere else?" Celexa asks. "Stay on the go? Head to Canada?"

"Walk to Canada?" Teagan asks. "It would take a week or more. I'm not being a punk, but we do have very limited options right now. We can't carry enough to get very far and can't rely on the ability to buy items we need. First of all, we have no money. Second of all, we don't know who to trust. Besides, there is a transmitter here in this prison. If we leave this building, I can't use the radio. I can't lose contact with my mom."

"We have to stay here," Lith confirms.

Teagan nods. "Until we hear otherwise. Or until something happens to force our hand."

"It's not safe for us to go outside or down to the basement. Let's start by bringing up all the food and supplies to this floor. That's a start," I say.

"But the showers," Celexa says, sorrow filling her eyes. "I love the showers."

"Today we all shower," I say. "And then we just use the bathroom sink."

"Teagan, are you sure there is no way to get into the main building from the basement?" Traz asks.

"I'm one hundred percent sure, but it never hurts to check again," says Teagan.

"Is everyone in agreement?" I scan the group.

No one objects. No one says a word. We just file out of the office and head toward the exit.

It takes the rest of the day to bring every supply we can upstairs. We pile it all in one of the cells, stocking the closet in the bathroom with toilet paper, paper towels, medicines, and toiletries like toothbrushes, soap, towels and washcloths, combs, and hygiene products. We even find trash bags and bring up the trash can from the kitchen and put it in the reception area.

"We need to be careful of rodents," Lith says, looking at the empty trash can. "We won't be able to risk taking trash outside."

"What have you done with trash up to this point?" I ask Teagan.

He glances up from the radio. "I've been burying it out in the forest. I don't generate much, obviously."

"But that's a good point." I turn to Lith. "We can assume that all trash has to stay inside which means it'll pile up."

"And then we will soon have visitors," Cass says, cringing.

"Gross," Emily says.

"Yeah. It will be gross. Not to mention we can't risk disease," I say.

"Put it in the farthest cell," Cass says, "on the top floor. And we can double bag. It's not like we're going to have a lot of waste anyway."

We agree that the cell at the end of the hall on the top floor will be our trash room.

"We have water," Cass continues. "We can rinse off anything that had food in it. That will help."

"Time for everyone to shower one last time." I look around. "Where are Traz and Celexa?"

Emily rolls her eyes. "They're already showering. Together."

"Didn't need to know that," Lith says. "And I'm not sure I want to be the one who goes next."

Two hours later, Teagan is the last one to shower. We don't have clean clothes, though, and all look the same save for the wet hair.

"We need to go back to the cabin," I say to Lith in the hallway, "and get the rest of our belongings. We have clothes, toiletries, medicines, some food. Bedding."

"Let's go tomorrow," Lith says. "I'd feel better if we hunkered down here sooner rather than later."

"How many of us should go? Should we all?" Emily asks. "We all have things there we'll want to have here."

"Maybe. Leave Teagan here. He has no need to go." I glance out the office's window, staring into the distance. It is a quiet landscape, void of any life that I can see. Not even the birds are out today. The tall grass is swaying gently in the mountain breeze, and the sky is covered in gray clouds.

"No need to go where?" Teagan asks, strolling into the room, water running down his neck.

"Dude, there are towels down there," Lith says.

Teagan laughs as he walks into the office. He picks up the radio and turns it on. Static hisses and pops. He fiddles with the antennae, ignoring his mom's advice about the batteries.

"We're going to the cabin tomorrow," I tell him, "to gather the things we want to have here. Any reason you can tell why we shouldn't?"

"No," Teagan says, "I guess not. But definitely go tomorrow. Get what you need. I'm sure nothing urgent will happen. You guys showing up here was the first sign of life I've seen in this area in months."

"But what your mom said," Cass says, coming out of the cell. "Should we risk it?"

"Everything is a risk," Lith says.

Cass nods.

"It's settled then," I say. "Whoever wants to can come tomorrow."

Just then, the static ceases, and a woman's voice comes on the radio.

"Shaun Treadway," the voice says. At first, I think it's Teagan's mom, but why would she know my name? The alarmed look on Teagan's face tells me something is not right.

"If you can hear me, this is Dr. Richter. I need to talk to you."

Teagan jumps to his feet, staring down at the radio.

Blood drains from my face.

"Shaun?" she says again, as if she's waiting on my response.

"We need to talk. Meet me at your grandfather's cabin. It's... Friday today. I'll meet you there tomorrow. After sunset. I can't say more now. I'll see you then. This is not a trick."

"What?" I whisper. "How?" I feel suspended, dissociated. "What just happened?"

Teagan stares at me, a hint of accusation behind the alarmed expression, and demands, "What's going on? I have never gotten a message from another person."

"That's not a message for you," Emily says. "It's for Shaun."

Teagan shoots her a look.

"Have you had contact with her before?" Teagan demands.

"No. Not since she waved at me the other day outside the asylum. But there's no way she could know about the radio, even if she knows about us being here."

"Unless she's gotten to my mom." Panic marches across Teagan's face. "Maybe she's got my mom! What does she want?"

"I don't know," I say, feeling frantic. "How could I know what she wants?"

"You have to go meet her and see what she says. You're going to the cabin anyway. See what she says." His panic turns to pleading. "I can't lose my mom."

Those last words remind me too much of Ryan's reaction after we left his sister.

I look at Teagan, steeling myself. "I don't know. I need to think about it. For now, seal the prison," I command, "and fortify the main entrance. Something is happening now whether we like it or not."

"They might not know we're at the prison," Celexa says, chewing a cuticle.

"Maybe not, but we're not taking any risks," I say.

Traz nods, jaw clenched. Lith crosses his arms across his chest, feet planted wide. Ryan stands in the shadows like a statue.

Teagan doesn't respond, stunned into silence. I'm sure he's wondering what this means. I know I am.

"Gather the weapons we have," I say. "Me, Traz, and Lith will do one last outing downstairs. We'll do one more lap around outside too. Then we'll lock the door."

"Should we stay downstairs instead?" Emily asks.

"I can't get reception down there," Teagan says. "Besides, it'll feel like a tomb down there, and we won't be able to see our surroundings. At least upstairs, we can see if someone approaches."

"The rest of us," Celexa says, "will guard the entrance while you're downstairs in case you all get ambushed. I think we're being paranoid, but we need to be."

"Can't take any chances," I agree.

Teagan rises to his feet and starts gathering weapons.

We split up as discussed.

Traz, Lith, and I are meticulous in ensuring there is no way up to the main part of the building from the basement. After that, we do one more look around to make sure we've gathered all the supplies and that none are left behind.

Teagan meets us outside. He wraps the chain through the lock, slams the combination lock into place, and uses the key to lock it. "This way no one can even get in the basement."

We glance at each other, silent confirmation passing between us that we are sure this area is sealed off, and we do a lap around the periphery.

We return to the main entrance. Celexa is standing there, holding the door for us, along with a long piece of chain and a knife. Ryan is by her side with another knife, looking far too checked out for comfort. Emily and Cass are in the reception area, armed and alert.

"Done?" Celexa asks.

"Done," I confirm, walking through the open door.

Teagan is the last one in, pulling the door closed and locking it.

"Now," Lith says, cracking his knuckles, "let's fortify this bitch."

17

Emily, Cass, and I are sitting in our cell, playing cards. The sun hasn't set yet, and we're using the last hint of daylight.

"Are you going to meet Dr. Richter?" Emily asks.

Isn't that the million-dollar question. I throw down an ace of hearts. "I think so. I mean, yeah, I am. Even with the risk."

"It does seem risky," Cass says, taking her turn, "but I still think it's best. There's too much we don't know."

"Yeah, and why not? She's known all along how to find me. Why lure me to her if the only goal is to grab me and put me back in the asylum?" I say.

"What do you think she wants?" Emily asks. "If you had to guess."

"I wish I knew. I can't even imagine what she'll have to say. And how did she know that she could get a message to me on the radio? If nothing else, I need to find out if Teagan's mom is safe, for his sake. Maybe the doctor has had a change of heart and wants to offer help now. Maybe she's helping Teagan's mom," I say.

Cass looks up from her cards. "Gibbon did—have a change of heart—didn't he? He tried to help you twice, right, Shaun? That last time is how you—we—actually escaped."

"He did," I answer, "but not before allowing his own two kids to be killed."

"It just makes no sense." Emily plays her card. "Why now, I wonder. If she has known where we are, why does she want to talk to you now?"

"Maybe because things are ramping up with the Agency." I look sideways at Cass. "What do you think?"

She plays her card, then looks at me with those stormy eyes. "I feel like this is all going to blow up soon, one way or another. I know we keep saying that. I think we need to keep saying that, not only to convince ourselves that this is actually happening, but to make sure we don't let our guard slip. Something is brewing. I can feel it. We can all feel it."

"What do you think it is?" Emily asks then laughs without humor. She throws up a hand. "I know, I know. This is all speculation, and all we do, over and over, is speculate. It just helps to talk about it, so bear with me."

"I don't know," says Cass. "Shaun seeing Dr. Richter. Her waving at him. The asylum up and running again. Finding this prison, Teagan, the radio. Dr. Richter on the radio. Change is happening. Things are coming to a head. Maybe she wants to warn us...you."

A chill marches over my skin, as if Cass has had a vision of our future. The chill multiplies as I realize she's right.

This will all be over soon, if not for the Agency, then for us. We can't go on living like this. I was already at a breaking point before we found the prison and caught the Hail Mary in meeting Teagan and learning about his mom. But still, eventually, we'll run out of supplies and have to leave this place.

Eventually, the Agency will find us and annihilate us. If their end game is truly the complete destruction of our generation, then it's only a matter of time. We're no match.

But we aren't giving up.

"It feels like the apocalypse is coming," I say, tossing down a card without really paying attention to the game.

"I think it is," Cass says. "I think this is it. It's all felt like a dream, or a nightmare, up to this point. Now, it's starting to seem really real. And final."

"What do you mean?" Emily asks, taking her turn.

"I mean, I was in the asylum. And before that, I was held prisoner by my own father. Escaped the asylum, thanks to you two." She lifts her eyes and looks at us in turn. "We have just existed for months without anyone trying to find us. Looks like they've known where to find us all along but haven't tried. That gave us a little cushion of security in an odd way. But now...now it seems like they're ready to just wipe us off the face of the planet. Hearing that from another source, an outside source like Teagan and his mom…I don't know. I'm having a hard time putting my words together, but…" She sighs. "Something has changed. And something will be decided soon, one way or another. The end is nigh."

"Poetic," I say, trying to lighten the moment.

"Unfortunately, I don't think we have control over how this is going to end, do you?" Emily asks us, not lightening the moment.

By this point we have abandoned the game and are now focused on each other. It's growing dark outside, and part of our lockdown plan is to keep the lights off, including flashlights, except when in the bathroom, which is fully interior anyway so it doesn't matter. But the lack of light isn't why we stop playing. Words are being spoken; our situation is being confronted in a blunt way it hasn't been to this point.

"I won't be taken by that asylum again," Emily says.

"Me either. That's why we have the insurance plan," I say. "From now on, we take it everywhere."

"Insurance plan?" Emily asks.

"Moonseed," I say.

"Ah," Cass says, her expression clouding over. Neither Emily nor I mention her past attempt to die by suicide, but her statement has a dark foreboding to it that makes my body grow cold. "I forgot about that. Does it need to be picked fresh to work?"

"I'll get some more when I go to the cabin," I say.

Lost in our own thoughts, we grow quiet. I can hear Lith and Teagan talking a few cells down. I can hear heavy breathing from Traz and Celexa's cell. Ryan, as always, is completely silent.

Ryan will never be the same, I think sadly. How could he be? His twin was the only person who meant anything to him, and now she's gone. Because we left her behind. I left her behind.

In truth, though, how will any of us ever be the same?

We won't.

We won't because life will never be the same again.

We won't return to school. Go to college. Go to work. Get married. Have a family. None of those are options for us. Period.

There is a sense of freedom that hits me suddenly and urgently.

I have nothing to lose.

"I'll be in control of my fate, not her. And besides, if she's known all along how to find me, find us, then why hasn't she tried? We were in that cabin for months," I say.

"Do you think they know we're here now?" Emily asks.

"I don't know, but I wouldn't doubt it," I say. "The Agency is like a giant eyeball, watching, knowing. And if that's the case, why haven't they just come and annihilated all of us?"

"I'm scared," Emily says, her dark eyes filling with tears.

I pull her hand into mine and grab Cass's with my other hand. They clasp their free hands together, and we are joined, the three of us.

"What do we have to lose?" I ask as emotions whirl around inside me. "What do I have to lose by going?"

"This," Cass whispers, looking at us in turn. "We have this to lose. I know we will eventually, but I'm not sure I'm ready to lose it just yet."

"Us?" Emily asks, seeking the clarification I want as well. "Meaning all of us here in this prison? Or...us...the three of us?"

Cass's eyes fill with tears. "Us. The three of us." She squeezes my hand, and I know she's squeezing Emily's as well. "It's been a strange push and pull between us."

Emily opens her mouth, but Cass shakes her head. "You know it's true, so please hear me out. We are together all the time. We even sleep side by side, the three of us, and always have. I have felt the attraction between the two of you, and I've felt the attraction to Shaun. What I hadn't fully realized is my attraction to you too, Emily. And it's more than sexual. You two are my people. Both of you. I don't want anyone to choose anything. I want the three of us to always be together." A tear rolls down her cheek. "At least for the time we have left."

Tears are spilling from Emily's eyes, and I feel my own welling.

These two people, Cass and Emily, have been vital to my existence for months. You can't go through something like we've been through and not bond in a way lifetimes of normalcy wouldn't allow.

We are merged, the three of us. I hadn't realized it until this moment. I had felt a pull toward Cass from the beginning. Then a pull toward Emily after our escape—even kissed her before I kissed Cass. I always felt in the middle, leaning toward Cass, but now I realize I've felt something for Emily too. I'm not in the middle. I'm part of this trio.

Warmth fills my heart like hot air in a balloon, and the air around us changes. Something tells me they feel it too.

I sit quietly, studying them as they look at me, look at each other.

Emily reaches out and wipes Cass's tears. Cass leans her head into Emily's palm. I reach out and brush off Emily's tears. She rests her hand on my knee, keeping her gaze on Cass.

Emily leans in and kisses her.

It's a chaste kiss. At first. But then Cass leans into her, and they deepen the kiss, lips parted, mouths suctioned together. Energy pulses through me.

They break the kiss.

Cass looks at me, holding my gaze. Leans toward me.

Our lips touch. It doesn't begin as a chaste kiss. It's hot and deep and full of emotion.

We pull apart.

I look at Emily. She's looking at me. I glance at Cass. Her eyes are shining.

I lean toward Emily as she leans toward me.

We kiss.

My body is so charged, I almost can't breathe. I pull back and glance at Cass. She smiles.

The sun sets outside, casting the cell in near complete darkness. It starts to rain, the sound soothing as it hits the glass.

Wordlessly, we lay out our bedding. And we lie down, letting the night, the emotion, our connection consume us.

18

Inside the Mind of Dr. Esther Richter

• • • • • •

Nausea twirls inside Dr. Esther Richter's stomach, acid burns in her throat. She looks in the mirror of the small bathroom and hardly recognizes herself. She was on a trajectory that she believed in.

Now she's drowning in an ocean of regret. Fear, remorse, rage, despair. So many emotions fight for space inside her, it depends on the minute which one holds court. Each one ends with the same question, though.

What have I done?

What happened to cause this change? She doesn't have to think too hard on that…

She had been to Washington, D.C., several times during her life. Having been born and raised in Philadelphia, she'd lived close enough to the capital of the United States for day trips or overnights as it was a mere two hours away. Several school field trips had landed her in this city, seeing all the museums, the government buildings, and even a professional ice hockey game.

Now she is in Washington, D.C., for a conference she had been excited about. That excitement was exterminated, though, over the past weeks, leaving her body filled with a darkness, a heaviness that makes her walk from the bathroom back to the cold auditorium challenging.

She yearns for those carefree years of her childhood before life and life's choices became so complicated.

The head of the Agency is standing at the podium, drawing his speech on the status of operations to a close. Dr. Richter looks around at the roughly two hundred and fifty colleagues who fill the seats. They are at a university in the city, inside the university's main auditorium where, in another lifetime or even a week ago, plays, concerts, and debates were performed. Today the stage is for the Agency's use as a platform to showcase the progress the doctors within the Agency are making.

She had been fortunate enough to present her own life's work at the last meeting, a month ago, and it was met with great fanfare. She'd received a standing ovation, even, and several doctors had wanted to talk to her directly to gather more information, share tips, and inquire about partnering for future research.

She'd been on top of the world.

But after the excitement died down, and the crowd started to dissipate, the true evil settled in.

His name?

Les Range.

She'd first met Les Range, the head of the Agency, not when she'd been brought on board, but when her work had started to show promise. He'd visited the asylum once and had seemed interested in her work. But he'd seemed even more interested in her. If it weren't for Cyrus being present during their meeting, she didn't know what would have happened.

And she would not have been a willing participant.

She hadn't heard from him since his visit and was less than thrilled to see him at the conference, hoping instead it was his fat assistant who showed, the same one who did the monthly visits to the asylum. He usually attended these conferences because Les could not be bothered. She didn't like him either, but he was less intimidating, less threatening even, than Les Range.

She tried to make herself small in the audience, but he'd found her anyway, staring at her throughout the entire meeting. Even when he was talking about other doctors' work.

She had yet to make friends in this group of doctors. Colleagues, yes, but they were all people willing to do anything and everything to get support, financial and otherwise, for their work. She was no different, though there was one thing she was not willing to do.

And that was just the thing Les Range seemed to want.

She'd made a point to not be left in the slowly emptying auditorium alone and attached herself to a group of doctors from Missouri as they exited. She made it all the way to the end of the hall, the exit to the parking lot just ahead, when she heard her name called.

"Dr. Richter, a moment, please. Dr. Richter."

At first, she ignored him. But the Missouri doctors spoke at once, all telling her that Les Range was calling her name.

She had no choice but to turn.

He strolled to her side. The Missouri doctors exited. The hall was empty.

"I'd like to see you in my office," he said.

"Oh. Okay. What about?"

"Come with me."

Her heart sank. It was so quiet in the hall, she swore she heard her heart pounding on its descent.

Without an excuse, and with his expression stating there wasn't room for one, she followed him back down the hall, past the auditorium, and up a flight of stairs.

A glance out the window of the office he led her into confirmed it was nightfall. She felt like they were the only two people left on Earth. Especially when he closed the door. And locked it.

Nausea whirlpooled in her stomach, rising like acid into her throat.

"I really need to be going," she said. "I have a long drive back to Blackthorn Peak."

"Sit," he said.

She paused. He raised his brows, challenging.

She sat on the edge of the seat.

He stood at her side, brushed her hair off her shoulder, ran a finger over her exposed neck.

"You're making very good progress, Esther," he said. "You can make more progress still. Get your name and your work elevated to be the shining achievement of the Agency's mission, leaps and bounds above the others."

He pulled her hair off her neck and held it in his fist.

"Everyone wants to be the one example the Agency uses when our work goes public. You could be that example. Not to mention the salvation to your grandfather's work and your family name."

Panic pulsed through her body. "No," she said. "Not like this."

He laughed.

Those memories are never gone from her mind. It was only four weeks ago, but it feels like it happened yesterday. The only difference is that she was in shock then. Now she's enraged.

19

"I'm going to meet Richter at the cabin," I declare the next morning. I'm standing in the office. Teagan is behind the desk, holding the radio, and Lith stands by his side. Traz, for once, is without Celexa, who is still asleep in their cell.

"Why?" Traz asks.

"She's known where to find us—me—this whole time," I say. "She doesn't have to set a trap to get us. It's probably pretty safe."

"Do you think it's possible she knows you've left the cabin, but she doesn't know where you went, and this is her way to find out?" Lith presses. "I know I'm playing devil's advocate, but we can't be too sure."

"I won't give us up if that's the case. I have the moonseed," I say.

Teagan's brows raise. Lith nods in understanding.

"I plan to gather more," I say. "I don't know how fresh it needs to be, but I won't be taken by the Agency again."

"Moonseed," Teagan says, "is poisonous."

"Deadly," I confirm.

"I see," Teagan says. "What do the others think?"

"Cass and Emily understand. I don't know about Celexa and Ryan. But we're still at a stalemate here. Yes, we've had gains in shelter and nourishment, but we still have no plan of action. We're stuck. Maybe Dr. Richter can offer some insight. If the Agency is truly in Phase II, they'll come looking for us sooner rather than later."

"Maybe she'll kidnap your ass and put you back in the asylum, or worse," says Traz, and I wonder if he would be happy about that based on the smirk on his face.

I say, "I will not let them take me back to the asylum. I don't know how much clearer I can be about that."

"I can go too," Lith says. "Take the long way around, huddle in the forest out of sight. In fact, I can go ahead and leave. They aren't meeting until sunset. It's barely past sunrise. At least you will have backup if something does go down."

Teagan watches me. "It would sure make me feel better if I knew what role, if any, my mom has in Dr. Richter having access to the radio. I need to know my mom is safe. Just don't lead Dr. Richter back here—in case she doesn't know where to find us."

"I'll be careful," I say.

• • • • • •

Soon after our conversation, Lith takes off to scout the area around the cabin. He'll hide there and wait for sunset. If he sees or senses danger, he'll turn around and come back to the prison. If it seems calm, he'll clamber up a tree that overlooks the cabin and wait. It's not a foolproof plan, but nothing ever is.

I wash in the bathroom, then return to my cell. Cass has packed a small bag of food and water. Emily stands there with my weapons. I'll take the sharp, wooden knuckles, a chain, and a knife. I don't know what Lith took, but knowing him, he's armed to the teeth.

I look between them. I'm distracted by my mission but tune in to any emotions they're exuding. Neither seem upset by what happened last night, but I ask anyway. "Are we good here?"

Cass glances at Emily. They offer each other a faint smile. A connection has grown between them, and I hadn't even been truly aware of it. I thought I was the connection, but seeing them look at each other, I realize they have one separate from me.

That comforts me, especially as I prepare to head into the unknown.

"We're good," Emily answers, looking at me. "Are you?"

As I look at them, something warm fills my chest. I feel a slight pressure at the back of my eyes.

"I'm good," I say.

I kiss Cass, then Emily, and I leave them behind as I head to the office.

"Anything new?" I ask Teagan, refocusing on the task at hand.

"Nothing. It sounds like she's trying to tune in, but I'm probably imagining it."

"Maybe it's something as simple as a storm in the area." I glance outside at the first sunny day we've had in as long as I can remember.

He offers the faintest hint of a smile, more for my sake than his. "Be careful," he says.

Traz enters the room as I move to leave the office. We eye each other before he rests a hand on my shoulder. "Stay safe."

I nod and walk out the door.

• • • • • •

It's only been a couple of days since we went into lockdown mode in the prison, but that's two days without fresh air or unfiltered sunlight, even filtered, cloud-covered sunlight. I take a minute and breathe deeply, my face turned toward the sky. Then I set off.

It feels like it takes longer for me to get to the cabin, but since I don't have a watch, there's no way to know.

I don't see any sign of Lith on the way. I feel modestly confident there's no one else here, or he would've warned me. Of course, there's always a chance that he was ambushed. That he was taken, or worse, killed.

I linger in the tree line, watching and waiting.

The temperature starts to cool, and the vibrance of the sun dims. Sunset is coming. My eyes sweep back and forth across the landscape. My ears are tuned and focused. My weapons at the ready.

I'll wait until I see her before I show myself.

So much time passes—the sun has dipped below the distant mountain—that I think she's not going to show. Then I hear the unmistakable sound of a car engine. She's driving.

I think back to the first time I came to this cabin in my old pickup. The road was a treacherous, potholed ascent straight up the mountainside. I wonder what she's driving.

I feel a pang of sadness over the loss of my truck.

It takes forever for the actual vehicle to appear even though I heard its first roar what feels like ages ago. But suddenly, the sound of the engine is blaring, and I know she's about to pull on to the property.

She's driving my old pickup.

I nearly forget myself but manage to keep myself from running forward. I want to pummel her until she's left lying on the grass, and I will drive away in my beloved truck that took me two years of saving to afford.

With overwhelming effort, I stay in the tree line.

Why is she driving my truck?

I search the forest for any sign of Lith, not expecting to find him, and he's nowhere to be found.

Dr. Esther Richter turns the engine off. I can see her through the windshield. She's looking around, likely hesitant to get out, unsure of what will be waiting for her. I realize then we both have reason to be alert.

I can confirm there is no one in the passenger seat—no one sitting up at least. Someone could be lying down to avoid detection.

The bed of the truck looks empty, but again, if someone is lying down, I won't be able to tell from this point.

I wait.

She finally opens the door and slides out. She closes the door but stays close to the vehicle. She waits. Glances at her watch. Looks around.

"Shaun?" I hear her call my name, softly, then more loudly, "Shaun? Are you here?"

Her voice sounds uncertain and shaky, like she's nervous.

Well, she should be. She knows my propensity toward violence better than most. She shouldn't feel comfortable in this situation. I'm not above killing someone when I have to or when I feel it's the right thing to do.

She leans against the driver's side door, arms crossed over her chest—for warmth or comfort, I don't know.

After several more minutes, and no sign of someone hiding, I step away from the tree I was standing behind.

Finally, I catch a glimpse of Lith. Our eyes meet. He nods. I nod back.

I step into the clearing. “Hello, Dr. Richter.”

20

It's almost as if she wasn't expecting me; the shock is so obvious on her face. She stands there, frozen, for so long that I'm tempted to dart forward and snap my fingers in her face. Or slap her. Or worse.

"Well," I say instead. "You asked for this meeting. What do you want?"

"How are you?" she asks quietly. She doesn't move to meet me halfway in the yard, choosing to stay near the truck.

"Why are you driving my truck?" I stop in the middle of the yard, leaving some distance between us.

"I thought you might want to see it."

"That's kind of sick, don't you think?"

She used to look confident and in charge. Now she looks small and insignificant.

I can't let my guard down. Can't forget that this woman has killed hundreds of my peers. Was going to kill me.

"What do you want?" I ask again.

"I've been wondering how you are."

"Why?"

"Well"—she throws her hands up, then lets them flop to her sides—"I don't know. I just…I always thought you might have been my first Redeemable."

"But I know there will be no Redeemables, isn't that right?"

The Agency had some sort of deluded system to separate teens into two categories: Redeemables and Expendables. Redeemables were the teens who they might keep alive after the surgery to work for the Agency. Not to enter society again. Expendables were, well, the obvious, and nearly all the teens were placed in that category.

She doesn't respond, so I continue, "You and the Agency are killing this entire generation, aren't you? Even though the procedures, yours and the other doctors', are ready for mass rollout. Tell me I'm wrong."

"You're not wrong," she whispers.

Uncertainty fills me. I don't understand what's going on here. Why did she reach out? Why does she seem so timid and frightened?

"What's wrong with you?" I demand.

"What's wrong with me?"

It's like she can't even understand English or has no recollection of our past. Or the trauma and death she's caused.

"Don't play dumb. Why did you want to meet me?"

Her eyes scan the forest, resting on the cabin, then the firepit. Me.

"Are we alone?" she asks.

"Why?"

"Anyone could be hiding anywhere."

"True."

"So, are we?"

"Is there anyone hiding in my truck?"

She looks surprised at the question. "What? No. No, there's no one in the truck. Feel free to look."

"Open the doors, both sides. Then open the hitch. You step away from the truck and go sit on the porch."

She opens the doors on the driver's side first, then passenger side. She opens the hitch, then moves to the porch where she sits on the top step, watching me.

Giving my old beloved truck a wide berth, I look in each opened area and see that it's empty. Even the trash I'd left on the passenger side floor is gone. It looks like the truck has been cleaned.

"Did you vacuum my truck?" I ask.

This is getting stranger by the minute, and I'm not sure if she's the one who needs lobotomized or if she's biding her time before she goes on the attack.

This is weird, and I don't like it.

"Empty your pockets," I say.

She's wearing slacks and a sweater, plus a heavy coat. She empties the pockets of the coat and the pockets of her trousers.

"Lift your shirt," I demand.

"You want me to lift my shirt?"

"You're not as smart as I would've expected. Yes, lift your shirt, and show me you don't have a gun in your waistband or a weapon strapped to your torso."

I glance over my shoulder to where Lith is. I don't see him, but I sense his presence. I wonder what he thinks about this situation.

She follows my instructions, even showing me the band of her bra. I could've done without that part but am grateful she did it anyway.

Slowly, I approach the cabin, keeping several yards between me and the bottom step. "I'll ask you one more time—what do you want?"

"I wanted to see you," she said.

"Now you've seen me."

She nods.

"What else?" I demand. "I'm not sticking around here all night. Is it possible you came here because you want to help me?" I think of Teagan's mom.

"Gibbon helped you, didn't he?"

"He did. Before you killed him."

Pain flashes across her face. "I have nightmares about that one."

"Not about the hundreds of teens?"

Her eyes drop to her lap. "Those too."

"So, you're here to confess? I'm no priest, so you can forget about absolution from me."

"I've made a terrible mistake," she whispers.

I heard every word, but I can't quite reconcile it, so I ask, "What did you say?"

"I said, I've made a terrible mistake."

"Too late for apologies, don't you think?"

"I do. But it's not too late to try and right the wrong I've committed and help."

"Help who?"

Her eyes lift. I keep waiting for an army to storm me from all sides. I put my hand in my pocket and pull a handful of moonseeds out. Ready access is imperative, as this situation seems to be teetering on a knife's edge.

"Are any of your friends still alive?"

My eyes narrow as I study her.

"The ones you escaped with?"

"Is Renee still alive?" I demand.

"Renee?"

"Don't play dumb."

She stands. Slowly walks down the steps until she's eye level with me. Those mismatched eyes are as unsettling as ever.

"What are you expecting me to say?" she asks.

"Is she dead?"

"No."

"Did you hurt her?"

Her eyes fill with tears. "I got my first Redeemable."

I feel sick and have to hunch over, take a minute to swallow against the rising vomit. Death would've been better than lobotomy.

"I believe in my work, Shaun. Despite everything that's happening with the mass annihilation, I believe in my work. The procedure I've perfected can change the world. I truly believe that. But I don't believe in the killings."

My mouth falls open.

"Not anymore," she clarifies. She wipes her nose with a tissue, puts it back in her pocket.

"What's changed your mind?"

"This is turning into a circus, no, a bloodbath."

"It's always been a bloodbath."

"I've realized something."

"Yeah? What's that?"

"That everyone is capable of evil." She pulls the tissue back out of her pocket but doesn't wipe her nose.

"You're just now figuring that out?"

"I am," she whispers. "I don't want my family name to be linked to any part of the Agency's work if this is how it's going to be."

"That's the stupidest thing I've ever heard—you're worried about your stupid family name when millions are set to die? Talk about narcissistic. Yeah, I took psychology my sophomore year." Pain shoots through my palms, and I realize I've been clenching my fists so hard my nails have dug into my skin. With effort, I force my fingers to relax.

"My grandfather created the lobotomy. He was a god in the medical world. Even in the regular world. Really on to groundbreaking psychosurgery. But then, the stardom went to his head. His name, my family name, became synonymous with barbaric malpractice and ridicule."

"I see you've carried on that tradition."

"I was trying to perfect the procedure. Help make the world a better place. I truly believed that was what I was doing. Please know I was also operating from a place of extreme grief." She raises the tissue to her eyes.

I don't tell her I know the story of how Emily and her friends stole that stop sign.

"Looking back…"

"Looking back?"

"I got caught up in something I didn't fully understand."

"For someone so close to achieving her goals, you seem awfully sad."

She wipes her nose again as she waits for me to continue.

"You have perfected this lobotomy, correct? And you're ready to shove an ice pick into the brains of countless children who don't fit the societal standard, isn't that right? And you say that you've changed?"

"Circumstances have changed. I have changed. I didn't know the full extent of what Les Range was capable of. I truly had no idea."

"Who the hell is Les Range?"

"The only person who matters at the Agency."

"I'm listening." I shove my cold hands in my pockets and wait.

"He is an evil man." She shoves her tissue into her pocket.

I raise my brows. "Only him?"

"You don't understand. The hold he has over people. The manipulation. The brainwashing. And if not that, the blackmail."

"Get to the point." My fists start to clench again. I force my palms to flatten, glancing down at my palms where I see the half-moon indentations from before.

"I came here today to see how you are and to see if there is a chance we can now work together. If I can help you and the others."

She's admitting she knows about the others.

"How would you do that?" I ask.

"I admit I'm not sure. I wanted to see you first to see if you would even talk to me. I would've understood if you didn't want to."

I snort. Glare at her.

"But I'm glad you came," she says. "Now that I know you'll allow me to help, I need to go back and think of a plan."

"Why me?" I ask bluntly.

Looking confused, she says, "Can you be more specific?"

"If I recall from my time under your oh so tender care, you thought I might be your first Redeemable. Why me?"

"I admire you. It's as simple as that."

"Why?"

"Because of your convictions. You were willing to do anything to save your mother."

"Yeah, I killed that asshole and ended up in the asylum."

"My sister was fleeing an abusive marriage, with her children, when her minivan was hit by the eighteen-wheeler."

I don't respond, but understanding starts to prick at my resolve.

"It lasted for years. It was devastating to watch. And I didn't do anything. You did do something. I so wanted to help you."

"By lobotomizing me?"

"You were also deeply troubled. Anyone who commits murder is. I wanted to give you a second chance at a better life." She inhales, then exhales. "I still admire what you did. Had I had more guts, I would've made her leave years before, and she never would've been on that road in the minivan with all of her children. Not on that day, because I would've had her go to another state. Far from that devil."

Several moments pass in silence as I try to process what she's saying. Finally, I respond. "But none of this matters now. The Agency is in the active killing phase, and you work for them. Your so-called change of heart doesn't really mean anything. Unless there's something specific you can offer me."

"No. Not yet. I can't. Today, I just wanted to see you. I can't talk more now. I have to be back." She looks around as if expecting this Les Range to walk out of the forest.

"You came all this way for...nothing? Just to *see* me?"

"How are the others? Your friends?"

"Who?"

"Emily, Cassidy, Ryan. And I believe, James, Carter, and Liza?"

I don't respond.

"And Teagan," she adds.

"How did you know how to contact me?" I almost forgot about Teagan's mom.

"I work with Teagan's mom."

"Is she safe?"

"As safe as any of us."

"Did she tell you about the radio? Tell you how to dial in?"

"She did."

"Why?"

"You all need help," she answers instead, "if you're going to survive. I believe she knows that."

"How many of you are willing to help when the time comes?"

"I don't have an answer to that yet. I wanted to see you, get a feel for how you would respond to me. If we can work together, if you'll allow me to help you, I'll return to the asylum and start doing everything in my power to right the wrongs I've done."

"How?"

"Meet me back here in two days. Now that I've seen you, talked to you, I want to talk to others. When we meet next, hopefully, I'll have guidance for you."

Her thin lips clamp shut. She's looking straight at me, but her eyes seem to lack focus, as if her mind is off and wandering. Or remembering. I know that look. That's a PTSD look.

"Did something happen?" I ask.

Her eyes clear and zero in on mine. "Yes. Something happened. And that something has led to my change of heart. To the veil being removed from my very naïve eyes."

21

Lith and I hike back to the prison, his questions coming at me rapid-fire.

"What did she want? What did she say? Did she explain why she wanted to see you? Does she still want to kill you?"

"Did you hear nothing of our conversation?" I demand.

"No. I was hiding, remember?"

"I thought our voices might carry."

"They didn't. Spill it."

Just before we come to the clearing of the prison, I stop him. "All I know is that she says she's had a change of heart and that she wants to help us. Something happened to her—"

"Did she say what?"

That's the fifth time he's asked me that question.

I sigh. "She alluded to something."

"What exactly?"

"She didn't say. Something has happened, though."

"Will you tell them you're meeting Dr. Richter again in two days?"

"Sure. Any reason why you think I shouldn't?"

Lith seems lost in thought. Finally, he says, "I don't think so. Let's just lay it all out on the table. We're past the stage of secrets. I just wonder how they'll react, and if anyone—I'm thinking of Traz specifically—will try to tell you no."

"I don't give a shit what Traz says. He's an ass."

"An ass who's managed to stay alive all this time."

"Yeah. Alive and doing absolutely nothing to change his situation."

Lith doesn't respond.

"I'm assuming," I continue, "that she'll give me more information at our next meeting. She said she wanted to see how I reacted to her. Hopefully I passed the test, and she'll be ready to actually help."

"Here's hoping," Lith says.

• • • • • •

We are sitting on the floor in the hallway, everyone awake and alert despite the late hour.

"Something happened to her," I tell the group. "She wouldn't say what, but she says she's had a change of heart."

"Do you believe her?" Emily's tone escalates with each word until every other syllable is a high pitch. "I mean, why…*how* could you believe her? This woman tried to kill us. Locked us in a room and pumped us full of medication. Killed our peers."

I'm slightly taken aback by the vehemence in her voice. Not that she's wrong…but I at least thought she'd wait to hear me out before jumping to conclusions. Cass pulls Emily's hand into hers and runs her thumb over her skin.

"I'm not saying I do one-hundred-percent believe her, so don't get me wrong. I'm just relaying what she said to me. She came alone. In my old truck, which was odd," I say.

"She was driving your truck?" Celexa asks. "Why?"

I shrug. "I'm not sure. Maybe to pull at my heartstrings. Associate herself with something important to me. I don't know."

"What else did she say?" Celexa's gaze is earnest, seeking, alarmed.

"She's known that we were in the cabin, and about Teagan, so I assume she knows about the prison."

"Did she say anything about my mom?" asks Teagan.

"She just said that your mom told her how to reach me by your radio," I say. "They're both interested in the same thing—helping us."

"Well, at least it's confirmed." Teagan releases a long sigh. "We'd assumed as much, but it helps to know for sure. Did she say if she or the Agency are coming after us?"

I say, "She confirmed that no one is safe and that they're kicking things into high gear, so to speak."

"Why now?" Traz asks. "They've been dormant for months. Spent years experimenting. Why start the mass killing now?"

"Phase II," Cass says.

I glance at her. "Phase II. Complete annihilation of our generation. We're no longer needed for experiments, so we're no longer useful. I assume they're ready for that complete reset of society. Dr. Richter didn't say much about that, though. Just that she's had a change of heart."

"I still don't understand," Traz says. "How will she help us?"

"She wants me to meet her again in two days," I say. "To talk more. That's all I know."

"Why?" Celexa asks.

"Why what?" I ask.

"Why you?" Celexa asks with more than a little accusation shaping those two simple words.

• • • • • •

Teagan asks for a break to check the radio again. Traz and Celexa head down the hall. Ryan never came out of his cell for our meeting. The remaining four of us stay seated on the floor.

"He's been checking that radio more often today," Emily whispers to me.

"Did he hear from his mom?" I whisper back, not sure why we're whispering. Every little noise travels, so the whole hall knows we're talking.

"She made contact earlier, but the reception was terrible, so it was a short conversation."

"Was she able to give any new information?"

Emily looks at Cass.

"What's going on?" Lith asks, not bothering to whisper. "Why the side-eyes between you two?"

Cass nods, eyes still focused on Emily, and Emily sighs before saying, "She did manage to give a warning."

"A warning for what?" I ask. I feel my body coil in dread.

"That there's a traitor."

"A traitor? Who?"

Emily watches me with unblinking eyes.

"Teagan?" I ask. "No way."

"A redhead."

"A redhead?"

She nods. Looks at Cass again. Cass just stares back at her. What silent exchange is going on between them is a mystery, but a dark feeling creeps into my soul.

• • • • • •

Cass, Emily, and I are sitting in a circle in our cell, our knees touching, connecting us. No one was interested in talking more after the redhead revelation, so we all went to our cells. Emily grabs the deck of cards, shuffles, and deals.

"That doesn't make any sense," I say to them.

Lith had gone to Ryan's cell. I could hear their low voices carry down the hall as they talked about old sports teams they played on as children.

"A redheaded traitor? I mean, first of all, it's ridiculous if anyone thinks it could be me. Second of all, did anyone wonder if it's Dr. Richter? She could be the traitor," I say.

"Why do you automatically think it was you?" Emily presses.

I roll my eyes at her. "Come on. I'm obviously the first one you all thought of. I could tell by the looks you all shot at me." I glance at Cass. "Or how you avoided looking at me at all."

Cass's eyes meet mine briefly before falling back to the floor.

Emily continues, "The reception was terrible, like I said. I think Teagan is staying by that radio so much because he's desperate for more information. We all are."

"Well, since I'm the only redhead in our group, and I'm not the traitor, it must be Dr. Richter," I say.

Cass shrugs, chewing on her lip.

Emily just says, "Hopefully, Teagan's mom makes contact soon."

"Did something else happen while I was gone, though?" I asked. "Besides the traitor comment? Celexa was acting weird, and I can't imagine that one comment has derailed everything we've all been through. Talk about jumping the gun. Not to mention, we've been living in very close quarters for months. How could I be a traitor?"

"She's always acting weird lately," Emily mutters.

"Really?" I ask. "I hadn't noticed anything. Cass, have you?"

"Not really," Cass says. "She seems preoccupied with Traz, but that's been going on a while."

"She seemed to think it was strange that Dr. Richter wanted to see me," I say.

"Well, it is strange," Emily says, glancing at the cards lying on the floor in front of her, untouched. "Why do you think she wanted to see just you?"

"The only thing she said was that she thought I'd be her first Redeemable and that she admired how I killed Rodger. Turns out, and I'm sorry to go here, Em, but her sister was leaving an abusive husband when the minivan was hit."

Emily pales, slapping a hand over her mouth to subdue a sob.

I continue, "And she wishes she'd been more aggressive in getting her sister to leave him earlier."

Tears spill from Emily's eyes. Cass reaches out a hand and rests it on her knee.

I think about Dr. Richter and how her entire demeanor was so different at the cabin than it was in the asylum. I wonder why any part of me would believe her, or even want to. Is that a reflection of how desperate our situation is? That I am now willing to overlook all the damage this woman has done over a vague commitment to help us in some elusive way?

I think about Gibbon, think about him often, actually. He was Dr. Richter's assistant. A huge man with a head shaped like a bowling ball and the IQ of a fifth grader, he had tried to help me escape more than once. He was vital in our final escape from the asylum, and I owe him my life.

He'd helped me when he wouldn't even save his own sons. I don't understand that. And since Dr. Richter killed him, I never will.

"Shaun, Earth to Shaun?"

I glance up at Cass. "Sorry. I was just thinking about Gibbon."

"I think about Trevor and Owen all the time," she says. She was the one who had found Owen's body half-buried in the forest behind the asylum, and the one who had lured Trevor into the asylum—much like she'd lured me. She hadn't really understood what was happening—her father, Cyrus, had never explained his demands of her, only commanded she do his bidding.

Owen and Trevor were Gibbon's sons. Why didn't he try to save them like he did us…me? Why doesn't Cass have more insight than she does?

I sigh. I'll simply never know.

I study Cass's bent head. Subconsciously, I study her hair. It's sprouting out of her head, making her look like a cool yet disheveled rock star. I feel a punch of relief that there is no trace of red in that brown hair.

She always said she didn't know anything about what was going on. That her father had such a tight hold on her that she never disobeyed him when he asked her to do things without explanation. And she had ended up in the asylum herself.

Maybe one day, after this is all over, more of her memories will surface. She was the only one of us with a connection to the asylum, whose father was directly involved.

Since there doesn't seem to be anything else to discuss right now, we huddle together under several blankets. It's nearing the end of October, and there is no heat in this building. It's still warmer than sleeping outside, but the cold is starting to creep in.

After several moments of shivering, we figure out a better way to keep warm.

22

Thus Speaks Cassidy Rutherford

• • • • • •

The warmth from Emily's and Shaun's bodies permeates far deeper than just the layers of skin between us. Their simple closeness, their existence, warms my heart and my otherwise cold soul. In fact, these two are the only parts of my life that are absolutely right. Puzzle pieces that fit together perfectly.

I listen as Emily and Shaun kiss, and instead of jealousy, I feel deep contentment. True *rightness*. When Emily kisses me, I feel charged and share that energy when I kiss Shaun. We are connected, the three of us, in a way far deeper and more profound than any human connection I've ever experienced.

Maybe it's the constant fear of death that has bonded us. The joint trauma that we've each experienced from the time in the asylum to our escape to these last months of extreme uncertainty. The threat of death is ever present, and it has created a unique opening for a merging of our spirits.

That's what it feels like—a merging of our spirits. I can't explain it. Don't feel the need to. I just feel it, and it feels right, and that is enough for me.

I cuddle into Shaun's shoulder, reaching over his chest to grasp Emily's hand. Within moments, our breath pattern merges until we seem to breathe as a unit. I can tell by their breathing when they are asleep, and I am almost there myself, these twilight moments the only purely blissful moments I have. I hold off on sleep a few extra moments to savor it because none of us know what tomorrow holds.

The words over the radio haven't stopped playing in my head:

redheaded traitor.

Surely Teagan's mom isn't talking about Shaun. Shaun would never betray us.

Yet, it was strange, those words Teagan's mom said, clarity chopped by static.

What a time for the reception to be so spotty.

Dr. Richter has red hair, that's true. Any of the rest of us?

No. Brunette and blond, but no red. I had mine dyed purple, or the tips at least, when I met Shaun, but my hair is brown.

Who could she be talking about?

I don't know. It can't be Shaun.

He did spend a lot of time hiking alone when we were at the cabin. That's true. But betray us?

Never.

Resigned to an unsettled feeling deep in my gut, I decide to focus on the two people beside me and their rhythmic breathing. I decide to take this twilight, and each and every one I'm given, and be grateful, for there is no guarantee of another.

23

I jolt awake. Shoot upright. Look around the darkness of the cell. Glance to my right, then left. At some point during the night, Cass and Emily curled onto their sides and were no longer lying in my arms. They're still asleep.

What happened?

Was it another nightmare?

Did I hear something? Maybe one of the others is awake and walking around. Lith. It's probably Lith. He never seems to sleep.

I listen. Hear nothing but the steady breathing of the girls. Carefully, so as not to wake them, I stand. I cover both with the blankets and pause to make sure they stay asleep.

I ease toward the window where gray-black light is pouring through, distant blips of gold from the stars adding an ethereal feel to the night. The moon is halfway through its latest journey. Fortunately, the cloud cover is minimal, and the unexpected light of the night helps me get my bearings.

There is nothing amiss outside that I can tell. I stand guard for several minutes to make sure. Then I tiptoe into the hall. I see no one and creep down to the office, careful to stay in the shadows.

I see Lith asleep in his cell, one arm flung over his eyes as if the gray light streaming in from outside is too blaring for his comfort.

Teagan's cell is empty.

It's so quiet, the sound of my own breathing is loud. I hold it and try to control it, which ends up making the urge to pant almost irresistible. I hold off hyperventilating as I ease forward.

Teagan is standing at the window, looking into the backyard. Does he see something I didn't?

I ease into the office.

He does not turn. "Someone is out there."

On silent feet, I move to his side, staying in the shadows, away from the window.

"One person or more?" I ask as quietly as possible.

"I'm not sure."

We wait.

"Go to the other side of the window," he says. "You watch that direction, and I'll watch this one. We don't want to be surprised. Or stand right in front of the window like a target."

"Should we wake the others?"

"Not yet."

"What makes you think someone is out there?" I ask, still seeing no sign that that's the case.

"I heard them. Whoever it is has been throwing rocks against the window."

"Of your cell?"

"Of the office. I never went to bed."

"I wonder who."

"Someone is trying to get my attention."

"You sure?"

"Yeah. Pretty sure. Though now I'm starting to second guess myself because I don't see anyone out there."

The fog is growing steadily, casting a white hazy sheen at the forest's beginning.

"What time is it?" I ask.

"Near dawn."

Suddenly, the sound of a rock pinging the window makes me jump.

"There it is," he says.

I strain to see. In this oddly enchanted area, the fog is like a set piece, coming and going as if on command. Now, it's growing steadily and quickly, our view becoming more and more obscured by the second.

"I can't see anyone," he says. "Can you?"

"I can't. Wait." There is movement along the forest line. I'm very aware that it could just be the shadows and mist, but I don't think so. "There's someone at the edge of the forest. Right in the middle."

The forest is close enough that someone could feasibly hit the window with a rock.

The fog needs to clear. The wind picks up, and the tall trees sway along with it.

The wind moves the fog.

There is someone standing there. I can see her more clearly now.

"Is that…" I squint, straining to see the face below the red hair. Is that Dr. Richter?

Before I can tell for sure, Teagan gasps. "That's my mother."

He darts for the door.

"Teagan, wait." I run after him through the reception area and grab his arm just as he grasps the knob on the front door. "You can't just run out there. It could be a trap."

"It's my mother. She wouldn't trick me. She wouldn't set me up."

"Why not?" I demand, thinking of my own mother. "Why wouldn't she?"

"Because she's my mother."

"That doesn't always matter. My mom is the one who set me up."

"What?" he demands.

"Look. You can't assume."

He wrenches his arm free.

"What's going on?" Lith appears in the reception area doorway.

"My mom is outside, and I'm going to see her," Teagan states.

"C-come again?" Lith stammers, caught between waking up and responding to chaos.

Teagan yanks open the prison door and darts outside before I can stop him. "Teagan!" I whisper-yell, but he's quickly lost to the thick fog.

I turn and look at Lith.

"Should we lock it?" he asks.

"For now. But let's not go far in case he needs inside in a hurry."

Lith nods.

I jog past him, up to the window in the office, desperate to catch a glimpse of Teagan and his mother. To ensure that it's just her. That he's safe.

For the longest time, I don't see him. Finally, I see a form running through the now very thick fog and disappearing into the tree line.

Lith and I wait.

• • • • • •

What seems like hours, though likely only minutes, later, Teagan can be seen crouching as he jogs out of the forest, heading back toward the prison. Lith hurries to unlock the door. Teagan walks in.

At some point, Traz joined us and now stands in the office. He's leaning against the wall, watching as Lith, Teagan, and I file in.

Tension tightens Teagan's features.

"Well?" Traz asks. "What's going on?"

Ignoring him, I ask, "What did she say? Is everything okay?"

"Everything is distinctly not okay." Teagan plops into the chair behind the desk. Turns and stares out the window as he continues, "She says we need to leave. Confirmed the Agency knows we're here and are further into Phase II than she knew." He looks at us. "They're coming for us."

"When?" Lith demands. "Did she say when?"

"Complete annihilation," Emily says weakly as she, Cass, and Celexa appear in the doorway.

"But where are we to go?" Celexa asks, pressing against Traz's side. He puts his arm around her shoulders. "Do we have to go today?"

"That's the problem," Teagan says, his voice monotone. "Nowhere is safe. She knows that, but she says being in the prison is a more immediate danger. Being in this area."

"She works for the Agency, right?" Traz asks. "How do we know she's telling the truth?"

"Because she's my mother," Teagan replies.

"With red hair," Traz says. Those of us who saw her from the window are all thinking it.

"She's the one who told us there's a traitor. She's not telling on herself. Don't be stupid," Teagan says.

Cass and I exchange quick glances. Both of our parents—my mom and her dad—were responsible for putting us in the asylum. We know better than anyone that parents cannot be trusted.

"This place is like a fortress," I say to get back to the point at hand. "I'm hesitant to leave it for the open vastness of the forest. It's going to be winter soon. Freezing temperatures. Snow. We'll never make it, assuming they also know about the cabin. Dr. Richter does."

"He's got a point," Lith says, rubbing his chin.

"Mom says that she's been talking with Dr. Richter and knows there are more here than just me," Teagan says. "She says if I can't convince everyone to leave that I should go to the local high school."

"The local high school?" Celexa asks. "Why?"

"Because the Agency is going to broadcast across the nation about all the 'good' work"—Teagan uses air quotes to emphasize the word—"that they're doing. They're ready to roll out their treatments to the masses. Take their show into every doctor's office. It's time for the great unveiling."

A cold, damp chill settles over my body.

"When?" Emily manages to ask.

Teagan says, "Tomorrow night."

"Does that mean…" Cass whispers.

Teagan looks at us all in turn. "That means that most of our generation are already dead."

Celexa bursts into tears. Traz punches the wall. Lith looks murderous. Emily starts to speak, quickly and with a shrill voice, words no one could understand in their jumbled mess. Cass looks like she's dissociated. Teagan and I stare at each other. My thoughts erupt in a flurry, and I can't grasp a single one. It's like chasing a snowflake.

After several moments of escalating hysteria, Celexa is led out of the office by Traz. He takes her down to their cell where her sobs can still be heard as clear as a bell.

"Let's take a minute," Emily says, gathering Cass into her arms. The two lean on each other as they walk down to our cell. I don't follow.

"Did she say anything else?" I ask finally.

"Not really," says Teagan. "I mean, it was a bit of a shock, so I'm not sure how much more I processed."

"Did she give you a time frame? How soon do we need to leave? I mean, if she's saying to stick around long enough to watch this spectacle, then the danger can't be imminent." I struggle to control my breath.

"She said to watch the spectacle if I couldn't convince everyone to go. Not to intentionally stick around for it," says Teagan.

"But where is there to go?" I slam my fist on the desk. "Dammit. There's nowhere to go."

There's no answer worth giving, so Teagan doesn't give one.

"When did you say this show is?" I demand.

"Tomorrow night," Teagan says.

"That gives me time to see Dr. Richter," I say. "Let's plan to stay here and take turns keeping watch, twenty-four hours a day. Let's keep weapons actually on hand at all times. We can use the top two floors as stakeout spots. We can see farther out that way. We'll barricade the door. I'll go see the doctor. She might be trying to help us. Some of us, at least, will go to the high school."

"You really want to see that?" Lith asks.

"No, I don't want a part of any of this," I say. "But…I have to ask, and I know you don't want to hear it. Teagan, your mom works for the Agency. What if it's a trap? If it's not true? Dr. Richter said the guy in charge of the Agency, Les Range, is a master at getting people to do what he wants."

"What are you saying?" Teagan's tone drops to a sinister level.

"Dude, don't come at me. We have to discuss all possibilities. This is, literally, a matter of life and death," I say.

Teagan's eyes narrow as he watches me, unblinking, deliberately and slowly moving from staring into my eyes to staring at my hair.

Finally, his eyes drop to the desk, and he nods.

"Listen," I say softly. "My mom put me in the asylum." The words almost get stuck in my throat like dry wood, but I swallow against the pain. "I know better than anyone except maybe Cass—whose dad put her in the asylum—what parents can do. It doesn't mean she doesn't love you. I think they get brainwashed or blackmailed." I sigh. "I'm just trying to cover all the bases."

He doesn't agree, but he doesn't protest either.

I continue, "Isn't it strange that she usually comes into the prison by the front door, and tonight lured you out?" Rage flashes across Teagan's face. I throw up my hands, placating. "Let's go to the high school and confirm this is true. She didn't say we had to leave right now, so we must have some time. I'll see Dr. Richter. We'll go to the show, and in the meantime, we'll create a plan to leave. We can't just head out of here and brave the elements. We won't survive. At least here we have a chance."

"I'll distribute the weapons," Lith says, "and barricade that door. Someone needs to create a schedule—we should have patrols on each floor around the clock. It'll be harder at night, but it'll also be easier to see if someone is approaching the prison with a flashlight." He seems to have grown in size, standing now with arms crossed.

"I'll create the schedule," I say. "And a to-do list. There's paper around here somewhere, right?"

Teagan nods.

"It's settled, then," I say.

Teagan is staring at me again. I purposefully ignore the look of despair on his face.

The air in the prison has become charged—I feel it inside my blood and on the surface of my skin. And I know, without a doubt, that this is it. That we are now stepping toward death, or life. The time for hanging in limbo is over.

24

"What if he's in on it?" Emily asks in a hushed tone. She, Cass, and I are walking along the top floor where we have the most privacy and where the windows in the cells offer wider views of the surrounding area outside.

"Who?" Cass asks.

"Teagan. Maybe he's the one being blackmailed or brainwashed or whatever, and it's a trick to lure us to the school," Emily says.

"Then he's in on it," I say. "I know that's not a great answer, but really, what other choice is there but to stick to the plan? We keep asking that same question over and over, and we're never going to get answers. Besides, I really don't think he's complicit in this. I really don't."

"I feel sick." Cass wraps her arms around her thin torso, hunching over as if she's trying to make herself smaller. Emily runs a hand over her back. I pull them both to me. For several moments, we just hold each other.

"Come on," I say after a while. "We're supposed to be keeping an eye out for intruders."

We pull apart. Slowly, we walk up to each window along the hall, pausing and watching.

"Why *wouldn't* his mother help us?" Cass asks after a long silence. "Why *would* Dr. Richter?"

"I don't know," I say.

"Could it be possible that there are others out there who would sympathize with us?" Cass wonders aloud.

"The doctor alluded to that," I say.

Cass pulls us to a stop in front of the window at the far cell. Here the trees grow almost up to the building. If I could open the window,

I'm sure I could reach out and touch the sturdy branch.

"What's most shocking about all of this," Cass says, "is that parents are in on it. I mean, aren't mothers supposed to protect their young? Like mama bears? Literally, how could so many mothers"—she glances at me with sympathy in those gray eyes—"sorry, Shaun. But how could so many mothers agree to this? Maybe the Agency's reach isn't quite as vast as we thought."

Neither Emily nor I knew our fathers, and Cass's father put her in the asylum, so we don't mention the male figures in our lives. Well, I killed the only male influence I knew, so it's best we stick to the females.

"Good point," Emily says, "but the problem is that, clearly, they are agreeing to it. Or if they're not, we have no way to find them. Not without exposing ourselves. There's no way to know who to trust."

"Can we reach out using Teagan's radio?" Cass asks.

"What are you getting at?" I ask, trying to jump ahead of her line of thinking.

"Can we reach out for help by using the radio? It's a long shot, I know, but maybe. Tune in to different channels. Cry out for help," says Cass.

"We could always ask him what he thinks about it," I say. "We just need to be careful not to give ourselves away."

"The Agency already knows where we are," Emily says.

"Yeah." I sigh.

"But it's true," Emily says, "that Teagan's mother helped set him up here and gave him access to that radio. She is someone who's helping. Dr. Richter might be someone who's helping too. We need a way to reach others, and I'd rather not put all our eggs in Dr. Richter's basket."

"Let's finish our rounds then go talk to Teagan." I give the landscape one final look before walking to the next cell, verifying from each window we've already been to that the world outside is still quiet. After going up and down the hall twice, as the group discussed, we head down the stairs to the second floor.

"I wonder," I say as we walk, our footsteps the only other sound, "if we can broadcast what happens at the high school out to the masses. If we broadcast live what we're seeing, and if it's as bad as Teagan's mother says it is, that might actually be the rallying cry we all need. And the hook to get someone to help."

"If anyone actually hears it," Cass says.

"And that's a big *if*." I release another heavy exhale. I'm not sure when I became someone who sighs, but it seems that I have. Just when we seem to take a teeny-tiny step forward, we're always pushed back twenty feet.

"Let's gather the group," Emily says, her voice taking on an intensity I haven't heard in days, months. "It's time we take action."

My next urge to sigh stops midway. I'm surprised by Emily's sudden burst of energy. I stop and look at her for a minute, then shrug. *Okay*, I think. *Why not?* But those weak words don't reflect my own surge in energy. I grab their hands, and we march toward the office.

• • • • • •

"We left some knives we didn't think we'd need down in the basement, in the kitchen," Lith says. "I think it's worth going back down there. I don't know why we didn't think about that before we barricaded ourselves up here, but we could use more of the knives."

"We didn't want to have excess utensils to dirty, because they would attract rodents," Emily reminds us. "I'm not sure a few more butter knives will help our cause."

"Everything little thing can help," Lith says.

"Good call," Teagan says. "Let's do one last search of the outside from each floor, and then two of us can go down."

"Lith and I will go," I say.

Teagan nods. "I'll man the watch with the others."

By that afternoon, we have more knives, and also forks.

"Might seem odd"—Lith laughs—"but I'm sure I can forge some kind of weapon out of these forks. If nothing else, they'll be useful in close combat."

We also grabbed matches, a can of propane that was in the pantry, cooking string—though I couldn't imagine what we'd need it for—scissors, the fire extinguisher, all the chili powder and pepper left, olive oil, and another box of trash bags we'd found.

We also discovered some walkie-talkies. I don't know how we overlooked them before.

"Look at all this stuff." Teagan actually laughs. "This reminds me of that scene in the Christmas movie with the kid who booby-traps his house."

Lith chuckles. "That's exactly what all this is."

No one mentions that this stuff is child's play against a force like the Agency, but it feels good in the moment, so we let it end there.

It takes the rest of the evening to booby-trap the main entrance with olive-oil slicked trash bags on the floor and a string barrier. We agree to go in and out the window at the far end of the hall if needed. Traz managed to unscrew the bars and replace them so it looks like any other window from the outside. In a hurry, though, we can just shove it aside and jump out. It's the closest point to the forest and the cover it provides.

That's how we'll leave when I go to meet Dr. Richter and when we go to the high school.

That evening, everyone is quiet. Traz and Celexa head to their cell. Cass, Emily, and I head to ours. I can hear Lith quietly talking to Ryan, though I don't hear Ryan say anything back. Teagan stays in the office with the radio that remains pathetically quiet.

No one knows what that means, and no one wants to know. Why not? Because the likely scenario is that Teagan's mom is right, and Phase II is almost complete. Meaning we might very well be the only ones left of our generation.

• • • • • •

We don't hear anything the next day from Dr. Richter or Teagan's mom. The radio's silence is astonishingly loud.

We play cards. Talk. Eat. Wash. Nap. Try to hold off the encroaching panic that creeps toward us anyway.

Emily tells the group about her idea of trying to broadcast whatever happens at the high school. Of course, there's no guarantee anyone will hear, but we weigh the possible harm with the possible benefit and decide *why not*?

I'm due to go see Dr. Richter this evening. Lith already left to scout out the area like last time.

Cass and Emily both kiss me before I leave. The others are quiet, as if we have to keep our voices down even while inside. A sense of suspended doom hovers in the air.

Armed with food, water, and weapons, I slip out of the window.

The air is charged. Frigid. Windy. The sky is gray, and it looks like it might snow. It definitely feels cold enough.

• • • • • •

"She didn't show," I tell the group as I crawl through the window hours later. Lith crawls through behind me. The group has gathered, waiting to hear any news. Even Ryan has come into the room.

"She schedules a meeting with you, then chooses not to show. What does that mean?" Teagan wonders.

No one answers.

"Any evidence she'd been there and left?" asks Celexa.

"None," I say, "but it's hard to tell."

"I was there early again," Lith says, "and never saw her."

"I wonder what happened." Emily pulls at her lip. "Did we get the days wrong? I, for one, lose track of time here."

"No," I say. "There's no way. She was clear about the timing, and we didn't mess it up. Tonight is the event at the high school that Teagan's mom warned about. They were the same day."

"Well," Teagan says. "I guess we plan on that little adventure and go from there. I'll stay by the radio today. Leave it on a little longer. Check it more often. Maybe she or my mom will try to reach us that way."

"Who's going tonight?" I ask.

"I want to stay here. If my mom is right, and they're already going into Phase III, we have no time to lose. Take the walkie-talkie and stream back to me what you're seeing. I'll take Emily's advice and go live on the radio. Or try to, at least. We have nothing to lose," says Teagan.

"Sounds like a plan. Do you think reception will carry that far? From the high school to the prison?" Lith asks. "I have no idea what the distance is between the two, but I doubt it's close."

"It should," Teagan answers. "As the crow flies, it's not that far."

"Then it's settled," I say. "We leave just before dusk. Whoever wants to go, be rested, fed, and armed."

"Do we know how to get there?" Traz asks.

"I do. I'll give you directions." Teagan hurries into the office. "It was one of the places I hid out before I came here. It's been abandoned for at least a couple of years."

25

When it's time to leave, it's Cass, Emily, Lith, Traz, and I who decide to hike to the high school. Celexa opts to stay with Ryan who is growing quieter and more withdrawn daily, which is really saying something about his mental state. Does he sense a change in the air? Does he sense our imminent demise?

I roll my eyes at my own dramatics—*Imagination, Shaun*, my mother used to say—but then the eye roll stops midway because this really isn't funny and there is a very good chance we'll be facing our demise very soon.

Just before dusk, we slide out the window and hurry into the cover of the forest. Following Teagan's directions, we stick to the shadows of the forest, rounding the prison and following alongside the dirt road. It looks like no vehicles have driven its path in months, as evidenced by the abundance of weeds and grass that interrupt what would otherwise be a smooth surface, and that brings some comfort, though we still stay inside the cover of the trees.

Twenty minutes later, we're at an old, seemingly abandoned, high school that is perched atop a large hill. We stop for several minutes, each scanning the area, rescanning, then rescanning again. There is no noise save for an occasional rustling of dried leaves in a brush of wind. Though it's a high school with typical high school campus attributes, the campus is small enough to see pretty clearly what the former students at this high school had access to.

There are chains on the doors to the main entrance. No school buses in the lots. No swarms of teens grumbling on their walk into the building in the morning, or in this case, cars squealing on their way out at the end of the day.

There are four tennis courts just off the back end of the small, paved parking lot. A baseball field rests just beyond the courts, the grass overgrown, the dugouts filled with dead leaves and fallen tree limbs that have blown inside with the wind.

To the other side of the parking lot is a soccer field, or what used to be a soccer field. The grass is so high in places, it's impossible to see the lines, but I see the goals, though the nets are ripped open in several places and flapping in the wind.

Ahead, down a slight decline, is the football field. It must be turf because it still seems to be intact. In fact, it gleams a shiny green and looks brand-new.

There is a gravel parking lot that leads into the stadium, and it's filled. There are two large tour buses, plus several cars, trucks, and vans. Two golf carts rest right inside the entrance.

"Something tells me they aren't here for a good ole football game," I manage to say. There is a stage set up right at the fifty-yard line.

Bleachers span the far side of the field. And they're filled. Not with teenagers, or families of players, or school staff. They're filled with white coats.

"Dear God," Cass whispers. Her hand shakes in mine.

"Keep your weapons ready," I say.

"Always," Lith responds.

We slide like snakes closer to the field, masked by the density of the tree line. As we draw nearer, we pause. Listen. Scan three-hundred-and-sixty degrees. Slide. Pause. Listen. Scan.

I can feel the energy from the stands, from the gathering of more people than I've seen together in a year.

There are no sounds like one would expect at a football field like this. Instead of hooting, hollering, taunting, and—in the case of my high school—fighting, there was a low hum, a cumulation of those hundred or so people talking.

The sun is close to setting, the sky orange at the tips of the mountain peaks, and I wonder how they plan to light up what's about to happen. Is it possible Teagan's mom got it wrong?

Oh, how I wish.

The sudden roar of the motor of a large truck in the distance overpowers the voices. Several minutes later, a large pickup turns into the high school, a flatbed trailer hooked to the back. On that trailer is what looks like an enormous screen. Not a television screen, but a projector screen.

They're going to show something on that screen.

My stomach coils.

"What now?" Emily asks to no one in particular.

The truck is followed by several white vans, exactly like the ones I saw at the asylum all those days ago.

"This can't be good," Lith says, and I almost laugh at the sheer understated-ness of that understatement.

I remain quiet, though, no words available to me right now.

I release Cass's and Emily's hands and shove my own in my pockets. Providing them comfort right now is not something I can do. I'm just trying not to collapse here on this ground and die.

We forgot the moonseeds.

My heart plummets.

We forgot our one way out of this if we're discovered.

I fight to regulate my breathing.

The pickup truck leads the vans through the parking lot and down the narrow road toward the football field. The vehicles pull on to the track and drive partway around the field before stopping. The pickup pulls on to the field and doesn't stop until it hits the fifty-yard line.

"We need to move around farther if we want to see that projector," Lith says.

We follow him on silent feet. Slide. Pause. Listen. Scan.

Soon we are facing the projector's screen.

Drivers exit the white vans, all wearing brown scrubs. Doctors, at least that's what I assume they are, in white coats get out of the passenger sides. The drivers walk around the vans and open the sliding doors.

Out of each van comes one teenager. I can tell by the way the teen walks that he or she is drugged.

I know that sight and that feeling all too well.

Dr. Richter not only used a medicine to put teens in a comatose-like state, but also created a medicine that allowed the teenagers to move in that state, which is how they were transported around the asylum without rebelling. The medicine freed their muscles enough that they could walk, but they still had no free will.

"What the hell..." The words come out of Traz's mouth with a long exhale.

While the teens exit the vans, a crew starts the process of taking the screen off the flatbed, using an enormous trolley to roll it onto the stage. Cameras are brought out, and what looks like a giant generator. The screen is lifted high enough for people to stand on the stage and not impede the video.

They're going to project on the screen what's happening on the stage.

The sky has turned from orange to reddish gray.

Two large standing lamps are wheeled onto the stage. Workers fiddle with long black cords until those lights come on.

My throat aches, and I find it difficult to swallow.

The teens are marched single file toward the fifty-yard line and stop just short of going onto the stage.

They look like statues.

They're dressed in brown scrubs, blaring white sneakers, and their heads are shaved. I reach up and run my hand through my new growth.

Not one of the teens moves. Not to scratch a nose or fix a strand of hair. Nothing. If they knew what was coming, they'd revolt and bolt. It's a testament to the power of Dr. Richter's medicine that they don't.

I see tears running down Cass's cheeks. Emily's skin is ghostly, her hand clasped over her mouth as if to prevent herself from screaming.

A hospital bed is pulled from somewhere—I didn't see from where—and is rolled onto the field, then onto the stage. Two metal tables are also carried out and placed by the bed.

As the sun finally dips away, swift and abrupt in its final descent as if it can't stand to be here when the show starts, the crowd's low hum grows. Excitement pulses through the air.

This is entertainment for them. At best, a curiosity. At worst, a tutorial on all the things these maniacal doctors can do to us. To anyone who doesn't act the way they want.

I look for Dr. Richter and easily spot her orange-red hair. She must've arrived in one of the vans because she's standing in front of one of the teens—her teen to sacrifice, I guess.

Lith talks softly into the walkie-talkie.

"You're going to have to be careful," I whisper. "We don't know who could be nearby or how much your voice will carry."

"I know," Lith says, but he lowers his voice anyway.

A man I don't recognize walks onto the stage, microphone in hand.

"Ladies and gentlemen, doctors, scientists, distinguished members of the Agency, we welcome you to tonight's very special event. My name is Les Range, and I am president of the Agency. First of all, please give yourselves a round of applause, because tonight we celebrate years of hard work."

The burst of applause sounds like a clap of thunder.

A cameraman walks along the line of doctors, capturing their faces while being careful not to focus on any of the teens standing behind them. Then he pans to the crowd.

We have a perfect vantage point, and that is not a good thing.

Les Range continues, "When we first started our work, we had one doctor, one scientist, one historian, and one assistant. We weren't sure that the goals we wanted to achieve could be achieved. I am humbled to announce that not only has that first team's work been approved for use in pediatricians' offices around the nation, but ten other teams' work has also been approved. We will be rolling out our procedures across the country in mere days."

Thunderous applause erupts again.

"Mental health and behavioral treatment as we know it will be forever changed. Thanks to your hard work." Les Range lifts his arm, sweeping it out toward the bleachers.

More applause.

"Since our teams are scattered across the United States, including Alaska, Hawaii, and Puerto Rico, we are hosting this event today to allow our teams to showcase the tremendous work they've done and to show off their immeasurable contribution to society, the field of psychosurgery, and mental health. They will also be taking the first step in teaching you all these valuable methods. Our ultimate goal is to provide widespread knowledge and competence in the field of psychosurgery and for every doctor to have this knowledge and these tools within their bag of tricks. Because in the end,"—Les Range pauses, looking across the crowd—"we know that the field of mental health treatment has stagnated to devastating effect. The work you'll see here tonight draws from history to pave the way toward a more peaceful future."

Applause.

Each clap of each pair of hands brings a new swell of nausea in me.

"We are worthy of a peaceful society, and now, ladies and gentlemen, a peaceful society is within our reach."

Les Range walks to the top right corner of the stage. "I know everyone is very excited, but before we get started with our first presentation, I want to remind everyone how this is going to work. Each team will come onto the stage and perform their groundbreaking procedure on a live specimen. The procedures will be projected on the screen behind me, as well as televised all across the country. After tonight's event, each of you, and all your colleagues watching from home, will be sent a packet—it should arrive within the week, so you can take notes now or simply observe and wait for the information that is coming in the mail. Inside this packet is a flash drive with videos of all the procedures performed tonight, written descriptions of the procedures, FAQs, relevant contact information, etc. Also included are dates and locations for all upcoming workshops where you can practice on live patients and then mingle with colleagues. We have ensured that each workshop location is in or near a large city with easy transportation access. Tonight's location being the exception."

Laughter from the crowd makes me murderous. How can these people celebrate what's going on here? Find humor in any part of this?

A woman dressed in a dark suit whispers something in Les Range's ear.

"Ladies and gentlemen," he says, "it's time. May I introduce Dr. Wolford and his team."

The crowd applauds as the doctor, the teen, and the assistant step onto the stage. Just as Les Range is about to hand the microphone to Dr. Wolford, he yanks his hand back. "I almost forgot—if you sign up for all ten workshops, you receive a ten percent discount."

Dr. Wolford takes the mic. The cameraman turns toward the crowd, documenting the spike in excitement, then turns it back to the doctor.

"Good evening. My name is Dr. Hans Wolford, and I am a board-certified doctor of internal medicine. The Agency bequeathed me with their first endowment because of a procedure I have long been interested in—bloodletting, sometimes known as leeching. This procedure is still used today and is a good gateway between modern and medieval medicine. Leeching began thousands of years ago with the intention of purging the specimen of whatever ailment they were experiencing. In short, the leeches are used to suck blood out of the specimen in the hope of purifying the blood and freeing the body from disease. I became interested in this procedure long before the Agency contacted me because of its ability to lower blood pressure and thin the blood. It's often used today in conjunction with certain microsurgeries."

The assistant guides the teen to take off his clothes, socks, and shoes, until he stands naked before the crowd while the assistant puts a hospital gown over his body.

The teen lies down.

They don't strap him down. They don't have to. The medicine makes sure that the teen has no free will.

Dr. Wolford continues, "There are two methods I use. Number one: leeching. Number two: bloodletting with an instrument that dates back centuries, but that I've adapted to be more precise, more user-friendly, and to have a higher rate of control. The leeches are, well, leeches."

Laughter from the stands.

"The instrument I use for bloodletting is called a scarificator. This specimen lying before you has a history of bipolar one disorder, or what used to be called manic depression. This condition is plagued with volatile mood swings, from mania to depression, from flying high and feeling like one has the ability to conquer the world to being unable to get out of bed. You can imagine the devastating impact on the quality of life this mental illness can have in all cases, and particularly when the patient suffers a psychotic break.

"Both methods aim to remove tainted blood from the body, lowering blood pressure in the body and in the brain. Both methods have been abandoned in the treatment of mental illness, but the removal of tainted blood forces the body to produce new blood, for one, and also results in the client succumbing to a state of relaxation."

The assistant opens the medical gown, the camera doing a body-length pan of the teen's nakedness. Then the assistant places a large jar filled with liquid and black leeches on the table, and he lays out an instrument, presumably the scarificator. There are several metal bowls laid out, and glass cups I assume are meant to be used for cupping over the open wounds. I know what cupping is because they tried that shit on me in high school when I pulled a muscle in my back unloading and carrying sacks of flour at work.

"I will show you both methods here tonight. For the sake of time, since I am the first of nine and we do not want to be here all night, I will perform the procedures with little commentary. As Mr. Range said, these procedures are being recorded and will be available later, along with further descriptive, supporting videos and files. Today is just the introduction."

With that, the crowd falls silent as the doctor gets to work.

Emily tucks her head into my shoulder when the doctor uses the scarificator to make cuts at a vein. Cass's face is pale, and her eyes are wide.

Lith's voice is the only sound as he gives a live play-by-play.

I feel numb, dumbstruck, and out of my body.

As Lith describes the use of the leeches next, I briefly think he would've been a good sports commentator in another life.

"You can look up now," I tell Emily as Les Range walks onto the stage to announce the next doctor.

"Excellent presentation, Dr. Wolford," Les Range says, returning to center stage. "Next up we have Dr. Samir Singh. His research is focused on the ancient art of trephination, which is the practice of drilling a hole in the skull to relieve pressure. As with Dr. Wolford, Dr. Singh has taken an ancient instrument and modified it for modern use, thus creating less room for error and more precision. I yield to Dr. Singh, and don't forget, as I'm sure you all have many questions, that we are not answering those questions tonight. Simply watch the procedures, reference your materials packet, and attend the subsequent workshops. Dr. Singh."

While he was speaking, a man and a woman cleaned the stage, preparing it for a stooped old man. He shuffles onto the stage, followed by a young girl who is short and skinny—I wonder how old she could possibly be—and an equally old assistant.

He shuns the microphone that Les Range tries to hand to him and lays his own instruments on the table while the assistant helps the young girl lie down. Fortunately, she is allowed to stay clothed. Her head is already shaved, as are all the others, so all the doctor has to do is prepare his instruments. It looks like he's already marked where to drill.

All too soon, the doctor is drilling a hole in the side of the young girl's head, the sound so jarring and terrifying, Traz vomits off to the side. Lith's voice takes on a tone of doom, and we all stand there, immobile.

There are no words.

"Thank you, Dr. Singh," Les Range says, returning to the stage. "Moving on to our third procedure. Allow me to introduce Dr. Esther Richter. She is our very own local celebrity, having taken over the abandoned Blackthorn Peak Lunatic Asylum—you were all given a tour of that facility earlier today—for her imperative research in the field of psychosurgery and the return of the transorbital lobotomy. May I just add that she too, along with the other two esteemed doctors, has taken an archaic instrument and reconfigured and perfected it for our use today in modern medicine." He moves to the corner of the stage. "Ladies and gentlemen, Dr. Richter."

Dr. Richter walks onto the stage, the camera panning in for a close-up. She looks directly at the camera, those mismatched eyes strangely off-balance. She is followed by a tall, lean girl, older than the last, and a new assistant.

I think of Gibbon and wonder if he would've been her assistant on this stage if she hadn't killed him.

This assistant is a young woman who looks oddly familiar.

Just as realization hits me, Emily yanks my arm. "Tell me that's not Renee."

"Renee?" asks Cass quietly, urgently. "Ryan's twin sister? Why would she be…"

"Dr. Richter was going to do that to me…" My words drop off as I try to organize my thoughts.

"Shaun, what?" Cass asks.

"Dr. Richter said that she thought I might be the first Redeemable, meaning someone she lobotomizes yet keeps alive. Not to return to society. But to have as a new assistant, like Gibbon," I say.

"No…" breathes Cass. "That can't be."

"You mean you think she's lobotomized Renee?" Emily demands.

"Yes," I snap.

"What do I do?" Lith asks. "What if he's listening with Teagan? I can't say she's down there."

"But he thinks she's dead. Wouldn't he be relieved?" Emily asks.

"That she's been lobotomized instead of killed? I guess," Lith says.

"Keep reporting," I tell him. "But don't mention Renee. We'll tell him in person when we get back. Besides, it's possible it's not her. Just someone who looks like her."

As if on cue, the camera focuses on the assistant's face.

It's Renee.

No one speaks but Lith, who slowly lifts the walkie-talkie.

"I can't watch this," Emily says, turning her back to the field and taking several steps away.

"This does hit a little too close to home," I whisper to Cass, feeling suspended from the horrific reality unfolding before me.

"I'll go check on her," she says, leaving my side.

Dr. Richter says a few words into the microphone, but my head feels like it's filled with water, and I can't quite process what's going on even though I know exactly what's going on.

Traz, Lith, and I stand in a row, barely breathing, fixated and unable to move or look away.

I feel a brief flash of gratitude that Cass and Emily have each other. And that they aren't watching this.

It's like watching a horror movie, even more horrific because we all came so very close to having this happen to us. We watch as the doctor positions the teen's head. She places something in the girl's mouth, and I assume it's an anesthetic of some sort. Something to make her patient not move while an ice pick comes toward her eye.

Whatever she gave her works, because the girl doesn't even flinch.

The long, shiny, thin pick is placed at the inner corner of her eye. The hammer hits the ice pick. *Chink!* It's done so quickly. Then she moves on to the other eye.

Chink!

It's done.

She lays the instruments on the metal table.

Somehow, we make it through her time on stage. Lith has to backtrack with his description, having gone mute during the atrocity, but manages to relay what happened.

Sometime during Dr. Richter's part, I think I heard Traz vomit again, but I couldn't pay attention to anything but that screen.

"Thank you, Dr. Richter," Les Range says. "If anyone is interested in a tour of our research facility, it's located on the grounds of the asylum you visited earlier and will be open to you tomorrow at noon. Next up we have…"

But I'm no longer listening. I stumble to find the girls, feeling completely out of my body. I need their warmth. Otherwise, I'll die from how cold the world can be right this second.

Lith continues to watch, as does Traz, but I don't watch or listen anymore. I'll get details later from Lith's report. Right now, I have hit my limit for how much terror I can cope with.

Instead, I turn my thoughts to this red-haired traitor, and I think we've found them. Dr. Richter was never going to help us. Does Teagan's mom know that?

Then why, though? Why meet me, try to convince me of her change of heart? I can't see the point of our meeting if it was all a farce.

Sickened and confused, I wrap my arms around Cass and Emily, comforting them while fighting against my own urge to break down and cry.

26

Inside the Mind of Dr. Esther Richter

• • • • • •

Dr. Richter moves through the motions as if in a dream.

This is not how it's supposed to feel, she thinks as she demonstrates the new and improved tools she's created, and then uses those tools to perform the new and improved lobotomy. Thoughts of her grandfather and her family name hover in the deepest recesses of her mind, as do any thoughts of glory.

She's distracted and can't quite bring herself to live in the moment, to relish her success, to savor the enormity of this occasion.

What's wrong with me? she wonders as loud applause swells.

The specimen will be driven back to the asylum where she will be monitored and will slowly start to be given daily tasks. Dr. Richter hopes and believes that within three days, she will be fully recovered. When she's ready, she will share duties with Renee, many of which Gibbon had, that have been too much for Renee on her own. Ideally, Dr. Richter would have lobotomized a male, as she needs a physically stronger aide, but she drew the female straw, so female specimen it is. She chose not to advocate for a change because that would have meant she had to talk to the head of the Agency about it.

She swallows the toxic bile that rises in her throat any time she thinks of…him. Instead, she focuses on the first daily tasks this specimen will start with.

So much has changed in Dr. Richter's daily routine, and her assistants' daily routine, since the research phase ended. Now Phase II is near completion, and Phase III is soon to roll out.

Everything is falling into place.

Then why does she feel like everything is falling apart?

She feels a stirring in her womb and knows what the problem is.

She is pregnant. She is growing a human life inside her body. She will give another human life.

She doesn't think of the father. Indeed, he has been written out of her consciousness out of sheer necessity—she cannot digest the way in which she became pregnant. The shame and embarrassment would be too great to manage. Not to mention the rage she feels anytime the memory pops up.

Les Range.

She would kill him if she could.

As she walks off the stage, she deliberately and completely shuts down any thoughts of him and runs a loving hand over her stomach.

It's her and this baby now. She will give it everything she has.

Still, as hard as she tries, her nightmares hold the memories, and their grip on her is more tenacious than she admits in the light of day.

27

Back at the prison, we climb through the window one by one. No one spoke on the hike back, and no one speaks now. Not even Celexa or Teagan, who are waiting for us in the office. Ryan doesn't come out of his cell. Several moments pass as we stare at each other, disbelief, distress, and even terror hanging in the air like a foul odor.

"This is unbelievable," Celexa says eventually, breaking the silence and moving to Traz, pulling him into her arms. "I'm sorry you had to witness that. It was bad enough hearing about it."

"It was surreal," Emily says. "And not in a good way."

"Were you able to broadcast it?" Lith asks. "I tried to balance talking into the walkie-talkie with not being loud enough to draw attention. You never know who could be lurking in those woods."

"It went as good as those things go," says Teagan. "I was able to sit back and let your words disperse across the airwaves. I knew I couldn't do it justice, trying to repeat or recap what you said, so it's actually just your voice, your play-by-play, that got broadcast."

"Any hint that someone heard?" Traz asks.

Teagan answers, "Not yet. I honestly don't know what that would look like, but it was worth a shot. Time will tell now, I guess. Before I signed off, I gave the location for the asylum in hope that, if anyone's alarms are raised, they'll know where to go to investigate."

"Les Range, the guy who seems to be in charge, said something about this being the hub for the research," I offer. "If someone comes and tries to put an end to things here in Blackthorn Peak, it would be a step in the right direction."

"But how will that help the rest of the country? Don't we owe it to every teen out there to try to stop them completely?" Emily asks.

"I don't want to be a punk about it, but these are questions we need to ask."

"I don't know that it will," I say.

Cass nods her silent agreement, though her expression seems less than agreeable. In fact, she looks like death itself. Pale skin. Glassy eyes. Black bruises underneath the gray orbs. Her lips droop. Her body hunched over as if she is trying to take up as little space as possible.

"You wouldn't believe what was going on there," I tell Teagan and Celexa. "I mean, I know you heard it, but…it's still unbelievable, and I was standing right there. The crowd was cheering and applauding like it was the Super Bowl."

"I guess for them it was," Cass says softly.

"I don't know how we'll ever fight this," Traz says.

"I don't either." Finally, Traz and I agree on something.

"I wish my mom, or even Dr. Richter, had told us where to go or what to do," Teagan says. "Waiting is the worst. It's torture."

Suddenly there is a knock at the door, quick bursts of three bangs.

We stop. Stare at each other. Hold our breath.

My heart pounds in my chest.

"Could that be your mom?" I whisper to Teagan.

"Is there any way to check who's out front?" Emily asks.

"I don't think so," Teagan answers. "There are no windows with direct line of sight to the front door."

"What do we do?" Celexa asks.

"Get your weapons," I say.

As silently as possible, we gather our arms.

We return to the reception area.

Someone calls through the door. The sound is muffled behind the thick wood, but it sounds like a woman's voice.

"If it's my mom, I need to let her in. She could be in trouble," Teagan says. He tiptoes toward the main entrance.

"We'll hide," I whisper. "But we'll stay close by in case it's not her, or if she's been followed, and they plan to ambush us."

The voice calls through the wood again, this time accompanied by a softer knock.

Lith and I stand against the wall on either side of the main doors. Traz stands by Lith's shoulder.

Celexa moves into the doorway of the bathroom in the reception area, just out of sight.

Emily and Cass go into the office, hiding just inside the door.

Teagan opens the door.

"Is Shaun here?" says a rushed voice. It's Dr. Richter. "I need to speak to Shaun right now."

I swing around until I'm standing face-to-face with Dr. Richter.

"Are you alone?" Teagan demands, scanning the darkness.

"Yes," she says.

"Is my mom okay?"

"Yes."

"Why didn't you meet me at the cabin the other day?" I demand. "And why are you here now?"

"Can I come in?" Her mismatched eyes dart around the landscape, surveying. "I feel exposed. Please." She plants that unforgettable gaze on me. "Shaun, please."

Ignoring the bristle of rage that brushes over me, I nod to Teagan, who steps aside and allows her to enter.

"You can come just inside this door, but no farther," Teagan says.

She slides through, and Lith closes the door behind her. He places his strong body in front of the door, feet planted, arms crossed. Traz and Teagan create a barrier in front of the entrance to the reception area. She is trapped between us, and I don't take my eyes off her.

"What are you doing here?" I demand again. "If this is a trick, so help me God, I'll kill you myself right now. We saw what you did. We were there. At the high school."

Dr. Richter glances down at the knife in my hand. She nods as if she knows I'll use it, and she's right. I will protect these people, especially Cass and Emily, with my life. Any sympathy or trust I might've started to have for her is gone.

"Start talking," I say again.

She looks at Lith and Traz as if she's trying to place who they are. It's possible she doesn't remember as they escaped before we did. Does she feel like she's seeing ghosts?

"It's… Things have gotten… I never understood…" she stammers. I've never seen her look so uncertain and vulnerable.

I can't let my guard down. I can't trust this woman. "Never understood what?" I ask, hostility clipping my words.

"That it's not as simple as it seemed," she says.

"You have to be more specific."

"There is evil everywhere."

"Yeah," I say with a snort. "You didn't know that already? Didn't realize you are part of that evil?"

"I did. But I thought…I wanted to create a better world and thought that was reason enough." Tears well in those odd eyes. She starts to sob, her chest heaving.

My guard shoots up at this display of raw emotion, and I raise the knife.

Her sorrow is not what I expect.

"But I don't see how that can happen now," she says. "A better world. It's all too far gone."

"What happened?" I ask.

She doesn't answer as the tears pour down her cheeks.

"Something happened," I press. "What?"

"I've seen it firsthand. Witnessed it firsthand." Her voice drops until I can barely hear her. I lean forward as she continues, "Because I've been a victim of it."

"You're talking in circles and not making sense. Get it together, or you can get out of here. I'm very thin on patience."

With that question, she pushes back the sides of the red cardigan she is wearing, displaying a pregnant belly.

"You're pregnant?" I ask.

The sobs spiral out of control until she's heaving and hiccupping.

I don't need to ask another question. The pain on her face is enough.

"Who hurt you?" Teagan asks. "Is my mom safe?"

"She's safe for now," the doctor manages to answer eventually. "This...was personal. But I don't know how safe any of us are, especially once Range realizes—"

"Realizes what?" Traz says through clenched teeth.

"Realizes that some of us want out. That some of us refuse to continue doing what the Agency wants. Once Les Range realizes this, he'll do anything he can to save the Agency's work and keep its mission intact," says the doctor.

"Who is this 'us' you're talking about?" I ask. "You're not making any sense."

She inhales a quivering breath and exhales slowly. "You have allies now, Shaun. I alluded to that the other day but have talked with more people since then."

"Like who?"

She replies, "Me. Teagan's mom. Others you wouldn't know—parents, grandparents. It's not a large group, and we have to be cautious about everything. We can't help if we're dead."

"I still don't understand why you're helping," I say. "You're pregnant and had a change of heart. Seriously?"

"I never understood. I never...I don't have children. Never wanted any. So, I never understood the heartbreak of losing a child," she says.

"Little too late after the hundreds you've killed," Lith snaps.

She nods. "Yes. It's too late for many. But not for you all. Not yet."

Rage colors my vision crimson. I step toward her. "Do you mean after all the blood that is on your hands that you're finally seeing the so-called injustice in all this?" My voice rises until I'm shouting.

"Oh, dear God," Emily says in disgust. "You're pregnant and don't want your kid to suffer what you've inflicted on the rest of us? On our entire generation?"

Dr. Richter stares at the floor.

"You disgust me," Emily says. "You only had a change of heart because it now directly affects you. What a load of bullshit."

"We should just kill you now," Lith says, a slow grin spreading across his face. "Put you out of your misery. Better yet, we can lobotomize you or drill a hole in your brain. That would be fun, wouldn't it? Or wait until your child is born and lobotomize them."

I put my hand on Lith's chest, feeling my own flash of fear because of my friend. There is a crazed look behind his eyes that I've never seen before, and I'd prefer to never see again.

"I want to help you," Dr. Richter says. "That's why I risked coming here."

"Help us how? Phase II is all but done, and they're rolling out Phase III. What can you do at this point?" Celexa asks. "You're doing a lot of talking but not about anything concrete."

"Truth," Traz says.

"How many teens are already dead?" I ask. "Mass killings have begun, right?"

She holds my gaze, her silence telling me I don't want to know the answer to my question.

"He asked," Lith repeats, seething, "how many are dead?"

"By the latest estimates, about a million," she says softly. "That is what we've been told. I have no way of knowing the actual numbers. Les Range controls all information. We only know what he tells us."

Lith loses it then. He has her neck in his hands before any of us can react. He slams her against the wall. Her eyes start to bug out, her face reddens, before Traz and I manage to pull him off.

"Calm the fuck down," Traz shouts, an inch from Lith's face. "She might be able to help us." He glances at Dr. Richter. "And then we can decide what to do with her."

Out of nowhere, Cass steps forward. Stands directly in front of Dr. Richter. "Where's my father?"

"I don't know, Cassidy," Dr. Richter says. "I haven't seen him in months."

"He's not part of this work now?"

"No. Not to my knowledge."

"Did you kill him?"

Sadness passes over the doctor's face. "No. I didn't. We aren't killing adults."

"You killed Gibbon." Cass's voice is deathly calm.

"I regret what happened to Gibbon. I was…a different person back then. I was angry that he'd tried to help you escape. It's remarkable how toxic and consuming pride and ego can be. It can destroy everything."

Cass doesn't respond. Just waits.

"I did hear that your father left town. I can't confirm it, though. It could all be rumor."

"Where do the rumors say he went?"

"I heard he went to Huntsville."

"What's in Huntsville?"

Sympathy flashes over the doctor's features. "Drugs, Cassidy. A way to forget."

"How do you know this?"

"Like I said, it's just what I heard. I don't know anything for sure. But it would make sense. The drugs. The need to forget."

I put a hand on Cass's shoulder, and she steps back to be by Emily's side. I can tell by her expression that she is lost in her own pain, hovering in a mental wasteland.

My mouth opens to ask about my own mom, but I can't do it. My mom is all but dead to me.

"So, what now?" I ask the doctor instead. "What are you suggesting we do?"

"One thing that would bring an end to this a lot faster is to kill Les Range. Chop the head off the snake, and then the Agency will wilt and die. Get rid of Les Range and it will all crumble. I promise," the doctor says.

"One man cannot have that much power," Traz says.

"Oh, but he does. Les Range is the keeper of secrets and the holder of blackmail. He has something on everyone, and that is how he gets people to cooperate. If it's not secrets and blackmail, it's manipulation. He's very good at it. A master." She looks at us each in turn. "It's how he ensures parents and loved ones are willing to sacrifice their own children. Or work for him to protect their own."

She looks at me. "You kill him, and the operation falls."

"Don't trust her."

I whip around to see Ryan standing in the door to the office, staring hard at the doctor. "Do not trust this woman. She killed my sister, and she will kill us too." His voice has a haunted tone I've never heard before.

"Your sister is alive," Dr. Richter says quietly.

A charged minute passes.

"What?" Ryan asks, breathless.

"Renee is alive."

Ryan's entire body starts to shake. Emily moves to his side, then Cass follows.

"You're lying," Ryan says.

"She's not," Emily says. "We saw her."

Ryan whips around, yanking away from Emily's outstretched hand. "You knew she was alive?"

"We saw her at the high school. During the show," Emily admits.

"Why..." he sputters. "Why didn't you..." Tears erupt from his eyes, sobs from his throat. "Why didn't you tell me?"

I was glad that he wasn't looking at me in that moment because I didn't have an answer to that. The show was so sickening that we had all hiked back in stunned silence.

I didn't know how he'd handle the news and couldn't think of a way to tell him that she'd been lobotomized and was working for the very doctor standing in front of us now.

Ryan charges Dr. Richter, and it takes me, Lith, and Traz to hold him back.

"She might be the only one who can help us," I manage to say, repeating Traz's earlier words.

"I'll kill you if you hurt her!" Ryan spits the words out.

No one mentions how his twin has already been hurt.

Ryan collapses into a ball in the corner, whimpering. No one moves to help or comfort him. That time very much seems to have passed.

28

Ramblings of a Sane Madman

• • • • • •

His nickname when he was in elementary school was "the worm." Not because he was slimy and shady but because he physically looked like a worm. Too long and too lean, from his face and the shape of his features—with eyes too close together and no chin to speak of—to his body that could never put on muscle or fat. Not to mention he was as hairless as a worm, having been born with the most unfortunate of defects.

It was a humiliating nickname, but one that didn't bother him too badly until he hit puberty and high school. Then he gained an understanding of the devastating effects of bullying.

It was during this fragile time of change that the bullying took on a purpose and an evolution that at first bewildered, then haunted him—and would until well into adulthood.

He'll never forget that day.

He was changing after gym class in the boys' musty old locker room. He didn't really sweat enough to need to change, but wearing a PE uniform was required, and so he changed along with everyone else.

He couldn't help but notice the changes in everyone's bodies during this time, but he was always sure to keep his gaze steadfastly rooted straight ahead or down at the ground. His peripheral vision, though, told him his body was different. Very different.

Whereas his body remained hairless, smooth and pale, his peers filled out by growing taller, gaining muscle, and sprouting hair. Les didn't even have hair on his head.

Nor did he anywhere else.

The nickname "the worm" took on a whole new meaning.

It was one thing to be hairless in elementary school. No one was really wise to what a grown-up body looked like, so though he didn't have hair on his face or head, it really wasn't too big of a deal.

But that day in the locker room…

Two soccer players, all muscle, hair, and sweat, were changing next to him. In the instances he couldn't be alone, he'd perfected the art of the lightning-quick clothing change. On this day, though, he was nude—completely nude—having grown flustered and frantic by the close proximity of the two athletes.

He ended up taking off his shirt, which wasn't too embarrassing, but when he took off his shorts, in his haste, he took off his underwear too, and before he could cover himself, they saw.

They saw him naked.

And they laughed. And laughed and laughed. They doubled over. Pointed. Slapped each other on the back.

Did you see that?

Look at him.

No wonder they call him "the worm."

The two athletes managed to stumble out of the locker room, the power of their laughter causing them to knock into each other and walk hunched over as if the sight of Les's naked body was so comical, they couldn't even stand upright.

The boys told the other boys who told the other boys who told the girls.

Les never did get hair on his body, on any part of it.

He threw himself into his studies as a distraction from the constant teasing, whispers, pointed fingers, and occasional incidences of his pants being pulled down while walking through the halls. This was back in the day when such bullying wasn't called bullying, and certainly wasn't punished.

He excelled at biology and chemistry, and was valedictorian of the high school. By the time graduation rolled around, he knew he was smarter than anyone else at that school, teachers included, and knew he'd make something of himself.

It felt good to be so smart. But he never forgot the shame. Or the hatred.

He cracked open his high school yearbook, always within reach for those times when he second-guessed his life's mission. The pages were faded, a few had even fallen out over time, and the spine was crumbling. He opened it now to his senior picture.

The young man staring back at him looked afraid, apprehensive, insecure…weak.

The man holding the yearbook now was none of those things. And he never would be again.

Now he was powered by that ancient notion of revenge.

And it felt so damned good.

And what was the best way to exact revenge? Go for the jugular of those who had mocked and tormented him.

Go for their children.

29

"How do you propose we kill Les Range?" I ask, ending the question with a derisive snort.

We are sitting in a circle in the reception room, staring at Dr. Richter. Ryan took off to another floor and hasn't been seen since. I felt more than a small amount of comfort that he could not throw himself out of any of the windows upstairs, and for the first and only time, was grateful for the prison bars.

"His office is in the asylum," says Dr. Richter. "He's been staying in the cottage. You'll almost certainly find him in one of those two places."

"The cottage I lived in with my dad?" Cass asks.

The doctor nods. "Yes. He settled in there a few months ago."

"Is he guarded, or is he alone?" Lith asks.

"He's guarded, though not heavily. He's usually just with other doctors or his assistant. It's a testament to how secure he feels, how untouchable, that he doesn't bother to have an armed bodyguard. But you'll need to have a plan because he's smart and conniving. Always seems to be one step ahead," says Dr. Richter.

"Why is he doing this?" Emily asks. "Why did he start this mission?"

Dr. Richter's eyes scan the group. "The most lethal of all reasons—revenge."

"Revenge for what?" I ask.

"He was bullied as a teenager. The shame he experienced has set him up to be merciless in pursuit of exacting revenge."

"Back to teens being the root of all evil, I see," Lith said.

"Why don't people revolt? It makes no sense," Emily said. "Does the world have no conscience? Do so many parents care so little about their own children?"

"It makes perfect sense when you think about it. He blackmails parents whose skills he needs, telling those parents—such as your mom, Teagan—that he'll keep their kids alive as long as they work for him," says the doctor.

"But it's unethical, what they're doing. Wouldn't people revolt at the sheer wrongness of it all?" Emily presses. "Even if they didn't have a kid who was affected by this?"

"Not when you surround yourself by others who were bullied like he was. Or were hurt by teens in one way or another." Dr. Richter looks around the group. "Like me. I was teased, yes, but—"

"Please don't say it," Emily begs. "I've never forgiven myself."

"What are you talking about?" Teagan asks.

"My friends and I stole a stop sign one night, for fun. Remember, I told you about it?" Emily's voice is barely above a whisper. She stares at the tile. A tear hits the brown surface. "A mom and her kids died. Got hit by a tractor trailer. It was the doctor's sister."

Pain flashes across Dr. Richter's face, but she doesn't condemn Emily. Not today.

Lith finally speaks. "This Les Range guy was bullied and now hates the world and rallies other people to work for him who hate the world too. Is that the gist of it?"

"And if they don't have a personal vendetta, they're blackmailed. To keep their troubled teen off the Agency's list, they have to work for the Agency. Then there are the doctors, they are more widespread across the country, who simply believe in their mission. I'm not sure how much these doctors know, though. It's possible they think they are doing research into psychosurgeries of the past and are not aware of what's actually going on around here," says the doctor.

"The murders," I clarify.

Dr. Richter nods. "The murders. It's possible the doctors you saw on the field don't know the extent of the Agency's mission. I'm not sure, but I wouldn't be surprised."

"Utopia isn't the final goal?" Cass snorts. "I can't get over how much that sounds like something straight out of a dystopian novel we read in ninth grade."

The doctor shakes her head. "That might be a secondary gain, but revenge is the first. The most powerful of all motivators."

"Revenge," Traz says.

"Revenge," the doctor confirms. "And those closest to him want revenge too. They feel righteous in their cause and have been lethal in the rollout of their plan."

"Let's say we manage to kill him. Why wouldn't someone else just step in and take his place? Don't some snakes just grow a new head?" I ask, thinking back to what she said a moment ago.

"There is always that risk, but his death will help even the playing field. Allow space for dissention among those of us who aren't happy with what's going on but have continued to do our jobs…for whatever the reason." She rubs her slightly swollen stomach. "An even playing field can turn the tide. Give us time to figure out who knows what; to figure out who, if any, will be our allies."

"A quick death isn't good enough for that bastard," I say.

"Burn him alive," Lith says as serious as a heart attack.

I nod. I could. And without regret or remorse. Just like when I burned my stepfather alive.

"He needs a dose of his own medicine," Traz says, eyes gazing off into the distance.

"Why don't you kill him?" Cass asks the doctor. "You work with him. Have the means. You certainly have no qualms about murder considering how many people you've already killed."

Dr. Richter rises to her feet. "He's the father of my child…as sick as that sounds." Her voice cracks. She clears her throat. "It's just not the same. I can't kill him."

"Why not?" Cass presses, her eyes holding an intensity I haven't seen before. "You've been complicit in the murder of hundreds of teens. Gibbon. God knows who else. Why can't you just kill him?"

Dr. Richter turns her back to us, staring at the main door, though something tells me she's not seeing the door. She's lost to a memory.

When I hear a sob escape her, I realize she's lost to a nightmare.

"We have a right to know," Emily says. "Please answer Cass's question." Her tone is less a plea than a firm command.

It takes the doctor several moments to compose herself. When she slowly turns back to the group, her eyes are shining with tears, and her hands are cupping her stomach.

She shakes her head.

"We need an explanation," Emily insists. "You owe us that."

So quietly I almost couldn't hear, the doctor says, "He assaulted me."

"Assaulted you?" Emily asks.

The doctor rubs her stomach.

Emily exhales loudly. "Ah."

Understanding descends.

"I can't be in the same room as him. Not yet. I—" Dr. Richter coughs to cover the sob. "I can't do it yet."

So, there you have it, I think. The tide has changed because she's become a victim. If Range hadn't assaulted her, getting her pregnant, she would likely still be killing teens without remorse.

I glare at her.

"You're a coward," I say.

Her eyes meet mine. "Yes."

After a beat of silence, Celexa stands. "What now?"

"For now," Dr. Richter answers in a quivering tone, "I have to go. If he discovers I've been here, then I'll be eliminated." She rubs her stomach again. "And he's been keeping a close eye on me, has had his cronies around me almost all the time, so I have to be more careful than ever. I have too much to live for to die now." She walks to the door. "I'll try to make contact again in twenty-four hours, either in person or via the radio. Try to check it as often as possible. I'll circle back with as much information as possible, like his whereabouts, when he'll be alone, anything to help form a plan. The sooner we do this, the more lives will be saved."

"Which is safer, here or the cabin?" I ask.

"Here."

"Why did you have my truck the other day?"

She turns. Looks at me. "I just thought you'd like to see it."

"Where is it now?"

"Parked on the grounds."

"Put gas in it and leave the keys in it."

She nods.

"Well," Lith says, looking around the room. "What do we do now?"

"We go back in there," yells Ryan, suddenly appearing in the doorway of the reception area. His face is red, eyes bulging. "We go back in there, and we rescue my sister!"

His body is shaking, and the grief that pours out of him leaves me shaken as well. It seems to fill the air like a noxious gas.

"Where is she?" Ryan screams, charging the doctor.

He lunges at her.

"Ryan, stop!" I grab him around the waist before he gets his hands on her.

"You bitch!" He's wild with fury and grief, and it takes the two of us and Traz to keep him off her.

"Where is she?" Ryan demands. "Where the hell is she?"

Dr. Richter's skin is pale, her eyes huge. "In the asylum. She has a room in the asylum," she says softly, her voice slightly scratchy. "First floor. Right hallway. Halfway down."

"I'll kill you if you hurt her," Ryan says, seething. Spittle drips down his lower lip.

"I'm sorry," she whispers.

Ryan goes for her again.

"Go," I tell her. "Go now."

She doesn't need to be asked twice and hurries out the door. I shut and lock it, then turn to Ryan.

He looks insane with rage.

"I'm leaving. I'm going to get her," Ryan declares.

"Ryan," Emily says. "We can't just waltz in there. It's too

dangerous."

"We are NOT leaving her in there!" Ryan yells. "I thought she was dead. Well, she's not, and I'm going to rescue her." He thrashes in Lith's and Traz's arms.

"We can't take on everyone in the asylum," Emily reasons. "Don't forget those in the red building. Some of those working there might be willing to help us, but not all."

"I am not leaving her there." Ryan manages to escape their grasp. Charges through the reception area and the rotating door before any of us can react.

"Wait!" I reach for him. "You can't just go out there."

He shoves me off and darts out the door.

"Ryan, wait." I run after him.

"No!" he screams. "I'm going. If they get me, fine. I don't want to live without my sister."

He starts to hyperventilate, pausing in the middle of the front lawn.

"Ryan, come back," I beg. "Let's create a plan. I'll even go with you. I was as responsible as anyone for her being left there. I'll go with you. I promise."

"I will too," Lith says, walking up.

Emily and Cass are outside now. Traz, Celexa, and Teagan stand in the doorway, watching.

"We can't go in there without a plan," I plead. "Please. Come back in. We can't be out here any longer."

As if possessed by a demon, Ryan starts to breathe heavily between clenched teeth, his lips pulling back to reveal his gums. Spit shoots out of his mouth. His fists clench.

Just as I fear he's going to charge me, he turns and runs off down the road.

"Ryan," I shout. Just as I'm about to break into a run and go after him, Lith's hand clamps on my shoulder. "Don't follow him. You're right that we need a plan."

I pull away from him. "It's partly my fault she's still there. You don't understand. We left her. I left her."

"I know you did. I heard the story. And I know how much it bothers you. But you can't go off half-cocked. It's a death sentence."

"I can't let Ryan go alone," I say.

I glance at Cass. She's shaking her head no.

"It's not a good idea, Shaun. Listen to Lith," Emily says.

But I turn and watch Ryan's retreating form. He's making good time and will soon pass out of sight.

With a burst of resolve, I run after him.

I don't shout for him to slow down. There's no way of knowing who might be hiding in the forest. But I'm faster than him, and soon I'm within several yards.

"Ryan," I whisper. "Ryan!"

He stops. Turns. "You're not going to stop me," he says.

It's cold enough outside to see his breath when he speaks. The sky is overcast with heavy clouds, and it feels like snow in the air.

"I'm not stopping you. I'm coming with you."

His eyes narrow.

"It's not a trick," I tell him. "I'm here to help. You can't do this alone."

"You think the two of us can do it together?"

No.

"I think we have a better chance if we do it together," I say, not revealing my true inner thoughts. "Maybe it's better that it's just the two of us and not everyone else. We can keep a lower profile."

"Three of us."

Ryan's eyes widen. I whip around to see Lith, burdened with weapons, coming to a stop next to me.

"They let you leave?" I ask.

"They don't control me. Traz tried. Didn't work." Lith smirks.

The three of us look at each other. Ryan nods his head. Lith distributes the weapons he brought.

"Any chance you brought food or water?" I ask him.

"Nope. I decided if I could carry another thing, it should be another weapon. Besides, this will come to a head tonight anyway. We can always decide to go back to the prison and regroup, but I don't see us just hanging out in the forest."

"No," Ryan says, adamant. "I'm going to the asylum, and I'm getting my sister back."

"Damn straight," Lith says.

"Let's go." I set off in a jog.

30

Thus Speaks Cassidy Rutherford

• • • • • •

Pressure grows in my chest as I stare at the tree line through the window. Shaun is gone.

"He's going to go with him," I whisper to Emily. "He's going to leave, and go with him to the asylum, and they're going to try and rescue Renee. He won't be able to talk Ryan out of it."

"They're fools," Traz says. "All of them, going off like that. They're just going to end up dead."

"You foolish coward." I turn on Traz. "Shaun has bigger balls when he's asleep than you do wide awake. He is a hero. Don't forget that we wouldn't be here if it weren't for him."

"Calm down," Traz says.

I launch myself at him with fists raised and teeth bared. "Don't you dare patronize me, James. Shaun is not afraid of you and neither am I."

"Whoa," Teagan says, coming between us, arms out. "What's going on?"

"He's got a big mouth for someone with such small balls," I say.

"Enough about his balls, Cass." Teagan pushes against Traz's chest. "Everyone take five, and then let's meet in the office. We need to talk about this, but with cool heads."

I glare at Traz.

Celexa doesn't look at me as she leads him down the hall to their cell.

"You okay?" Teagan asks me.

"I'm fine. I just can't stand his pompous ass."

"I didn't know you had it in you, girl," Emily says. "You go hours, days, without saying much and then suddenly you go after Traz? I think you're the one with the balls."

"What if something happens to him?" I manage to say, just now fully realizing the reason for my rage at Traz. "What if—"

"He's like the cat with nine lives," she says. "He's a survivor. Look at all he's been through."

"Until he's not. Until those lives run out."

My gaze returns to the tree line as if I can still see the shadows of Shaun and the others, as if they'd only just left a moment ago. They left the safety of the prison, but for what? Nothing good can come of this.

Emily rubs my shoulder. It brings little comfort.

"I can't believe this is our life," I whisper, blinking back tears. "Some days everything seems…fine. Am I right? I mean, we're here. We're safe. We have shelter, food, each other. Some days it feels like I've never been so happy, and I don't want anything to change. Then I remember…"

"Remember?" she asks softly.

I look into those big brown eyes. Touch my fingertip to her tattoo. She wipes a tear from my cheek.

"Remember that we're on borrowed time. That we're practically dead. And if we don't die soon, we'll always be running." I sigh. "The hatred. The betrayal." I think of Cyrus. "The simple yet deadly misguided notion that by killing our generation, everything will be okay."

Emily offers me a soft smile, and I'm struck by how beautiful she is. "I've never heard you say so many words."

She watches me to make sure the soft joke lands, and I crack a smile in return. Kiss her gently, then turn back to the window.

"We have to go get him," I say.

Teagan clears his throat.

Emily's hand slips into mine.

"Y'all ready to chat?" he asks.

I look at him, this guy I barely know, but somehow am aligned with now. "We need to go after them."

He nods. "Come into the office, and we'll make a plan."

Teagan walks away. Emily and I stand there a minute longer, hands entwined.

"Why do I feel like this is the end?" I whisper.

"It has to end sometime. No better way than by trying to save a friend."

I look at her. "I love you. I love you and I love Shaun, and I'm so grateful for you both."

"I love you, too."

"I'm ready to end this."

"Me too."

Emily smiles. We walk into the office, hand in hand, united.

31

Dr. Richter says to kill Les Range.

Ryan is going to find Renee.

There are three of us, two huge buildings, countless adults, no plan. What the hell are we thinking?

Do we just focus on getting Renee back at this point? Will there be another chance to kill Les Range if we get her and run, then make a plan to kill him in the future?

This feels awfully similar to the debate we had when we tried to rescue Renee the first time. We failed then. We marched off to the asylum only to find the entire building empty. Save for Cyrus, of course, and Gibbon's dead body.

That was when we found the computer file that stated all of us were dead. Including Renee.

What are the chances that we can actually get her and run? How can we flee with her and not try to kill Range?

We have to kill Range.

If there is any hope of us having a future, he has to die. Hopefully, someone has heard Teagan's broadcast, and help is coming. Hopefully, Dr. Richter is correct in her belief that there are people willing to help.

Range needs to be dead before any help arrives. Otherwise, won't he just start the blackmailing all over again? If he's astute enough to create and orchestrate this whole operation, he cannot be underestimated.

These questions whirl around in my head like a tornado as I struggle to keep up with Ryan. He's setting such a fierce pace, both Lith and I are winded. We can't be far from the asylum, though. The only problem? It's going to get dark soon.

And it's starting to snow.

The temperature is plummeting. We can't hide out in the forest tonight. We'll die from the cold. We have to get in and get out.

Maybe we should've taken time to plan. I keep these thoughts to myself as snowflakes start to land on my eyelashes.

Then I look at Ryan, still visibly pulsing with energy. I look at Lith. His expression is stony and focused. As we walk, something overtakes me too.

Fury.

Determination.

Focus.

And a deep-seated feeling of injustice. Of *how dare they*?

Single file, we stay hidden in the cover of the forest. Just ahead I can see the tree line, where the thick growth of arbors ends and the red building looms just beyond. On the other side of that mass of red bricks rests the asylum. From this vantage point, I can only see the side of the clock tower, the heavy beige stone tinted gray with the darkness of a snowy night. To get to the entrance, we have to travel around the red building, cut between the two, and walk half the length of the asylum to get to the main entrance.

There is no way to stay hidden once we step out of this forest. We can stay close to the buildings, but when we move from one to the other, we'll be exposed. Not to mention, the red building faces the asylum. Anyone gazing out a window will see our movements.

The air beats with a heavy energy, emanating from that massive building.

A resting dragon. What horrors will unfold if we awaken it this time?

What the hell am I doing back here?

"Dr. Richter said Renee is likely in her room on the first floor of the asylum. The main entrance is the quickest and most direct route to those rooms." I recap what I remember, focusing on the task at hand to keep from spiraling. "Maybe we should try the back entrance, though. That's how we got in before."

"I walked out the front door," Lith says.

"Actually, that's how we left too," I say. "Do we dare just walk in the front door now?"

"Yes," Ryan says. "Because the door in the back leads to the basement. We need a straight shot to Renee. We get her and we get out. We regroup, and then some contingent can return to kill Range. I'm not sacrificing my sister again." He looks at us both pointedly. "Get her and get out."

Lith and I glance at each other, at Ryan. We nod.

In and out.

Regroup.

Kill Range.

Best laid plans and all that...

• • • • • •

The night is full of darkness and shadows and snow. The ground is covered, which means we will leave footprints with every step we take.

There doesn't seem to be security patrols. It's as quiet as it was when we escaped all those months ago.

No one patrols the grounds that I can tell. No cameras set up that I can see. No lights on outside the entrances to the two buildings.

How could they not have security?

Because they don't need it.

They aren't afraid of us, not even the least little bit.

This simple fact frightens me to my core.

Evil hovers in the air, a merging of past and present demons, dead and alive, using this space for death and destruction. Righteous death and destruction.

Shadows hover around every corner of the two buildings. There are a scattering of lights on in both buildings, but mostly, they look like the hollowed out eye sockets of a long-dead skeleton.

Dr. Richter alluded to there being people other than her and Teagan's mom who might be willing to help us. Can we trust her? Trust them? Trust anyone?

I glance at Lith and Ryan, their eyes intent on the buildings.

"Our plan is to walk through the front door," I confirm. "Go down the hall to the right. She's in one of the rooms there."

They nod.

"We need to keep moving," Lith says. "It's so cold we'll freeze to death. Won't do anyone any good then."

Our threadbare clothing leaves us with chattering teeth and shaking limbs.

"Should we wait for all the lights to go out?" Shaun asks.

"No." Ryan's voice is hard as ice. He straightens. "We go now. I'm not waiting another minute."

"We're with you," I say.

Lith nods.

Without another word, Ryan marches out of the forest's cover.

Lith and I lock eyes, and then follow.

It is quiet like only a snowy night in a rural forest can be. The moonlight reflects off the snow-covered limbs, making them sparkle like crystals. My breath comes out in white wisps, reminding me of the cigarettes I smoked in juvie. What I'd give for a cigarette now.

Our footsteps crunch against the cold, snow-covered earth. We're leaving an obvious trail, but that can't be helped right now. We push forward, weapons at the ready.

We come upon the red building. I constantly scan the area, the building, for any hint of awareness of our presence. There is none that I can see.

We press against the side of the red building, moving toward the asylum, resting in all its menacing glory yards ahead.

At the corner of the red building, we stop. We will be exposed from this point until we enter the asylum. Three pairs of eyes are alert, scanning, ears listening. Snow melts against my skin, dampening my shirt. Adrenaline pumps through me, and I feel the weapons shaking with my hands.

I clutch them tighter.

Without looking back, Ryan steps into the openness.

The asylum soars upward before us, the heavy beige stone seeming to expand and retract with my breath.

We press against the building, covered now by the asylum's shadow. We pause. Listen. Scan.

Ryan starts along the front of the building. Cyrus's red roses, once vibrant as newly drawn blood, now thorny and brown, direct us toward the main entrance.

Just before we come to the main entrance's concrete stairs, flanked by snarling dragon sentinels, we pause again. Listen. Scan. The angel fountain to our right, hovering right in the middle of the grounds like a weeping goddess, seems to exude a sense of despair and sadness that pierces something deep inside my soul.

I look up at the clock tower. Those long black hands pointing to the twelve and six.

Thirty minutes past midnight.

This is it. This is the moment when we willingly and intentionally return to the innards of this diabolical building.

What are we thinking?

Ryan walks up the stairs, his footsteps the only sound.

I follow. Then Lith.

The front door is unlocked.

How can they not have security? The question runs through my mind over and over.

Is Range so confident we can't get to him that he isn't taking any precautions?

This doesn't feel right on so many levels.

A tsunami of panic erupts throughout my body as Ryan pushes the right door open. The last time I walked through these front doors, I was following Cass. She had warned me over by the angel fountain on the front grounds of the asylum. Told me to run. I didn't. She'd gone into the asylum. I started to follow her. But I stopped, deciding at the bottom of the stairs that I would use common sense, for likely the first time in my life, and leave.

But then she'd screamed.

And I ran in, through these heavy black doors, to what awaited me. When they shut behind me, I was cast in darkness.

At first, I'd called her name, trying to hold off the panic that threatened to consume me. But then instead of me calling her name, someone else started calling mine. I never did find her. Never saw her again until days later when we were trying to escape, and I found her unconscious in a patient's room. In a straitjacket.

Ryan steps inside.

"I can't go in there," I whisper.

Lith grabs hold of my arm, and I let him pull me inside.

The foyer is dark, just like last time. The stained glass window at the opposite end does nothing to help lighten the area. The shadowy grayness of the world outside pushes at our backs.

It's hard to breathe. The oppressive weight of this building, all this stone, and all this tragic history pushes against my lungs, restricting and confining them until I'm on the verge of hyperventilating.

Out of nowhere, I remember the breathing techniques from juvie.

I gather my resolve. Realize that we're dead anyway. It's only a matter of time. Why not try to rescue Renee?

But we forgot the moonseeds again. Just as I remember this, my safeguard against ever being held in this prison again, Lith shoves something in my pocket.

I whip around, brows raised, demanding.

"Moonseeds," Lith mouths.

"Thank you," I mouth back.

The door closes behind us, casting us in darkness.

As my eyes adjust, I see that there is a little bit of light coming from underneath a closed door off to the left, behind the nurses' counter.

We start forward in a single line. The sharpened wooden knuckles in my right hand cut into my skin.

My breath comes in spurts as the memories punch at my brain. The whispered *Shaun, Shaun, Shaun* the day I was taken. The prick of the needle before losing consciousness. Waking up in a straitjacket chained to the floor. The doctor. Gibbon. Cyrus. The terror. The "room."

The room.

My worst nightmares came to life in that room, where four walls of teenagers stood, comatose, behind a glass wall. Waiting for lobotomy. Waiting for death.

We tried to burn down that room, but a stone building is hard to burn, so it was more symbolic. More of a message.

A big *Eff You*.

Where was the bravado of that message now?

We've been hiding in the forest for months, half-starved and barely alive, with no prospects for change or long-term survival. Now we're slinking around this godforsaken building looking for someone who will likely never be the same, even if we do manage to get her out of here.

Have they already won?

There's a sense of freedom and boldness that comes with feeling like you've already lost. Nothing else to lose. Right?

We turn right and start down the hallway.

There is no sign of another person—awake, that is. The doors of the patients' rooms are open, offering a clear view inside. Each one has a single twin bed inside, with a single person asleep on top. Someone is snoring softly, but other than that, there is no sound. From humans, that is.

There is a sound that comes from the building, an ancient wheezing moan that permeates the walls, the halls, the air. It has always seemed like the building was alive and breathing. A distinct character all its own in this horror story.

A distant moaning creak sets my teeth on edge.

Dr. Richter said she thought Renee's room was halfway down on the right.

A faint light flips on in one of the rooms.

We stop. Listen.

Tiptoe forward.

Could it be Renee? Did Dr. Richter tell her we were coming? Did she give her a flashlight to help guide us?

My heart pounds.

The asylum moans.

In the dark rooms, it's impossible to tell who is in the beds, if anyone. A few doors down, Ryan starts stepping into each room to get a better look. He weaves in and out until we come closer to the room with the light.

It goes off. Turns back on. Goes back off.

Is it a sign? Why wouldn't she come out of her room if she knew we were coming? Maybe she's in a straitjacket, unable to move? Hurt and bedbound?

The light is from the next room down.

On. Off.

We haven't found her yet, so it's seeming more and more likely that she's in that room.

Can we trust Dr. Richter?

We stop just outside the door.

Ryan glances back at us. I don't look at Lith, so I can't know what he's thinking, but I leave it up to Ryan. If he wants to go in, we got his back. We've come this far down the hellish rabbit hole. Too late to turn back. Besides, Ryan would never turn back without his sister.

We're committed. Even if it's to death.

I think about the moonseeds in my pocket.

I lift the knuckles. I hear Lith's chain scrape against the floor.

Ryan steps around the corner and disappears into the room.

• • • • • •

I listen to his footsteps cross the room. Even the asylum is quiet.

I can hear Lith's breath, and it's as fast as mine. I try to slow my heartbeat as I listen.

"Renee?" Ryan whispers. "Is that you?"

The light is off. I wonder how he'll be able to tell without the light on.

"Renee," Ryan says. "It's me."

It must be her.

I step around the corner. Lith's breath is on my neck he's so close.

Cardboard covers the window, just like when I was in one of these rooms, preventing any moonlight from seeping in.

"Come on," Ryan whispers. "Get up. You have to get up."

But then the most maniacal laughter erupts from the bed, a cackling, witchlike sound that sends arrows of terror shooting through my body.

"Renee?" Ryan says, voice shrill.

What's going on?

The flashlight flips on, held underneath a demonic face, pale, hairless head, hairless face. Sharp teeth, bared, the lips pulled back in laughter.

It's not Renee.

It's Les Range.

"Hello, boys," Les Range says.

Something is jabbed into my neck.

I try to grab the seeds. They fall from my hand.

Then darkness. Total darkness.

32

Inside the Mind of Dr. Esther Richter

• • • • • •

The door to her office is locked from the outside.

Panic makes everything she sees burn a yellowish orange.

She has to get out of this office.

She can't get out of this office.

She slams her palm against the metal door. "Help me!" she screams. "Is anyone there?"

Since Les Range took over her office in the asylum, she's had a small, windowless interior office in the red building. When he orchestrated the renovations in preparation for the new labs and more office space, he installed metal doors on all the rooms. With outside locks.

She hadn't thought much of it at the time. Always wary and on guard around him, she missed the more dire signs and never thought he'd use those doors to imprison her.

Whether she is hyperventilating or there is really a lack of oxygen, she can't say, but her skin starts to tingle. Black spots appear in her vision.

"Help!" she screams again. "If you can hear me, open the door!"

She's not sure how she got here. She was walking down the hall, going from the lab to her office, when the power went out.

Seconds later, something had been placed over her mouth. She vaguely remembers falling, but then…nothing.

Fortunately, the power is back on. Otherwise, her office would be pitch-black without windows.

She runs her hand over her belly.

The power goes off.

Terror rises in a swell. She can't see anything. Not the door. Her hand against it.

Surely, it's just a power outage, and the backup generators will kick on soon.

Any minute now.

She knows this is not true. Can still smell the faint remnants of ether.

She needs to stay calm for the baby. Someone will come by soon. If the lights don't come on, someone will check the rooms to make sure everyone is okay.

Surely, he won't leave her in here to rot. She needs to calm down.

Desperate, she practices breathing techniques. Feeling her legs weaken anyway, she knows she needs to sit down.

She feels her way over to her desk. Finds her chair. Pulls it out and gently sits down.

Counts her breaths. Practices a mantra.

"I'm okay. I'm okay. I'm okay."

She feels her sense of control start to return, piercing through the fog of her mind.

She places her feet firmly on the floor, trying to ground herself.

She places her palms on the cool surface of the wooden desk. Focuses on the points of contact.

Breathes.

"I'm okay. I'm okay. I'm okay."

She runs her palms over the surface, focusing on how the wood feels against her skin.

Where she expects to find her keyboard, monitor, mouse, papers, and stapler, she feels nothing.

The surface of her desk has been wiped clean.

Except for her instruments. Two cool metal extensions of her own hands.

Why are they here? She distinctly remembers putting them back in their case after cleaning them.

But here they are.

On her desk. She's locked inside this room. In the dark. With only her two instruments.

Deep breathing no longer works as terror consumes her.

33

Thus Speaks Cassidy Rutherford

• • • • • •

It's been six hours. They should've been back by now.

Unable to sit still, I've been pacing up and down the hallway of the prison ever since they left. I can see an imaginary line worn into the floor.

"Where could they be?" asks Emily, who has been talking the entire time I've been pacing. Her voice is starting to grate on my nerves.

I don't bother to answer.

Why not?

Because those answers hold too many catastrophes to acknowledge.

As hour seven begins, I stop pacing. "I'm going after them."

"What? No," Emily says. "You can't. It's too dangerous."

"We can't just leave them."

"It's the middle of the night. And snowing. When we talked to Teagan, we agreed to go in the morning at first light. It's too dangerous to go now."

"I don't care."

"What if you get caught?"

"Moonseeds."

Emily's dark brows arch. "You're ready to die?"

"If they're already dead, or kidnapped again, it's only a matter of time until the Agency comes for us and tries to lock us away again… or kill us."

Tears fill Emily's eyes. She finally seems out of words.

"I know it's hard to hear," I say, "but this is the situation we find ourselves in. I'd rather go down fighting. And I don't mean go back into the asylum. I mean dying. I'd rather die fighting for what I believe in."

"Which is?" she whispers.

"Shaun."

She doesn't respond, but I can tell her mind is in a whirl.

"Emily, Teagan's mom said there is a traitor. It has to be Richter. She might've given them bad information from the start, like where to find Renee. She might have sent them to their deaths." I stare out a window, past the tarnished bars to the shadowed forest. Snow is falling steadily now. In another time, another world, the landscape would be beautiful. Now it looks taunting and evil. "I'm leaving," I say after a beat. "You don't have to come with me."

"You're not going alone." She wipes her cheeks and stands.

"No, you're not," Traz says, coming out of his cell. I study him, skeptical. I've never been sure this guy was trustworthy, and not just because Shaun has never meshed with him. He just isn't someone I like.

I cross my arms, plant my feet, and stare at him. Challenging him to try and tell me I can't leave. If that's the case, I have a few choice words for those pretty boy ears.

"It's too dangerous," he says.

"I'll go with them," Teagan says, coming out of the office.

"You're ready to deliberately go to the asylum, risk everything, to try and help them?" I ask, needing confirmation that he knows what he's signing up for.

"Yes," Teagan says. "My mom is there. I need to get her away from that place. I can't sit still any longer either."

"This is a suicide mission," Traz mutters. "At least don't be so stupid as to go now. It's freezing outside. Wait till the sun is up."

"No," I say. "I'm not waiting."

"You're so stupid," Traz says.

Celexa shoots him a look.

"And you're a coward," I snap.

Emily steps to my side.

"I'll stay here and man the radio," Celexa says, breaking the tension. Traz's eyes cut her way, but she doesn't look at him.

"That's a good idea," Teagan says. He darts into the office and grabs the walkie-talkie. "This way if you learn something or need to warn us, we at least have a way to communicate. Leave the radio and the walkie-talkie on."

"Fine," Traz says with a huff. "I'll stay with her. She shouldn't be here alone."

"The three of us can go," Teagan says.

I look at Emily. "Yes," she says.

Without breaking eye contact with Emily, I say softly, "Let's go get our guy back."

34

No. No. No. No.

Sorrow rolls through me like waves crashing against a rocky shore.

My body yearns to crumble to the floor, roll into a ball, and die.

My mouth yearns for that moonseed, and the reprieve it will bring.

I can have nothing I yearn for.

I'm in the asylum. Sitting at the table where I was the last time. In the exact same chair.

There are no teens held behind the glass wall, unlike the dozens and dozens who were trapped behind that glass barrier the last time I was here. It's just me.

Sitting with Lith and Ryan. And Renee.

If they are alert, I can't tell. This medicine is so potent, I can't even be sure I'm blinking. I'm probably not. Maybe I'm not even awake. I'm dreaming. Or maybe I'm already dead and this is what the first minutes in the afterlife are like.

Terror tumbles around inside my brain, which is at least alert enough to know that I've been played a fool.

I'm back in the asylum, the room, sitting at the same table.

Once again, my foolish need to help has resulted in my imprisonment.

The word makes my heart weep.

Ever since juvie, I've been terrified of being locked up again. Absolutely terrified. Yet somehow this is the fate I keep finding myself in.

What have I done?

Was Dr. Richter the traitor all along?

What is wrong with me that I believe people? That I think I can save people?

Am I the narcissist?

Does my core belief that I can save everyone actually make me pathological?

I can't believe this.

I can't believe this.

I can't believe this.

Maybe I deserve to be in here. Deserve to die. If I'm stupid enough to repeatedly make catastrophic choices, maybe I don't deserve to live.

I don't fight the medicine and allow it to carry my thoughts off into a very welcome void.

35

"Well, well, well," says a male voice. "If it isn't the wondrous Shaun Treadway and his fellow escapees."

Sitting in the exact same chair as last time allows me to see the balcony that overlooks the room out of my peripheral vision.

A long, lean man is standing there, leaning against the railing.

At first, I think it's Cyrus, who was also long and lean like that, but the voice is different, and I know it must be Les Range.

"You people are absolute fools," he says, his voice light and teasing. "To think you were so stupid as to come back here. But, of course, Renee is here, and if there was one thing I knew Shaun Treadway couldn't resist, it was rescuing a damsel in distress. It was smart of me to keep her alive, wasn't it? I knew you'd learn she was here at some point and return."

He starts walking down the stairs into the main part of the room.

"It's too bad the others didn't come with you. It would've made my job easier to have you all gathered here."

I'm alert again, consciousness creeping in like a fog, terror making it black and ominous.

"But I know where they are and can easily go get them. I would've thought you teenagers, so self-righteous and convinced of your own superiority, would have fled the area by now. But, alas, you made the ill-fated decision to stay, not that it matters."

He's standing by my side now. I can smell his cologne. He puts a hand on my shoulder and leans down into my face. He is a very ugly man, more reptilian than human, with skin paler than any I've ever seen, nearly colorless eyes, and a hairless head.

"Tell me, what were you thinking?" he says.

We were thinking there was nowhere to turn, asshat. I want to scream but can't even swallow my own saliva.

He laughs. Removes his hand from my shoulder to place it on Lith's. He moves around the table, touching each of us as he goes.

"I'll tell you what you were thinking, you stupid teenagers. You were thinking there was nowhere to go for help, that the Agency's reach—my reach—was so widespread that it encompassed the entire nation. So, you thought you had nowhere to turn. Which meant you had to end this the only way possible—by killing me."

He throws his head back and howls in laughter.

"What fools. So easy to manipulate. All I had to do was insinuate that there was nowhere to turn, and *poof!* You believed there was nowhere to turn. So, you return to the asylum, the one place you should have put in your rearview mirror. You should've never looked back. But you did. All because you believed a great big lie. Stupid, stupid children."

He grabs the only empty chair, the one across the table from me, and sits, crossing an ankle over his knee. "Ever wonder what exactly was going on here? Did you ever question whether or not you knew the truth? Well, you don't. You've been so easy to manipulate, it was almost a pity to involve you all in my little experiment.

"What is true, you ask? Well, I don't have anywhere to be. Do you?" He laughs again. "I'll assume not. So let me tell you. The part about annihilating your generation was a desire rather than an actual plan.

"Seriously, how could I, or the Agency—which is just me by the way—and a few ignorant men, like Cyrus Rutherford—I hear he's addicted to meth now—kill millions of people? Did you actually believe that the world would be okay with that?

"I just wanted to eliminate those of you who…" He taps his chin, gazing off into the corner of the room. "How do I say this…who are evil or are born of evil. Bullies with no merit to society. People who think it's okay to act without understanding the consequences to others." He grins like the Joker.

"The past is the past, isn't it? Or is it? Anyway, there may be fewer teenagers in this area of the country, but they're alive and well throughout the rest of the country. My reach isn't that long, and I wouldn't want it to be.

"All I care about are the teens in this area of the country. Mostly West Virginia, of course, but other nearby states as well. And you all played right into my"—he looks down—"hairless little hands."

He slams those hands on the table and leans forward. "I went to high school with all your parents. How unfortunate it was for me to be exposed to such vindictive, hateful people. I thought they had ruined everything. With their perfect bodies, athletic skills, good looks. Perfect hair. They thought they were so worthy, that it was okay to tease those who weren't like them."

He sighs, stares off into the distance. "I wanted to end my life at one point. But, alas, revenge is far more entertaining than doing something so banal as hurting oneself."

I feel his eyes on me.

"I'm sure you're curious as to how this all comes back to you. Some of the teens here, most of them, truly, had no fault in this other than they were born and raised in an area that creates bullies; mean people who thrive on demeaning others. Their only fault is they lived in the wrong place at the right time for me and the Agency's mission. Revenge isn't fun if it's one and done, is it? No, it's not. I can attest to that. Plus, I needed specimens for experimentation. Oh, by the way, that part is nationwide...the part about reinventing old procedures to create new procedures. That's still a noble effort. The mental health care system in this country is broken."

He sighs again, as if he's growing bored. "Anyway, how does this all come back to you?" Contrary to the heavy sighs, his eyes are like lasers, hot and deadly, pointed straight at me.

"It wasn't just the boys who were bullies. No, they spread the word about what they saw in the locker room, or offered shoves and punches here or there. But it was the girls who were the most lethal. The ones who would recoil, sneer, *ignore*." He emphasizes that last word with a weightier tone. "Sometimes being ignored, literally not being seen, is the worst part of bullying. Because they make you feel like you don't matter. Oh, but I matter. In fact, I'm the only one here who does matter."

He relaxes back in his chair. "But I showed them anyway, those high school tormentors of mine. Where are they now, you ask? Well, some are in the cemetery—those who didn't have children. Some work for me. Thank the stars for such a rural area, forgotten on a national level and isolated beyond measure. One can get away with anything here. There is no protection. No one protected me when I was younger. No one has protected them, or their children, now."

He stands. "I have work to do, and I'm growing bored. I do appreciate this little reunion. Yes, you have seen me before. Or I've seen you. I was here when you were all here the first time. Of course, I only came down here after you were pumped full of medication. I like a specimen who isn't aware of what's happening to them."

He laughs and laughs.

"I may come back later. I may not. I may never see you again. Or rather, see you again *alive*." He laughs again as he bounds up the stairs, skips across the balcony, and disappears through the doors.

Despair blackens the world around me.

How could we be so foolish?

Since the medicine is still running thick in our blood, there is nothing to do but sit. Sit and wait. And pray the sorrow consumes us before the fate Les Range has planned does.

36

It's not Gibbon who comes around with the next dose of medicine, but Dr. Richter. She looks pale, gray almost. Her hair is oily and unkempt, like she hasn't washed it in days. Her clothes are rumpled, stained under her arms.

She stops by the table and starts to cry.

"I'm so sorry," she says, weeping. "I didn't mean for this…for any of this… I tried to help. I really did." She blows her nose. Stuffs the tissue in her pocket. Her hands are shaking. "He's evil. And we know what he'll do to those who don't do what he wants, and he threatened my—" She hiccups and cries at the same time. "My baby. He knows about the baby. What do I do? What choice do I have? He only let me out of that office…"

She is sobbing hard now. "That office. I was terrified."

"Esther," a man's voice says in warning. Les has reappeared and is standing on the balcony, just inside the doors.

She cries the entire time she prepares the syringes and shoves them into our arms.

The darkness is welcome…

• • • • • •

I'm walking. I know I'm walking. I'm very aware of it, but I have no control over it.

I've never had the medicine they give to make teens move without will, but now I know I have.

I'm following someone. Who it is, I don't know.

He looks young. But from behind, it's hard to tell. He's muscular, an inch taller than me, with closely shaved hair.

Is this the new Gibbon?

My thoughts feel like they're happening in the deepest recesses of my brain, but I thank a God I no longer believe in that I'm having them at all.

That means I am still alive. For now.

I try to use these thoughts to make my body react, but it's impossible. The medicine is in complete control.

I'm led down several flights of stairs into the basement.

Even my eyes are not under my control—can I even blink?—but my peripheral vision takes in the basement. The last time I was here, we were sneaking back into the asylum to rescue Renee.

Why don't I ever learn?

Why do I think that I am everyone's savior when I can't even save myself?

I saved my mom. At least I saved her. Even if she did this to me in return.

The basement looks the same as it did the last time I was here, with discarded furniture and other items from the days when the asylum was used to house the mentally ill. Hospital beds, desks, chairs, bathtubs, other equipment.

I follow the guy toward the left.

To Dr. Richter's patient room.

I want to scream.

She's going to give me a lobotomy.

Please kill me instead. *Please. Please.*

I can't control my body, and I follow this guy, knowing what's going to happen. I feel a sharp stab of sorrow, knowing now that all those teens sent in here for the procedure were mentally alert and likely aware of what was happening.

So sad. So very sad.

I'm led into a room that is an exact replica of a typical pediatrician's room. Blue walls. Stickers. Patient table. Swivel chair resting under a small desk.

The ultimate goal was to have lobotomies performed in pediatrician's offices. Pop in. Get a flu shot. Get a lobotomy. Go on your merry way.

The guy helps my body lie flat on the patient table.

Out of my peripheral vision, I see the metal table with the metal tools. The ice pick and the hammer.

My soul cries even though my body cannot.

I don't understand what's going on. I thought they were done with the experimentation part of the program. Why not just kill me?

Please just kill me.

The guy leaves.

I'm there all alone. Waiting. Mentally understanding what's happening. Physically unable to move.

I'm trapped in my own body.

Despair settles into my bones.

I lie there for what feels like hours before I hear footsteps.

My fingertips start to tingle, whether from the medication wearing off or anticipation of what's about to happen to me, I don't know.

The door opens, and Dr. Richter rushes in.

"Are you awake?" she asks in a hushed rush of words. She leans close to my head. "Blink if you can."

I try.

"Okay. Good. I see some movement of your eyelids, even though I doubt you can tell. We need to get you out of here. I will not let this happen to you."

I feel like I have no ability to speak or move.

She straightens, motions for someone.

Cass, Emily, and Teagan pop into view.

What the hell is going on?

"I've been working on a counter medicine," Dr. Richter says, her words rushed, "that is meant to undo the effects of the original medicine. It's not really been thoroughly tested, but I don't think we can wait."

"No one else has been given this medicine?" Cass asks.

Dr. Richter looks grave. "No. But we can't wait for him to become mobile." Out of the corner of my eye, I see her start to prepare the syringe. "No one knows about this counter med. I've had to be quite resourceful and strategic about developing it."

She looks at Teagan. "Your mother was a big help."

I think Teagan's eyes fill with tears. He coughs into his hand.

Dr. Richter glances at Cass. "Any objections to me giving Shaun this medicine? In place of his family, I'm asking you."

"I *am* his family," Cass says, voice hoarse.

"Right," says Dr. Richter.

"Give him the medication."

A horn suddenly starts blaring, like something you'd hear announcing an air raid.

"What is that?" Emily demands.

"We have to hurry," Dr. Richter says. "An alarm system was put in place after you all escaped. It was disarmed when Shaun and the others arrived, but Range must have reset it."

"What happens?" Cass asks.

Dr. Richter shoves the needle in my arm. "It'll take several minutes for full effect, but he should be able to move in a few."

"What happens when the alarm goes off?" Cass asks again.

"I'm not sure," the doctor says. "We should go, though."

"We gotta get out of here," Teagan agrees. "There's no telling what'll happen. And I want to find my mom." He grabs me under the shoulders. "I'll carry him."

The alarm rattles my eardrums.

We go out into the main section of the basement. Dr. Richter starts toward the stairs to the main foyer.

"Shouldn't we go out the back?" Emily asks, pointing. "We can run right into the forest from there. It goes straight outside."

"No," Dr. Richter says. "That door has been sealed shut. Everyone coming in or out of the asylum has to funnel through the front doors."

By the time we get to the top of the stairs, I can stand on my own. Teagan keeps an arm around my waist, my arm around his shoulders. The foyer is empty. Without warning, the lights shut off.

"No," I whisper, terror everywhere. "Not again."

I know what happens when the lights go out in this evil place.

"Please," I plead.

It must be midday because there is light, albeit dim and filtered, that breaks through the stained glass window.

We head toward the door.

"Who is waiting for us out there?" Cass asks. "Are we walking into an ambush?"

"I'm not sure," says Dr. Richter. "The sirens have never gone off before. But there is not a lot of security here, none that I know of actually, so the sooner we get out of here the better. Before Range can call in reinforcements."

The sirens remind me of those from a World War II documentary. I wait for the sound of bombs dropping. Maybe that would be best, anyway. End it all here and now.

With each passing second, I regain more strength. "Wait."

Dr. Richter turns. I pull my arm from Teagan and stand on my own.

"We're not leaving the others," I say.

Dr. Richter grasps the doorknob. "We'll come back."

"No." I turn and start back toward the stairs, shaking my limbs to make the blood pump faster. "They're in the room. Lith and Ryan. And Renee."

"I'm coming," Cass says. I hear her footsteps behind me.

"Let's go and regroup," Emily says, eyes huge. "We've been here too long already."

"She's right, Shaun," Dr. Richter says. "We have to go."

The sirens continue.

Ignoring them, I start up the stairs.

The first few steps are a labor to get up, but the more I move, the easier it is until I'm sprinting up the stairs to the top floor. I don't know if anyone is behind me, other than Cass, and I don't care. Then I realize with a jolt, that's foolish. I do care. I need the doctor, and her medicine. If we have any hope of getting out of here, they'll need to be able to move on their own.

"Go in through the balcony," Dr. Richter says, coming up behind me.

I whip around. Look her in the eye. About to demand the medicine when she holds up a syringe. "I have it," she says. "Enough for three."

She, Cass, and I run down the hall so fast I don't have time for a trip down memory lane.

I throw open the door to the balcony. Hear footsteps. Turn to see Teagan and Emily rushing toward us.

In the deep recesses of my brain, I question why security or Range or someone hasn't come yet. Are they just waiting outside, not bothering to exert themselves by hunting us down while we're in the asylum? They'll just grab us when we try to run out?

One problem at a time, Shaun.

I dart through the doors and look down over the room.

The table is empty.

"Where are they?" I whip around, grabbing Dr. Richter's arm. "Where did they take them?"

"I don't know," the doctor says. "Maybe to the basement."

"We were just in the basement."

"Maybe to the red building."

"Let's go. We'll follow you."

I leave nothing up for discussion. She opens her mouth like she's going to protest but doesn't. *Good decision*, I think as we follow her out of the room. Back down the stairs. Stopping in the front hall.

"Shouldn't we check this building first before we go barging outside?" Teagan asks. "I mean, I'm all for a showdown, but we have to be smart about it."

The siren is muddling my brain, making it hard to concentrate.

Why don't they turn it off if no one is coming?

"I don't understand," Cass says. "Why the siren if there is no police or army or whatever to find out what set it off in the first place?"

Dr. Richter shakes her head, looking as confused as everyone else. "Maybe to simply unsettle us. And it's working."

"What's the best way to get to the red building without being seen?" I ask.

"We can't ensure we won't be seen," the doctor says, "but I have a suggestion. Shaun and I go, just the two of us, and he acts like one of the patients."

"No," Cass says.

"Hear me out," Dr. Richter continues. "I know it sounds risky, but no one knows I'm helping you. Well, Range does, or did, but he'll think his threats were enough." She runs a hand over her belly. Exhales sharply and drops her hand. "We can't go charging in there without a plan. I can get myself and Shaun in right under their noses. Find the others, or at least rule out if they're over there. And let's pray they aren't."

"Why?" Teagan asks. "What's over there? Is my mom over there?"

The doctor doesn't respond.

Guess we don't want to know.

"At least take me too," Teagan says. "That way there's one more person."

Dr. Richter studies him while she thinks. Eventually, she nods. "But no one else."

"What are we supposed to do then?" Cass asks. "Stand here in this building and wait…for what? To end up in the room again?"

"Check the floors. They should be empty, but just ensure they are," Dr. Richter says.

"What happened to all the teens I saw that one day?" I ask. "When the vans first returned to the asylum?" I pause. "When you waved to me."

Her nonresponse is answer enough. That must mean there are about one hundred more graves newly dug out back.

I feel sick.

"Les Range's office is on the first floor," Dr. Richter says to Cass. "There's a chance he's in it. If he is, kill him. Can you kill him?"

Cass, Emily, and I exchange glances. No one here has intentionally killed another person. Except me.

"I'll kill Range," I say. "Can you take Teagan, Cass, and Emily to the red building?"

"I'm coming with you," Cass says to me. "I can provide backup."

I nod.

"Me too," Emily says.

"I'll go with the doctor," Teagan says.

"Shaun—" the doctor starts to say.

"Go," I say. "We don't have time. Find the others. Get them out and meet at—where is the best place to meet?" I ask the doctor. "The cabin or the prison?"

"The prison," Teagan answers. "That's where Celexa and Traz are."

He reaches into his back pocket. "Wait. Let me see if they've tried to reach us." He turns the walkie-talkie on, only to hear static. "Celexa?" he says into it before releasing the button to wait for the reply. "Traz?" He glances at us. "Nothing."

"We need to go," Dr. Richter grabs Teagan's arm. "Shaun, you three be careful."

"We will," I tell her. "You too."

"And kill him." Her mismatched eyes are too bright, almost possessed.

"I'll do my best."

She and Teagan set off for the red building.

Once they've slipped out of the front door, I look at the girls. "Are you ready for this?"

"Why wouldn't we be?" Cass asks.

"Of course we are," Emily responds.

"I don't have a gun. I'll have to kill him up close. If he's even here," I say.

"We're with you," Cass says. "No matter what."

I look between them and wish they were not here. But I'm so grateful that they are.

"Let's end this," I say.

37

The siren stops abruptly, the sudden silence almost as blaring.

I lift my finger to my lips. *No more talking. No sound.*

Cass and Emily nod. Before I turn for the hallway, Emily tugs at my shirt. Lifts her hand. Gives me a single moonseed. I nod. Grateful.

The doctor said that Range's office is on the first floor.

I count the doors as we go down. Stop when the door that should be the office is a few feet away.

"Ready?" I mouth.

Both nod. Raise their weapons.

I listen for any sound. Typing. Talking. Walking.

Nothing.

Then I hear it. Breathing.

My own stops.

He's in there.

The sound of breath is so faint, there's no way it's a room full of people.

I point to the door and nod.

Understanding, they return the gesture. Their eyes are huge. Cass is chewing her lip where the silver ring used to be. Emily's black tear-drop tattoo is overly dark against the paleness of her skin.

Time stands still in that moment, as if the universe wants me to take stock of this moment. In case I never see them again.

"I love you," I mouth, looking at Cass. "I love you," I mouth, looking at Emily.

Both respond to me. To each other.

I hold up my fingers. Countdown.

One.

Two.

Three.

I step around the corner and stop in the doorway. "Hello, Range."

38

Inside the Mind of Dr. Esther Richter

• • • • • •

This is a suicide mission, Dr. Richter thinks. She's tried so hard to protect the baby growing inside her that she can't believe she is now actively seeking out death, or at least the likelihood of it.

But something changed inside her with the planting of the little seed. A pregnant woman, soon to be a mother to a child, becomes a kind of universal mother and can't allow other children to be victimized. Why did it take her assault and pregnancy to realize what was happening? That rampant killing was not the answer?

She can't think about that now, and she shuts down those thoughts. Her comeuppance will come soon enough. What kind, she doesn't know, but she has no doubt that it will. And she will deserve everything she gets.

The only thing to do now is to help the best she can.

Soon she is walking across the grass with a robotic Teagan trailing behind her.

They walk toward the front door of the red building.

It's cold out, winter not far away. Snow is falling, and her steps leave prints on the white ground. She wipes the edge of her nose.

When they arrive at the main door, she uses her key card to get in. The unlocking mechanism is loud as it turns.

Thank goodness the siren stopped. That was enough to drive anyone mad.

"Hello, Winston," she says to the young man, one of her first Redeemables, who helps with transportation of bodies. He holds the door open while Teagan follows her in.

"Hello, Dr. Richter," says Winston.

She glances at his eyes, all evidence of his lobotomy long healed.

She turns left and walks down the hall toward the lab where she thinks the others might be held, hoping it's not too late. The overhead lights are fluorescent and glare off the white walls, ceiling, and floor. There are no windows in this building. Well, none that haven't been boarded over with Sheetrock, making the tracking of time difficult. It's almost like a Las Vegas casino where one loses all sense of time while lights are bright and oxygen is pumped in.

I'd like to go to Vegas someday, she thinks as she continues down the empty hall.

If the others are in this building, they are likely in one of two places.

Gibbon penned her room in the basement of the asylum the "kill room" because that was where she administered the fatal doses of medication after she'd performed her procedure. That kill room had nothing on the one here in this building where a dozen teens could be put to death within minutes. If the others are in that room, hope is already lost.

She will go to the other room and keep hope alive for just a few minutes more. The "experiment room," for lack of a better description.

This room is huge, walls having been knocked down to create a large, open space. It resembles a school cafeteria in size, but instead of tables, there are hospital beds. No curtains or walls divide the space—everything is visible to everyone.

Machines of various sorts help fill the space. Cabinets of medicines, carts of instruments. Hospital gowns, paper towels, cleaning supplies.

There are only a handful of people in the room—three assistants and two Redeemables.

She does feel a flash of pride at how well her procedure works now. The two Redeemables are pleasant, with stable moods and appropriate social engagement. Their emotive skills have been slightly reduced, and she's been monitoring their emotional well-being, but so far, she is very pleased.

If things had turned out differently, her procedure could've actually, truly, been an asset, a miracle even, a gift to the world. Now, she can't imagine it ever rolling out to the masses. Certainly, after her part in all these deaths, she won't have a role in her procedure's future.

Sorry, Grandfather. I couldn't redeem the family name. I only harmed it more.

A lump forms in her throat.

She never meant for things to go this far.

She'd been humiliated in medical school because of her grandfather's past. So desperate was she to overcome that humiliation, to show them, so to speak, that she'd lost everything that it meant to truly be a doctor.

Do no harm.

Shame makes her cheeks burn.

She can at least redeem herself a little if she helps end this now.

She wonders if Shaun and the girls are still alive or if Les Range has killed them. Range cannot be underestimated.

If anyone can kill Range, though, it's Shaun.

She feels a tug to her heartstrings. She always had a soft spot in her heart for Shaun Treadway. And a murderous spot for Range. He was the one who trapped her in her office and was also the one who let her out—under the order that she continue to carry out her work and medicate, then lobotomize Shaun and the others, or he'd force a miscarriage. At first there'd been no option. She'd given the teens the medicine in the room. But then, when it came time for the actual lobotomy, there was no way she could do it. What kind of mother would she be? She'd have to fight for these teens and her baby. *That* was the only way to redeem her family name.

When Cass and the other two had shown up to help, it was as if she'd been given a sign. That it was time to do right. Not continue the wrong. Where they came from, she didn't know. But she was done flip-flopping. She was team teen now, for better or worse.

She shuts down all extraneous thoughts and focuses on the beds in front of her.

There are bodies lying on beds, covered in white sheets up to their chins.

She wonders which doctors are planning to do which experiments on them, likely not until tomorrow. The doctors had ended up staying in town after the show the other night to record their procedures for other doctors to use for training and reference. Fortunately, none of those other doctors are in this room right now.

An assistant comes forward, a middle-aged woman with graying brown hair.

"Hello, Dr. Richter. Do you need a bed for your specimen?"

"Yes, please. But I don't want him given any meds just yet. Hold off on that."

The assistant looks at her a minute too long. This request is out of the ordinary. The assistant's job, once a specimen is brought in, is to immediately inject them with a dose of the medicine that they use in the room in the asylum.

Keeping the teens comatose is the best way to ensure order.

But the assistant doesn't object, simply nodding and indicating to Teagan to follow her.

When Teagan is settled on a bed, and the assistant has left the room, Dr. Richter moves toward the closest beds.

With faces uncovered, it's easy to rule out identities quickly.

Within minutes she has spanned three-quarters of the room and is headed toward the far end where the remaining beds and bodies lie.

She glances over her shoulder, ensuring no one new has entered the room, ensuring that no one has raised an alarm.

She stops at the foot of a bed and gazes down.

39

Les Range glances up, peering at me over the bifocals that sit low on his nose. They're rimless, adding a strange quality to his already vanilla-pudding face.

He straightens, tosses his pen onto the desk. Smirks. "If it isn't the altruistic one himself."

"If it isn't the murderer himself."

He shrugs. "I could say the same about you, couldn't I?"

"I hope to find out."

His brows raise. "You're here to kill me?"

Why isn't he alarmed?

He's cornered. I'm blocking the door with Emily and Cass behind me. I'm also younger, stronger, and have killed before. Surely, he knows I'm not above killing again. The weapons in my hands, not to mention my past, should indicate my seriousness.

"Yes, I am here to kill you. And won't feel a bit bad about it."

"What makes you think that killing me will have any bearing on the Agency's work?"

"The head of the snake and all that."

He cedes the point. "Noble thought." He folds his fingers under his chin, peering over the rimless lenses. "It's so funny, isn't it? This big joke."

"What big joke?"

"You idiot teens staying in the area, convinced that the entire country was in on the Agency's work—that nowhere was safe. What's that song..." He taps his forehead. "Something about being ironic..." He flips his hand through the air, dismissing the thought. "Anyway, bad song, so bad I can't remember the title, but good idea. Because it is ironic."

I stay silent, my pulse pounding in my ear.

"Ironic that you stayed under our noses all along. I couldn't have played it out better myself. And now you're here to kill me. Always plagued with thinking you're better than you are."

Rage makes my pulse pound even harder. I struggle to keep my eyes focused. All I can see, though, is red blood. Brown earth. Graves. Hundreds of graves. The room. Dozens of teens awaiting execution after being brutalized for a science experiment. The cabin. The prison. My mom, who sent me down this path.

"Because you were bullied?" I taunt. "That's the reason for all this? That's pathetic. You're pathetic."

Anger, mixed with pain, flashes across his face. "What would your mom say about your rudeness?"

"Don't you dare mention my mom."

"Why not? We were friends once upon a time."

"You knew my mom?"

"Jeannie? Yes, I know her well. Have known her for a very long time."

I can't speak suddenly. Can't think. Process. It's as if he's just shot me full of the medicine, even though he hasn't moved.

Mom. My mom put me here. After I saved her. After I killed my stepfather who beat her mercilessly. After I knew one more beating would kill her, so I killed him instead. She put me here, is the reason I am in this situation, about to murder for a second time.

Because that's exactly what I'm going to do. It might cost me my own life, but I will kill this man. But first, I want more answers.

"Prove it. How did you know her?"

Dark shadows fall over his face, and I know I've hit a nerve just like he did. I watch as he struggles to control himself. If I hadn't been studying him so astutely, I would've missed the distress.

"We went to high school together."

"You grew up in this area?"

"I did."

He watches me as closely as I watch him.

"And…?" I prompt, tapping the sharp end of the knife with my fingernail.

"And your mother…" His voice drops off, his eyes losing focus. He is quiet before suddenly raising his eyes, venom shooting out of those pale orbs. "She was a friend before she became a slut."

I lunge forward.

He's quicker than I expect. He jumps to his feet. Backs toward the wall. I stalk around the desk, the urge to murder pulsing through me.

I lunge again.

He darts around the desk. I'm behind it. He's halfway to the door. A maniacal laugh erupts from his rotten insides.

"Cass, shut the door. You and Emily wait outside. If he tries to run, hurt him."

"Cass?" Range laughs demonically. "Such a pretty girl."

The door slams shut. But Cass is standing inside it, not on the other side.

Where's Emily?

"Why thank you," Cass says in a mocking tone.

Range stands between us.

"Cass, leave," I tell her.

"No." She shakes her head.

Range's head sweeps between the two of us several times.

I take stock.

Can I stab him in front of Cass? Can I stab him at all? It's different killing someone in close range versus setting a house on fire with them asleep inside.

I keep my knife raised. Cass is holding a smaller knife and a crowbar.

Range watches Cass.

He's going to grab her and try to use her as a hostage. Since she's looking at me, that's possible.

While his face is turned to hers, I pointedly glance at the crowbar. Motion, quickly, for her to throw it to me.

I might not be able to kill him with a knife, but I have another option. A better option. The timing has to be perfect, though.

Sweat breaks out on my forehead. A bead runs down my back.

At first, she doesn't understand. Range looks back at me. Sees that I have not advanced. Looks at her. He raises his hands. She's closer to him than to me, and he can do it.

I jab my finger at the crowbar.

She understands.

He lunges toward her. She throws the crowbar. He grabs her arm. I swing the iron pipe across the back of his knees.

He collapses, howling.

He grabs for Cass's ankle.

She jumps back.

Emily throws open the door.

I lift the crowbar. Slam it against the back of his shoulders. He slumps to the ground.

"Kill him," Emily says.

I toss Cass the crowbar and tie his ankles and wrists with duct tape that was lying on the desk.

"Help me," I manage to say, breathless.

"Help with what?" Emily demands.

"You two grab his shoulders. I'll get his feet."

"Where are we taking him?" Cass asks.

"To the room," I answer.

The three of us look at each other, understanding flashing between us.

Range starts to catch his breath and begins thrashing. The girls have a hard time holding on to him, but he is weak, lacking any muscle or strength to speak of.

We drag him down the hall.

He slips from their grasp. Thrashes and kicks.

I punch him in the face.

He slumps.

We pick him back up.

Start down the hall. Go up the stairs.

We come to the room.

Drag him inside.

Shove him behind the wall. The fob that controls the glass is conveniently in his pocket.

He's not able to stand on his own, so I close the glass wall just enough to wedge him inside so we can stand him up without him falling, trapping him against the corner and the glass. He can fall to his right side, but he's gaining consciousness now and manages to stay upright as his eyes focus.

He realizes where he is.

His ankles and wrists are still taped. Fury, then terror, flashes across his face.

I hit the button, and the glass door starts to close. Just before he is stuck inside, I reach in, use my knife to cut the tape around his wrists, shove something in his hand. Barely get my own hand out before he grabs me.

His screams fog up the glass, distorting his face.

He can't move anywhere except to the side. But the glass is closed now. There is nowhere to go. He can't even turn around.

I think of all the teenagers kept behind that glass wall.

"Let's go get the others," I say.

"Are we just going to leave him there?" Emily asks.

I glance at Cass. She knows exactly what I put in his hand.

"Yes," I answer, walking away.

I knew I couldn't kill him outright, with a knife slice to his throat. But I sure could make it impossible for him to live. The moonseed will make sure of that. And if he chooses not to eat it?

I turn just inside the door.

When I was held in this room, the wall was packed with teenagers, standing shoulder to shoulder, unresponsive, unaware. They stood there until it was time for Dr. Richter's lobotomy, and then death.

I look at Range, now, the only body behind that wall.

And I feel good.

This is the end of him one way or another. My parting gift is he gets to choose.

40

"Let's go," I say to Cass and Emily.

"Where?" Emily asks.

"The red building. Let's get the others and get out of here."

Neither asks the million-dollar question—get out of here and go where? We'll cross that bridge when we get to it, I guess. I can only hope Range was right, and that it was all a sick joke. That it's not a nationwide program, and that there will be help. If we can only find it. And stay alive long enough to do so.

I stumble over my feet. But help for who? Maybe for the others. But what about me? I'm still wanted for Rodger's murder. Celexa, whose own mother put her here too—what will happen to her? A known drug dealer. Emily, who was partly responsible for the death of a mother and her children. Technically, I'm a minor. Celexa turned eighteen this summer, but what does that even mean? Emily will be eighteen in a few weeks.

If we find actual help, what risk is that unexpectedly causing us?

We have no money. No family. No resources. Hell, I haven't even graduated high school. Several of us are wanted for crimes we've committed.

"Shaun?" Cass puts her hand on my arm.

"Let's go," I say again and start jogging toward the main entrance. I'll help save the others, then decide what to do.

"Are we sure no one else is out there?" Emily asks.

"We're not sure of anything, but we're not leaving the others." I glance at them over my shoulder. "Keep the moonseed handy."

I shove open the door.

Three different camera crews are setting up just outside the entrance. Tripods, microphones. Lights. Another two vans are coming down Main Street.

"What the hell?" I throw out my arms to stop Cass and Emily. We don't move off the landing, keeping the five concrete steps between us and whatever the hell is going on down on the lawn.

"Shaun!" a female reporter shouts, scurrying toward us. "Are you Shaun Treadway?"

"Who the hell are you?" I demand. I scan the grounds. Where is Dr. Richter?

The reporter has the good sense to stop at the bottom step, resting a hand on one of the dragons. "I'm Debbie Stanton, a reporter with News 4 out of Philadelphia, and want to ask you some questions. Is this Cassidy Rutherford and Emily Howard?"

I do another sweep of the grounds. Look for vans of teenagers. Men with semiautomatics. Doctors, assistants, instruments. I see nothing but the reporters.

"What are you doing here?" Emily demands.

The other two reporters and crew crowd in behind Debbie Stanton, microphones thrust outward. So far, they are allowing her to ask the questions.

"We're here to interview you." Debbie's eyes have that slightly manic look and stern-lipped expression you often see on reporters' faces. Her voice takes on that pretentious lilt they also use, as if that superficial tone elicits trust.

Not with this crowd, I think. Trust does not come easily to us.

"Word has spread," Debbie continues, speaking into the black microphone in her hand, "about what's been going on here at the asylum. People are *dying* for information." She smirks. "No pun intended."

I shoot her a look. She straightens. Clears her throat. Changes her expression. Removes her hand from the dragon to wipe imaginary dirt off the skirt of her moss-green suit.

"What do you want?" I ask, voice low but deadly serious.

"Can I ask you three a few questions?" Debbie asks.

"Why? What is the point of this?" I ask.

"Don't you want to get your story out there? Tell the world what has been happening here at the Blackthorn Peak Lunatic Asylum?" Debbie says.

How much do they know?

Whose side are they on?

I glance over at the red building where there is no indication of life.

I'm tempted to spill my guts. Tell this annoying woman everything. But I've learned to not trust. To be defensive. To never assume.

Clamping my lips shut, I watch a van enter the property, then come to a stop. The crew quickly hops out, scurrying toward us.

"I'm not sure I like this," Cass says under her breath.

"This is the help we wanted. Finally," Emily answers. "The break we need. Maybe they heard the broadcast from the other night."

Emily steps forward, staring down at Debbie. "I'll talk."

"Emily, wait," I caution.

Those huge brown eyes look at me, defiant. "No. I'm done with this. We finally have people here to help, to get our story out."

"But the things we've done..." I reach for her arm. She pulls away before I can remind her that she and I are both wanted for murder.

"My name is Emily Howard, and the Agency tried to kill me and my friends. They have already killed hundreds of teenagers."

"How did you escape?" a young male reporter asks, thrusting out the microphone.

"Where are the others?" an older woman asks.

"How long have you been here?" a middle-aged man asks.

"Where is Les Range?" Debbie asks, her voice rising above them all.

Emily stops. Turns back to look at me. We've left Les Range in the room to die.

One more murder on our list of murders.

We can't confess that right now. Maybe never.

Emily finally finds her discretion and presses her lips together.

Cass steps forward. "He's inside. Likely dead from poison. From moonseed found in the nearby forest."

"Is his death self-inflicted?" Debbie presses. "Or was he poisoned?"

Cass stares directly into the camera. "It was self-inflicted. We arrived too late."

Cass slides her hand into mine, and I slide my other into Emily's. We stand in a line, defiant and secure. At least from one more murder charge.

• • • • • •

Shortly after the arrival of the reporters, several police SUVs arrive, the words STATE POLICE splashed on the sides. I see five black SUVs also pull on to the property, and men and women with blue jackets that read FBI across the back spill onto the lawn.

I try to go to the red building to find the others, but the officers won't let us move from the steps.

"This is a crime scene, now," the young officer says.

He barely looks older than me.

Another officer walks up, this one oozing authority, puts a hand on Debbie Stanton's shoulder, and urges her to step back. "I'm Detective Barber," he says, his gaze zeroing in on us, "and I'll be the one in charge here."

Exhausted, Cass, Emily, and I sit on the top step to the asylum. It's been roughly fifteen minutes since Debbie asked her first question, and no one has walked out of the red building.

I feel like I'm stuck in some alternate universe. None of this makes sense. And even though it looks like help has arrived, I feel unsettled, guarded, and defensive.

I can never forget that I am wanted for murder…of a police officer. In the eyes of people like Detective Barber, that's an unforgivable sin, regardless of why I did it.

"Your names, please?" the detective asks.

"Emily Howard."

"Cassidy Rutherford."

Detective Barber looks at me. He has naturally arched brows, not slightly rounded but pointed, almost like a caricature. He's not dressed like a police officer but his comrades are, milling about in green uniforms and those offensively wide-brimmed hats state troopers wear. One stands by the detective's side but doesn't speak. Just watches us.

Barber raises those brows even higher.

"Shaun Treadway," I answer, watching closely for his reaction.

He gives nothing away. If he knows me, he doesn't show it.

"Where are the others?" he asks.

"What others?" I ask.

His eyes narrow. "You help me. I help you. That's how this works."

"It's a valid question," I state. "Are you talking about the staff who tried to kill us or our friends? You have to be more specific around here."

"Where are your friends?"

"In the red building." I point. "I assume. We were on our way to find them when you showed up."

"Why were you in the asylum?"

My lips snap shut again. Because the truth is that I went in to kill Les Range, but that's not a truth I'll divulge here.

"We went in to look for our friends," Emily offers.

"And they weren't in there?" asks Barber.

"No. That's why Shaun just said they might be in the red building," Emily snaps.

That earns raised brows for her benefit.

"You're quiet," he says to Cass.

"I'm a quiet person," Cass answers.

His arched brows purse.

If what Les Range said is true, that it was all a farce, then these people are likely here to help. But how can we know that for sure?

Detective Barber is staring at me.

I force myself not to get in his face. Or fidget. Or squirm. Or punch him.

He turns to the officer standing behind him. "Check both buildings."

That officer gives the command, and the other officers fan out, several sprinting up the concrete stairs, bypassing our sedentary forms.

The detective turns his back to us and talks to the remaining officer so softly I can't hear what he's saying.

"This is strange," Cass says. "I don't know what to think. After all this time, help is here? It's too weird."

"They *are* here to help us," Emily says. "You two are crazy for doubting it. We finally have help. Yes, after all this time."

I want to remind her that *we just murdered Les Range*, not to mention the murders in our past, but I don't. Fortunately, Cass isn't wanted for murder, so maybe she'll get away.

But where will she go? We haven't seen her father, Cyrus, since we escaped the asylum. She's only seventeen. What kind of life is out there for her?

I'm starting to think that rescue doesn't sound quite as appealing as it used to, back when I yearned for it more than anything else.

Am I just trading one prison for another?

41

Inside the Mind of Dr. Esther Richter

• • • • • •

Dr. Esther Richter is in the process of reviving Renee with her experimental medication. Ryan and Carter are already sitting upright, sipping water, regaining their strength.

She glances between the three teens. Ryan struggles to his feet and manages to walk to Renee's side as she starts to slowly regain consciousness. She's disoriented and, at first, seems to think that Ryan is a ghost. But he speaks to her softly until he convinces her otherwise, and the two embrace, not letting each other go. Carter is standing now, arms crossed.

"Is everyone ok?" Teagan asks, joining us. "Where's my mom?"

Just then his mom, Nancy, darts through the door. She skids to a stop when she sees her son. Then she bursts into tears as she runs forward to embrace him.

"Mom, what's going on?" he asks.

Nancy looks at the doctor. "Do you know?"

"Know what? I'm so confused." Dr. Richter rests a protective hand on her stomach.

"Police are here. Range is dead," says Nancy.

Oh, thank goodness.

She holds her breath, waiting for Nancy to say the others are dead too. She doesn't.

"You all need to leave," Dr. Richter says. "Right now. Go outside. Go to the prison. Get away from this area. Shaun's truck is parked out back with keys and gas. Don't be associated with me."

Five pairs of eyes stare at her.

"Nancy, go. This is your chance. You're innocent enough in all this, but it's not a chance worth taking if they start asking questions. And they will start asking questions. Get them out of here, and don't come back. Any of you."

"What about you?" Nancy asks, concern and sympathy imprinted on her face.

Such a kind soul. She had no business being mixed up with this.

"I'll stay," Dr. Richter says.

Nancy opens her mouth to say more, but the doctor waves her hand. Shakes her head. They hold each other's gaze a moment, then Nancy nods. Motions for Ryan, Renee, and Carter to follow her and Teagan.

"I'm not leaving without Shaun," Carter states.

Ryan looks at his sister. How they haven't already bolted, she'll never know. But they stand firm beside Carter.

"Go," Dr. Richter urges Nancy. "Just go."

Nancy and Teagan slip out the door.

Dr. Richter feels unsettled and curses the boarded-up windows that prevent her from seeing outside, an attribute she had praised not so long ago, relishing in the privacy this building offered her and her work.

She sits on a stool and waits, thinking.

She thinks of the work she's done—of how proud she is of her accomplishments. She still believes in the lobotomy. She doesn't believe in killing the entire generation. But those hundreds of graves behind the asylum? Those that lie beyond the original cemetery, in the more freshly disturbed earth?

She's responsible for those.

Mass murder.

She doubles over, her head in her hands.

"What have I done?" she asks herself.

She had been so convinced of her work. So convinced that the world needed a drastic and radical change. Had gotten swept up in Les Range's ambition for the world.

His desire for utopia.

Anyone who had suffered pain couldn't help but buy into the novel idea.

Every person he recruited to work for the Agency, for him, had been hurt by a teenager and their poor choices. Every single one. He was a master at finding weakness in people and exploiting it. Creating a situation where revenge could be had and a better world could be cultivated at the same time.

"Sadistic sociopath," she calls him, "but then what am I?"

42

I'm not going back to prison. Not juvie. Not adult prison. Not the asylum.

I keep an eye on Detective Barber and the other officers, my mind reeling.

How do I get out of this?

No matter what has happened to me here, I've still killed a man. I still killed my stepfather. Can they let me off because I've had a hard life since? Because I have survived the unimaginable?

How could they? I killed one of them in cold blood.

My blood turns to ice as despair—and desperation—rise.

I have to get out of here. I can't let them take me into custody or allow them to question me. If I leave the open space of this expansive asylum lawn, the safety of this vast forest, I'll never escape their grasp.

Struggling to control the rising panic, I glance at Cass and Emily. Both sitting to my right with Cass in the middle.

"I can't be questioned," I declare.

"I told the detective that Range took the moonseed himself. Not that you gave them to him," Emily says.

"But I killed Rodger. There's no mistaking that. And they know my name—I'm sure they know what I did to get in this situation. To end up here. They know what I've done. And Rodger was a policeman, just like them. You know how they rally around each other."

"You have a point," Emily concedes. "Do you really think after what we've been through that they'll still punish us? I mean, haven't we been through enough?"

"I don't think that's how it works," I say.

"What are you saying?" Cass asks. "That you're worried you'll be arrested?" Her voice rises several octaves with that last word, granting us a glance from a group of officers nearby who are talking about how they've secured the crime scene.

Crime scene.

They're probably going through a process similar to the one the officers in Baltimore went through when they investigated the house fire that killed Rodger.

What am I going to do?

"I can't stay here," I whisper, watching three more police cruisers drive on to the property. "I just can't. I won't be locked up again."

"What are you saying?" Cass asks. I wonder if she's thinking of the seeds.

"I'll eat the moonseed," I confirm. "Shit! I gave it to Range. Do either of you have yours?"

"I'm not giving you a means to kill yourself," Emily says. "I'm wanted for murder too. I don't want locked up either, but I cannot imagine they will lock us up. They can't. Not after what we've been through."

That's her story, and she's clearly sticking to it. I don't buy it, though.

"I wonder why the others aren't out here. Do you think they're okay?" Cass offers a change of subject.

"That's a good question," I say. "Maybe they're keeping us all separate to question us?"

"What if something is wrong? What if Dr. Richter wasn't on our side and ended up killing them? Or worse, lobotomizing them?"

"Way to stay positive, Em," I say.

"I'm serious," Emily says.

There's nothing to say, so we sit there quietly. I don't know what the girls are thinking, but I'm thinking of a way to escape.

Just then, Dr. Richter is led out of the red building, her hands cuffed behind her back.

Behind her comes Lith, also in handcuffs, and Ryan and Renee, not cuffed, but surrounded by police. That makes sense as Ryan and Renee didn't do anything wrong other than be born to drug-addicted parents who lost custody, which sent them into a foster care system that didn't want them. But Lith was wanted for grand theft auto. I remember so clearly how much he liked the video game and tried to recreate that in his otherwise boring life.

Where is Teagan? I pray he found his mom.

I jump to my feet.

Run, Shaun. Go now. But how? I'm fast, but also severely malnourished. If I run, they'll catch me. Or shoot me in the back.

That would be better than capture. Arrest. Imprisonment.

"Give me the moonseed," I demand, eyes flipping back and forth between the two people closest to me in the world. "They'll arrest me, and I can't be imprisoned again."

"They'll arrest me too," Emily cries, "but they'll have to let us off."

"Shaun, if they arrest you"—Cass looks between us—"either of you, I'll do what I can to get you out."

"You're seventeen, for God's sake, with no contacts and no money. You'll be almost as bad off as we will be," I say.

"You can't kill yourself," Cass says.

I shake my head. "I can't let them take me. No way."

I hurl myself down the stairs and make it to Cyrus's first rosebush before I'm easily grabbed by an officer and cuffed.

"Shaun Treadway, you have the right to remain silent…"

• • • • • •

It's like I'm suspended in air, watching myself from on high.

I see the officer cuff me.

I see my body thrash and fight. Scream for the moonseed. Plead for death.

He wrestles me to the ground. Knee on my back.

No. No. No. I release a guttural wail that feels like it comes from my stomach.

Cass is screaming, too. Yanking at my arms, the officer's arms. At one point she punches him in the face.

She is cuffed too.

Emily is cuffed. Wanted for stealing that stop sign that resulted in the death of Dr. Richter's sister and her children.

Renee and Ryan stand in the distance. Ryan is talking to another officer. Lith is walked toward a different cruiser.

I watch the officer shove me into the back of an SUV. Watch as the officer reaches in and punches me in the face. I hear him say, "That's for Officer Steele."

Rodger Steele.

The devil of a stepfather who beat my mother repeatedly.

He's still plaguing my life, long after his death.

• • • • • •

We're driven about thirty minutes away to some other town in this rural area, one I don't recall passing when I drove into this state all those months ago. Maybe it's farther down the road. Who the hell cares?

I'm thrown into a holding cell.

I see Cass and Emily, brought in from a different car, led to a cell down another hall. Fortunately, the glass allows me to see that they're at least intact. I'm thankful they don't see me, or they would see the bruise on my eye.

If they brought Lith here, I don't see him.

Where did Ryan and Renee go? Did they have anywhere to go?

What about Dr. Richter?

Shouldn't she be in here too? Why is it always the teenagers who get the bad rap?

The bench is hard beneath me. That's all that's in this room. A bench and a toilet/sink combo. Not even any toilet paper. Or blanket.

This must be where I stay before booking.

They checked me for weapons, but I haven't had to change clothes yet. I look around, see no one through the bars, and stand. Slap my pockets.

One more seed. One more seed, please. I can't be imprisoned again.

I start chanting "one more, one more, one more" under my breath like a mantra.

Turning my pockets inside out, my panic grows.
I can't stay in here.
My breath comes in spurts. Sweat breaks out on my brow.
One more.
One more.
I need one more.
I find one more.
Squished deep in the corner of my jean's pocket.
I collapse to the ground, desperate with relief.
"Thank you, God," I whisper.
I lift the seed.
"Shaun?"
I look up. Drop the seed. "Mom?"

43

"Shaun, I am so sorry."

The woman before me looks like my mom. Or a sobbing version of her. A version without a bloodied and bruised face. A version who is a healthier weight with a healthier glow about her.

But my mom...she handed me to Les Range on a silver platter.

And now she's sorry?

I'm so confused, I just stare at her.

"Are you okay?" she asks, clutching the bars, pressing her face between them. "Shaun, say something. Please."

"What are you doing here?" I manage to say.

"I came...I came to rescue you."

"A little late for that, isn't it?"

"I've been here for months."

"What?" I bolt to my feet, lunge for her. She jumps back. I grab the bars she just held in her hands. "You've been in Blackthorn Peak for months?"

"I've been working with the others, trying to end this the right way."

"The right way?" I yell. "You gave me up for this diabolical experiment, for death, and then come after me only to sit by and let it almost happen again?"

An officer walks up. "Everything okay, ma'am?"

My mom nods. "Everything is fine."

"Son, watch it, or I'll ask her to leave if you can't maintain control," the officer warns.

I throw my hands in the air. "Controlled," I snap sarcastically.

"Your smart ass should stay locked up," he says under his breath and walks away.

Mom studies me a moment.

I almost don't recognize her. Even the whites of her eyes are clear, making the color brighter.

I wonder if she's still taking her medicine. I haven't taken mine in months. Clearly, I wasn't bipolar. Maybe she's not either.

"Are you ready to talk?" she says. "Or I can come back. I'm sure this is all very confusing for you."

My mouth falls open as I stare at her. Confusing?

"Would you like me to come back another time?" she asks.

"And just leave me in here?" I wail.

"I can't get you out. Despite what happened to you at the asylum, you still killed your stepfather. There will have to be a trial."

Her eyes fill with tears. She pulls out a tissue. Wipes her eyes, then her nose, before tucking it back into her pocket.

"I never had a chance to say thank you, though," she says.

"If you're so thankful, why did you put me on that list?" Venom shoots out of my mouth with every word.

"It was all so shocking at the time. I don't expect you to understand, but I have to state my piece anyway. I had a concussion. He'd beaten me worse than he ever had. He was going to kill me the next time. I was in shock, from this knowledge and from the injuries. A man showed up at the hospital."

"Cyrus Rutherford," I say. A piece of the puzzle I didn't know was missing just clicked into place.

"How do you know him? I'd only just met him."

"Long story," I answer dryly.

"He told me about this program for troubled youth. I knew that if I didn't do something, you'd be arrested and tried as an adult. Maybe even get the death penalty. This man had a brochure, and it all seemed so legit."

She inhales, exhales, then continues, "I was so afraid for you. I knew how hard juvie was for you. The thought of you being in regular prison, the risk of the death penalty, was too much. I knew you'd be convicted. You'd already tried to kill him twice. I saw no hope."

My chest hurts, pressing and squeezing in a way that makes me want that heart attack that is unlikely to come.

"When I was driving that night, you called me. Tried to get me to turn around. Why?" I asked.

"After you left, that man, Cyrus Rutherford, returned. I was slightly more lucid. They hadn't given me my next dose of meds, and even though I was in pain, I had a clearer head. Something didn't add up. I mean, Shaun, I've never been a good mom to you. If I had, I never would've gotten with Rodger, and I'm so sorry for that.

"But I tried to become strong from that point on. I tried to warn you. I understand why you didn't listen. When I was discharged—it took longer than they expected to discharge me because they found bleeding on my brain. Anyway, I drove to Blackthorn Peak, but you weren't at the cabin. I could tell you had been, but you weren't there anymore.

"Then I ran into someone I knew from high school." A shudder runs violently down her body until she's left gasping, and she grasps the bars again.

"Let me guess. Les Range. How did you know him?"

She nods. "He was…picked on in school. Called 'the worm' and mocked mercilessly in the locker room, around the whole school, and even in the community. Anyway, he had a crush on me that I didn't return, but he wouldn't leave me alone. Called my home several times a day. Followed me from school to work. He was the reason I left Blackthorn Peak."

"Not to follow my father?" A strange feeling makes my chest tighten.

"No. Not to follow him. But I set up a life in Baltimore and stayed."

"I thought for a minute you were going to tell me Les Range was my father."

She looks like I just punched her in the face. "Why do you say that?" she manages to say eventually.

My hackles are raised. There is something unsaid resting just out of my reach. What is it?

"Mom?"

She starts shaking her head back and forth, staring at the ground. I watch her hair flip around her face. Tears fall to the ground.

"Mom! The time for secrets is over!"

Then she lifts her eyes, so slowly I want to reach out and grab her chin, but her gaze finally meets mine. She sniffs. Snot runs down to her lips anyway. Her face has taken on a swollen quality with her crying.

And I suddenly know I don't want to know what she's on the verge of telling me.

"No..." I say, backing up, going deeper into the cell. "No. Don't say it. Don't even think it. It can't be true."

She's sobbing so violently now, as if all her past traumas have shot to the surface and she isn't equipped to handle them.

This time it's a female officer who comes to check on us.

"Ms. Treadway? Is everything okay?"

She's still shaking her head.

"Don't say it," I demand. "Just don't."

"Don't say what?" the officer asks, her brows pursed, eyes brimming with concern.

"That Les Range is Shaun's actual father. That he..." She collapses. The officer catches her, holds her.

"That he what, Ms. Treadway?"

I lose it. I start slamming my head against the bars, screaming and screaming. I want Les back in my grasp so I can choke him to death with my own bare hands.

A doctor comes in with three huge police officers. I land several blows before I'm given an injection and succumb to the void.

• • • • • •

I'm strapped down again. I'm just lucid enough to know this, but incoherent enough to not be able to fully grasp it.

"Hi, Shaun. My name is Dr. Peters. If you promise to stay calm, I'll undo these restraints."

I think I nod. I must, because my wrists are eased out of the straps. I lift my hands and try to focus my eyes on my fingers.

"The sedative is wearing off. You'll feel funny a little longer but will be back to normal in no time. Can I get you anything?"

"Water," I croak, caught between the memory of waking up in the asylum in a straitjacket and waking up here in restraints.

Dr. Peters gives me water in a huge plastic cup with a lid and a straw. "Can you hold it?" he asks.

I grab it, not trusting that he's not taunting me with it like Dr. Richter had done that first day all those months ago.

He's not. He releases it easily. I gulp it down.

"Take it easy," he cautions. But he doesn't try to take it away from me.

"Where's my mom?"

"She's actually next door. You're in the medical section of the prison. You two must've been having quite the discussion as you both needed to be sedated. But don't worry, she's okay. She's been asking for you, and when you're ready, I'll bring her in."

"I'm ready." I sit up in the bed, confirming my wrists and ankles aren't tied. I can get up if I want.

"Shaun?" My mom peeks around the corner. Her face is blotchy, but she's no longer crying. She comes to my bedside and pulls the plastic cup out of my hands. Holds the straw to my lips. Allows me to drink as much as I want without yanking it away.

It's a surprisingly loving thing to do.

"I'm ready to hear more," I tell her.

She sits by my bedside, pulls my hand into hers, and talks.

• • • • • •

Les had been stalking her for months. First, they were friends, or acquaintances, really. They'd been lab partners. But then, his behavior changed. The teasing started at school, and he became obsessed with her, like he thought that if she liked him, he would be saved from the bullying. He wouldn't leave her alone. She'd told friends, teachers, her dad. My grandfather, Earl Pickens, had believed her but couldn't make anyone else do so.

Then, the assault.

She didn't go into the details. I didn't want the details.

But Earl found out. Range had already disappeared, and Earl couldn't find him. When he found out his daughter was pregnant by assault, he couldn't handle the pain, the feeling that he'd failed her, and eventually hung himself from a tree by the cabin in the woods. The very cabin we'd stayed in for months.

Mom had already moved to Baltimore by that point. My dad, the man she had told me was my dad, had lived in Blackthorn Peak and had moved to Baltimore. They were friends, though. Nothing more.

To avoid suspicious questions about the truth of my conception and birth, she'd made up the story about following my dad. When he married, she made up the story about him choosing another woman. And so on.

Ancient history now as I never knew the guy anyway.

But I did know Les Range. And I had all but killed him. I killed my stepfather, and now I've killed my father.

Maybe I do deserve to be in jail. On death row.

"I have a good lawyer," Mom is saying.

"How can you afford a lawyer?"

"Insurance money. From the fire damage to the house. It burned to the ground."

I can't tell if there's a twinkle in her eye or if I only imagine there is. I don't know, and I don't care.

"Where are my friends?" I ask her.

"Emily is here, in this building, as is your friend Carter. Your friend Cassidy, well, I'm not sure where she is. I believe she was released, but I can't say."

"Have Emily or Lith, I mean, Carter, had anyone visit?"

"Not to my knowledge."

"Is the lawyer willing to represent all three of us?"

She looks confused for a brief moment, then says, "We'll make sure he does."

"What about Dr. Richter?"
"We're not paying to help her."
I hold her gaze a minute, then nod.

44

My mom made a very strategic move at that point and went to the press all over the eastern United States—Charleston, Richmond, Pittsburgh, Charlotte, Philadelphia, Washington, D.C. While me, Emily, and Lith stayed behind bars, she rallied for the most important court of all: the court of public opinion.

No one had seen Traz or Celexa.

Teagan's mom became Mom's ally in this fight. Together, Mom and Nancy preached their gospel all the way to the Midwest, to Chicago, in fact, where a certain famous television personality lived and worked.

Three weeks later, when it came time for our trial, everything was settled out of court. All charges were dropped under the condition that the three of us engage in intensive counseling every week—one session of individual and one session of group. If our therapists deemed us a threat in any way, either to ourselves or others, we'd be remanded to prison and await new prosecution.

It was anticlimactic as these things go, but I was free, and there was no way in hell I was ever being locked up again.

• • • • • •

Dr. Richter was charged with the murder of three hundred and eighty-four people. I didn't reach out to her, though there was a part of me that wanted to thank her. If it weren't for her, we would not have escaped.

But she was also responsible for horrible crimes. And so many deaths...

Her trial went ahead two weeks after our case was settled, and created far more interest. Maybe because she was pregnant with her own child, ironic considering how murderous she'd been toward others' children. Maybe it was because there was some sympathy for why she'd stepped down the path she had: having lost her sister and her nieces and nephews to that wreck had broken something in her. The court of public opinion vilified her, but also sympathized with her. Those who sympathized with her had been hurt, or had a loved one hurt, by a teenager's impulsive actions. It was appalling to learn how many people have been hurt by the actions of my generation. Eventually I stopped listening to the news.

After a three-week trial, Dr. Richter was sentenced to life in prison. She would serve her time in Charleston, the state's capital.

Maybe she could do good while in prison. Teach others to read. Start a small medical clinic.

I wondered what would happen to her baby. Her sister was dead. I didn't know anything about her parents, if they were dead or alive, or if she had other siblings.

If she didn't, and she couldn't have her baby in prison with her, one more child would land in the foster care system.

The other doctors were in varying levels of trouble, depending on what they'd done and what they knew. None had committed murder like Dr. Richter, who'd been so caught up in trying to redeem her grandfather's name in overcoming the bullying she herself had received, and in trying to please a diabolical Les Range, that she'd lost all human decency.

A few of the doctors lost their medical licenses. A few were reprimanded. A few are still practicing. It turns out Les was speaking the truth when he said it was only this area where teens were being killed. The doctors across the rest of the country were truly working on psychosurgeries only.

• • • • • •

I haven't seen Cass in weeks.

• • • • • •

While waiting for our release, Mom rented two hotel rooms near the courthouse, one for her and one for Ryan and Renee. Teagan and his mom rented a small apartment nearby. Once we were released and our case was settled, we stayed on during Dr. Richter's trial but didn't go to court other than when it was our time to testify.

Mom wanted Emily and Renee to stay in a room with her, and me, Ryan, and Lith to stay in the other, but we couldn't be separated—neither me and Emily, nor Ryan and Renee. Mom understood and got a third room.

Lith stays in the room with Ryan and Renee, though we spend every waking moment in one room, huddled together on the beds, talking, remembering, lingering in silence…remembering.

We talk on and on about Cass. Worry. Fret. Obsess.

Where is she?

My instincts tell me she isn't hurt. But why hasn't she tried to find us?

"Maybe she went to find her father," Lith says one night over a bucket of fried chicken from the nearest gas station.

I stare at him a moment. "I bet you're right." It makes sense. Cyrus Rutherford is one question we don't have answers to.

Well, one among a hundred, but one that matters to one who matters to us.

45

Thus Speaks Cassidy Rutherford

• • • • • •

There is an opioid crisis in Appalachia. I've heard about it. My father had preached to me about it. And now I'm seeing it firsthand. In my father.

I'm standing on the corner of two of the main streets in one of West Virginia's biggest cities, which is to say it barely makes the status of a city because this state is so rural. But there are more people here than most other places in this mountainous state. And this is where I found Cyrus Rutherford.

How did I get here?

I knew I couldn't help Shaun and Emily and Lith. I have no money. No resources. Nothing. I'll return to testify on their behalf if it comes to that, but I have something I need to do first.

I found Cyrus two hours away. How did I get here? Hitchhiking.

After what I've been through, one doesn't tend to be afraid of anything.

The first person to stop and give me a ride was a man driving an eighteen-wheeler. He said some flirtatious things. Tried to reach over and grab my thigh. Sharpened wooden knuckles to his hand stopped him in his tracks. He dropped me off on the side of the road but didn't press charges. What would he say anyway?

The next car to pick me up was a car with four college girls in it, passing through the state. They were high as kites, but fun, nonthreatening, and willing to share their weed.

I partook willingly.

Freedom is a beautiful thing.

The final ride I got was from a high school boy, leaving a visit to his grandma at an old folk's home.

He was sweet.

He kept stealing sideways glances at me, but it didn't bother me. We talked. I could tell he wanted to kiss me, but I told him I have a boyfriend, and he was respectful of that. I didn't tell him I also have a girlfriend.

He dropped me off downtown.

How did I know my father would be here? Call it a little hint from Dr. Richter.

"Huntsville," she'd said. "At least that's what I heard."

After her arrest at the asylum, I never saw her again.

I didn't see Shaun and Lith again either after we were taken to the jail. It was all very surreal, and Emily and I had clutched each other and not let go. That earned us some inappropriate comments from one of the officers, but I had an inappropriate retort, and he left us alone.

Then, soon after we arrived at the station, the police had let me go. I wasn't in the system for any reason, so they couldn't hold me. Guess my weak punch hadn't been enough to charge me with anything. The odd thing was that they didn't ask for a parent to pick me up or sign me out or anything. I just walked out the front door.

And was terrified. I'd never felt so alone.

I'd walked around the town, starving and without money. I went into a local diner to use the restroom, and I must've looked a mess, because the lady behind the counter fed me a huge plate of chicken and dumplings.

I was in a haze.

Those I loved more than anything had suddenly been taken from my life, and I couldn't get to them. They were gone, at least for the near future. Cyrus was gone. I was in a town thirty minutes from Blackthorn Peak. I couldn't even get to the prison or the cabin if I wanted.

I thought about my cottage, suddenly desperate to return to the small stone building I shared with Cyrus. I managed to find a ride back to Blackthorn Peak with a kind, elderly man who grew up near the asylum and who was eager to see it again after all the news coverage. He talked the entire ride, and I was grateful that there seemed to be no need for me to engage in conversation. When he stopped the truck on Main Street, I thanked him for his help and hopped out of the truck before he could offer to accompany me. I walked straight onto the grounds of the asylum, then straight through the front door of my old home.

My bedroom was still the same. So was Cyrus's, which was odd considering Les Range had been staying here.

I still didn't know the connection between Range and Cyrus. Would I ever have all the answers?

I didn't know. But I did know that I would go to Huntsville and try to find Cyrus. Then I'd return to find my true loved ones. I had no doubt about that. But I couldn't be with them while they were behind bars. At least, that's where they were when I left. They would likely be there awhile if I knew anything about the justice system.

I needed closure here first, though, before anything else.

As I stand at the corner in Huntsville, watching Cyrus, the shift in power is so powerful I almost fall to my knees. This man who had controlled and tormented me for years, as punishment for what he felt my mother's sins were, was nothing but a shell. He'd ruined my childhood. Almost ruined my life when he had me put in the asylum. Look at him now.

Drugged out on something so potent, he can't sit up straight, can't open his eyes, can't close his mouth.

He's filthy, like he hasn't changed clothes, much less showered, in days, if not weeks.

I smell his body odor from here.

He has no idea I, his own daughter, am standing before him.

"Cyrus?" I say, staring down at him.

He grunts. Doesn't move otherwise.

"Dad?"

His head shoots up. Or, rather, does a slow ascent upward until he manages to also lift his eyes and look at me.

He doesn't seem to recognize me in his drug-induced haze. I have to admit, it hurts. But then, oh yes, then he recognizes me.

"Cassidy?"

I don't respond.

"Cassidy?" he says again, tumbling into such pathetic weeping, I recoil, take a step back. He swipes his hand in the air as if reaching for me. "Cassidy?"

"Look at you," I say. "And you thought I…we…my generation was the threat to society." I shake my head. "Pathetic."

"Cassidy?" he cries and slumps forward, making a weak weeping sound. "Cassidy."

He urinates on himself, turning his light gray trousers dark.

I turn and walk away. Hitchhike back to the town where my friends were taken, to those who really matter to me. They need my attention, my help, my support. Those who truly love me. My true family.

EPILOGUE

Spring in Appalachia brings soft rain, blooming wildflowers, allergies, and green. Life sprouts in every possible way. I breathe in deeply before sneezing and then vowing to buy allergy meds next time I head to the pharmacy.

It's late April, one year since we were first in the asylum, six months since Range's death. Cass, Emily, and I actually returned to Blackthorn Peak and fixed up my grandfather's cabin with help from Mom's insurance money—which she all but forced me to take—our jobs, and my unexpected inheritance.

Since the asylum closed, people started returning to the area. Well, once the EPA came in and said all the water pollution rumors were false. How Range managed to pull all this off is still under investigation, but he had garnered a fortune from investors who had little to no idea what he was actually doing and used that fortune to lie, manipulate, threaten, and kill.

Since he had no will that anyone could find, and since I turned out to be his only remaining family, I inherited a vast amount of blood money. I am constantly thinking of ways to use it for good. I think about Dr. Richter's child and wonder if anyone knew Range was the father. One day I might visit her and ask. If the child needs anything, I can help. For now, though, I can't worry about a half-sibling.

Range is buried behind the asylum, but not in the forest near the cemetery where his victims rest. Rather, he's buried all by himself in a particularly shadowed and cold part of the forest where a certain plant called moonseed grows in abundance. I planted it myself early one cool spring morning.

I finished high school online, as did Cass and Emily. It turns out it was not difficult at all to get Wi-Fi to the cabin, despite the isolation. Well, the money helped overcome some of the obstacles.

After our graduation, a small ceremony that consisted of a trip to a restaurant in a nearby town, we all went to work.

Cass works at a tattoo and piercing parlor. I've never been happier to see that silver hoop back in her lip. Giving it gentle tugs with my lips is one of my favorite pastimes. She's thinking about cosmetology school but is taking time to settle into a life free of her father, the asylum, and the night terrors, which are finally starting to wane.

Emily works as a waitress, waiting on the fall semester to start at a community college thirty minutes away. She wants to be a nurse.

Me, I'm going to return to school too and was granted a scholarship at an annex of the state university where I'll study psychology. I want to be a therapist for troubled youth. I didn't get to the point I did last year when I landed in the asylum without having made huge mistakes along the way. I hope some other teen can benefit from my missteps. Isn't that what it's all about? Making mistakes, learning, helping others? Preferably without the constant threat of death or lobotomy.

Lith went back to his hometown where he's working as a mechanic. But he's not far, and often comes to the cabin on the weekends. He's dating a handsome guy named Thomas, but it seems casual.

We never saw Traz and Celexa again. They must've fled from the prison and never looked back. I didn't miss Traz and only missed Celexa a little, though I do think about them often.

Ryan and Renee also finished school online and are planning to start college in the fall, maybe at the same place Emily is going or maybe at a community college a little farther away. Both are talking about becoming social workers and going to work in the foster care system. Renee has had trouble concentrating since her lobotomy, though, so they are talking with the schools' counselors to determine which college can provide her with the best support. Ironic that she had never been on any meds before the lobotomy but now is encouraged to take pills for severe ADHD. I guess her nickname would be Vyv for Vyvanse.

They've been renting space in the house my mom bought in Blackthorn Peak—Mom lives on the main and second floors, and they turned the basement into a two-bedroom apartment. Mom didn't want to return to Baltimore. Too many memories. Besides, we didn't have a house anymore thanks to my twitchy fingers.

Teagan and his mother decided to remain in the area as well, continuing to stay in the small apartment they rented. Shortly after the end of Dr. Richter's trial, they were both killed by a drunk driver. The driver was nineteen with a history of addiction.

It's odd, and oddly healing, to live in this town that has brought me so much grief. But it's because of that that I can't leave. I'm tied to Blackthorn Peak now, and the only way to move on is to make this place mine. That means being part of the revitalization of an area that was the seat of so much pain, suffering, and death.

Cass wants to eventually open a tattoo parlor in town, an endeavor I support one-hundred-percent. I can see her being part of the reopening of the shops on Main Street, and the thought of life returning to that dreary drab of abandoned businesses makes me happy. She's getting really good, too, showing an artistic talent I never knew she had. She tattooed both me and Emily and then had her friend tattoo her. We all have a pine tree on the inside of our right wrist.

Mom suggested that I renovate the asylum since I now own it—another odd and unexpected part of my inheritance—and reopen it as a hospital or group of clinics to serve the surrounding area's desperate need for medical care. At first, I thought the idea was terrible. There is no way any of us could handle that place being operational. Not after what we went through. If anything, I wanted to burn it to the ground, smash it to bits, obliterate it from the earth. But then her idea started to make sense.

She and I met with a realtor and a lawyer to see what we would need to do to pull this off.

In the end we decide it will be a hub for primary care, urgent care, mental health, dental care, and on and on. It will draw people in from a wide radius and help revitalize the town in no time. It will be up and running within a year.

I still can't drive by the asylum, though, without a cold shiver marching down my spine. Maybe I never will be able to. But maybe the building, like us, needs a second chance.

I can give it that, and I plan to work there after I've earned my degree. Help give second chances to troubled teens. I can't think of a better use of my time, or money, or a better use for that building.

We are working with the town council, which now consists of my mom, a few locals who stayed deep in the mountains, and a few folks newly returned, to turn the cottage into a museum and to create a memorial near the cemetery's entrance.

Never forget is the motto we all practice as we revamp an asylum meant for experimental psychosurgery and murder. But we vow to use the painful past as a means to create a better future.

Ironic that that seemed to be the goal of the Agency from the start. Well, not Les Range's goal. But those other doctors, including Dr. Richter, who worked for him all had the goal of creating a better future with less suffering. Their goal was admirable even if their means were a bit archaic.

Before her death, Teagan's mom confirmed the traitor was Dr. Richter. She'd seen firsthand the push-pull the doctor was caught in—between wanting to perfect and share her new and improved lobotomy with the world and wanting to protect us. Throw in the warped and tragic relationship she had with Range, and it was no wonder her loyalty was all over the place…especially once she became pregnant. In the end, she'd chosen us, but she had gone back and forth so many times, Teagan's mom hadn't trusted her. Hearing this information from Nancy didn't really change anything, but it added a level of understanding of Dr. Richter.

I think about her often, still confused and unsure about whether or not she was a victim or a perpetrator. I guess because she was, truly, both.

• • • • • •

I look up from the grill to see Cass and Emily coming out of the cabin. Cass is carrying a tray of hamburgers and hot dogs to go on the grill. Emily is heading toward the table we set up in the middle of the yard, arms filled with paper plates, paper cups, and plastic utensils.

There are nine chairs around the table, even though we are only expecting the three of us, Mom, Ryan and Renee, and Lith and his boyfriend. But we always leave an empty chair to remember the victims. Owen. Trevor. Gibbon. Teagan. His mom. My grandfather. All those who call the ground behind the asylum their home.

That chair will always remain empty, because we will never forget. But that's not what we focus on as our family arrives and settles around the table. We focus on each other.

And we are grateful.

ABOUT THE AUTHOR

Tracy Hewitt Meyer is an award-winning author of young adult thriller and contemporary fiction. She doesn't shy away from tough topics that teens face such as mental illness, domestic violence, self-harm, and pregnancy, but her characters always tackle tough life events with resilience and hope. When not writing, Tracy is a mental health therapist, working with adults and couples. She is a member of SCBWI, the Virginia Writer's Club, and International Thriller Writers. Tracy lives in the mid-Atlantic region with her family and pups, Lila and Leonard.

Milton Keynes UK
Ingram Content Group UK Ltd.
UKHW040716120924
448172UK00004BA/34

9 781643 974002